LOVE LETTERS TO THE DEAD

LOVE LETTERS TO THE DEAD

AVA DELLAIRA

HOT
KEY
BOOKS

Originally published in United States of America by
Farrar Straus Giroux Books for Young Readers in 2014

This edition published in Great Britain in 2014 by Hot Key Books
Northburgh House, 10 Northburgh Street, London EC1V 0AT

A CIP catalogue record for this book is available from the British Library.

ISBN: 978-1-4714-0288-3

5

Printed and bound by Clays Ltd, St Ives Plc

www.hotkeybooks.com

Hot Key Books is part of the Bonnier Publishing Group
www.bonnierpublishing.com

For my mother, Mary Michael Carnes
I carry your heart

LOVE LETTERS TO THE DEAD

Dear Kurt Cobain,

Mrs. Buster gave us our first assignment in English today, to write a letter to a dead person. As if the letter could reach you in heaven, or at the post office for ghosts. She probably meant for us to write to someone like a former president or something, but I need someone to talk to. I couldn't talk to a president. I can talk to you.

I wish you could tell me where you are now and why you left. You were my sister May's favorite musician. Since she's been gone, it's hard to be myself, because I don't know exactly who I am. But now that I've started high school, I need to figure it out really fast. Because I can tell that otherwise, I could drown here.

The only things I know about high school are from May. On my first day, I went into her closet and found the outfit that I remember her wearing on her first day—a pleated skirt with a pink cashmere sweater that she cut the neck off of and pinned a Nirvana patch to, the smiley face one with the x-shaped eyes. But the thing about May is that she was beautiful, in a way that stays in your mind. Her hair was perfectly smooth, and she walked like she belonged in a better world, so the outfit made sense on her. I put it on and stared at myself in front of her mirror, trying to feel like I belonged in any world, but on me it looked like I was wearing a costume. So I used my favorite outfit from middle school instead, which is jean overalls with a long-sleeve tee shirt and hoop earrings. When I stepped into the hall of West Mesa High, I knew right away this was wrong.

The next thing I realized is that you aren't supposed to bring your lunch. You are supposed to buy pizza and Nutter Butters, or else you aren't supposed to even eat lunch. My aunt Amy, who I live with every other week now, has started making me iceberg lettuce and mayonnaise sandwiches on kaiser rolls, because that's what we liked to have, May and I, when we were little. I used to have a normal family. I mean, not a perfect one, but it was Mom and Dad and May and me. Now that seems like a long time ago. But Aunt Amy tries hard, and she likes making the sandwiches so much, I can't explain that they aren't right in high school. So I go into the girls' bathroom, eat the kaiser roll as quickly as I can, and throw the paper bag in the trash for tampons.

It's been a week, and I still don't know anyone here. All the kids from my middle school went to Sandia High, which is where May went. I didn't want everyone there feeling sorry for me and asking questions I couldn't answer, so I came to West Mesa instead, the school in Aunt Amy's district. This is supposed to be a fresh start, I guess.

Since I don't really want to spend all forty-three minutes of lunch in the bathroom, once I finish my kaiser roll I go outside and sit by the fence. I turn myself invisible so I can just watch. The trees are starting to rain leaves, but the air is still hot enough to swim through. I especially like to watch this boy, whose name I figured out is Sky. He always wears a leather jacket, even though summer is barely over. He reminds me that the air isn't just something that's there. It's something you breathe in. Even though he's all the way across the school yard, I feel like I can see his chest rising up and down.

I don't know why, but in this place full of strangers, it feels good that Sky is breathing the same air as I am. The same air that you did. The same air as May.

Sometimes your music sounds like there's too much inside of you. Maybe even you couldn't get it all out. Maybe that's why you died. Like you exploded from the inside. I guess I am not doing this assignment the way I am supposed to. Maybe I'll try again later.

Yours,
Laurel

Dear Kurt Cobain,

When Mrs. Buster asked us to pass our letters up at the end of class today, I looked at my notebook where I wrote mine and folded it closed. As soon as the bell rang, I hurried to pack my stuff and left. There are some things that I can't tell anyone, except the people who aren't here anymore.

The first time May played your music for me, I was in eighth grade. She was in tenth. Ever since she'd gotten to high school, she seemed further and further away. I missed her, and the worlds we used to make up together. But that night in the car, it was just the two of us again. She put on "Heart-Shaped Box," and it was like nothing I'd ever heard before.

When May turned her eyes from the road and asked, "Do you like it?" it was as if she'd opened the door to her new world and was asking me in. I nodded yes. It was a world full of feelings that I didn't have words for yet.

Lately, I've been listening to you again. I put on *In Utero*, close the door and close my eyes, and play the whole thing a lot of times. And when I am there with your voice, it's hard to explain it, but I feel like I start to make sense.

After May died last April, it's like my brain just shut off. I didn't know how to answer any of the questions my parents asked, so I basically stopped talking for a little while. And finally we all stopped talking, at least about that. It's a myth that grief makes you closer. We were all on our own islands—Dad in the house, Mom in the apartment she'd moved into a few years before, and me bouncing back and forth in silence, too out of it to go to the last months of middle school.

Eventually Dad turned up the volume on his baseball games and went back to work at Rhodes Construction, and Mom left to go away to a ranch in California two months later. Maybe she was mad that I couldn't tell her what happened. But I can't tell anyone.

In the long summer sitting around, I started looking online for articles, or pictures, or some story that could replace the one that kept playing in my head. There was the obituary that said May was a beautiful young woman and a great student and beloved by her family. And there was the one little article from the paper, "Local Teen Dies Tragically," accompanied by a photo of flowers and things that some kids from her old school left by the bridge, along with her yearbook picture, where she's smiling and her hair is shining and her eyes are looking right out at us.

Maybe you can help me figure out how to find a door to a new world again. I still haven't made any friends yet. I've actually hardly said a single word the whole week and a half I've been here, except "present" during roll call. And to ask the secretary for directions to class. But there is this girl named Natalie in my English class. She draws pictures on her arms. Not just normal hearts, but meadows with creatures and girls and trees that look like they are alive. She wears her hair in two braids that go down to her waist, and everything about her dark skin is perfectly smooth. Her eyes are two different colors—one is almost black, and the other is foggy green. She passed me a note yesterday with just a little smiley face on it. I am thinking that maybe soon I could try to eat lunch with her.

When everyone stands in line at lunch to buy stuff, they all look like they are standing together. I couldn't stop wishing that I was standing with them, too. I didn't want to bother Dad about asking for money, because he looks stressed out whenever I do, and I can't ask Aunt Amy, because she thinks I am happy with the kaiser rolls. But I started collecting change when I find it—a penny on the ground or a quarter in the broken soda machine, and yesterday I took fifty cents off of Aunt Amy's dresser. I felt bad. Still, it made enough to buy a pack of Nutter Butters.

I liked everything about it. I liked waiting in line with everyone. I liked that the girl in front of me had red curls on the back of her head that you could tell she curled herself. And I liked the thin crinkle of the plastic when I opened the wrapper. I liked how every bite made a falling-apart kind of crunch.

Then what happened is this—I was nibbling a Nutter Butter and staring at Sky through the raining leaves. That's when he saw me. He was turning to talk to someone. He went into slow motion. Our eyes met for a minute, before mine darted away. It felt like fireflies lighting under my skin. The thing is, when I looked back up, Sky was still looking. His eyes were like your voice—keys to a place in me that could burst open.

Yours,
Laurel

Dear Judy Garland,

I thought of writing to you, because *The Wizard of Oz* is still my favorite movie. My mom would always put it on when

I stayed home sick from school. She would give me ginger ale with pink plastic ice cubes and cinnamon toast, and you would be singing "Somewhere Over the Rainbow."

I realize now that everyone knows your face. Everyone knows your voice. But not everyone knows where you were really from, when you weren't from the movies.

I can imagine you as a little girl on a December day in the town where you grew up on the edge of the Mojave Desert, tap-tap-tap-dancing onstage in your daddy's movie theater. Singing your jingle bells. You learned right away that applause sounds like love.

I can imagine you on summer nights, when everyone would come to the theater to get out of the heat. Under the refrigerated air, you would be up onstage, making the audience forget for the moment that there was anything to be afraid of. Your mom and dad would smile up at you. They looked the happiest when you were singing.

Afterward, the movie would pass by in a blur of black and white, and you would get suddenly sleepy. Your daddy would carry you outside, and it was time to drive home in his big car, like a boat swimming over the dark asphalt surface of the earth.

You never wanted anyone to be sad, so you kept singing. You'd sing yourself to sleep when your parents were fighting. And when they weren't fighting, you'd sing to make them laugh. You used your voice like glue to keep your family together. And then to keep yourself from coming undone.

My mom used to sing me and May to sleep with a lullaby. Her voice would croon, *"all bound for morning town..."* She would stroke my hair and stay until I slept. When I couldn't sleep, she would tell me to imagine myself in a bubble over the sea. I would close my eyes and float there, listening to the waves. I would look down at the shimmering water. When the bubble broke, I would hear her voice, making a new bubble to catch me.

But now when I try to imagine myself over the sea, the bubble pops right away. I have to open my eyes with a start before I crash. Mom is too sad to take care of me. She and Dad split up right before May started high school, and after May died almost two years later, she went all the way to California.

With just Dad and me at our house, it's full of echoes everywhere. I go back in my mind to when we were all together. I can smell the sizzle of the meat from Mom making dinner. It sparkles. I can almost look out the window and see May and me in the yard, collecting ingredients for our fairy spells.

Instead of staying with Mom every other week like May and I did after the divorce, now I stay with Aunt Amy. Her house is a different kind of empty. It's not full of ghosts. It's quiet, with shelves set up with rose china, and china dolls, and rose soaps meant to wash out sadness. But always saved for when they are really needed, I guess. We just use Ivory in the bathroom.

I am looking out the window now in her cold house, from under the rose quilt, to find the first star.

I wish you could tell me where you are now. I mean, I know

you're dead, but I think there must be something in a human being that can't just disappear. It's dark out. You're out there. Somewhere, somewhere. I'd like to let you in.

Yours,
Laurel

Dear Elizabeth Bishop,

I want to tell you about two things that happened in English today. We read your poem, and I talked in class for the first time. I've been in high school for two weeks now, and so far I had been spending most of the period looking out the window, watching the birds flying between phone wires and twinkling aspens. I was thinking about this boy, Sky, and wondering what he sees when he closes his eyes, when I heard my name. I looked up. The birds' wings started beating in my chest.

Mrs. Buster was staring at me. "Laurel. Will you read?"

I didn't even know what page we were on. I could feel my mind going blank. But then Natalie leaned over and flipped my Xerox to the right poem. It started like this:

> The art of losing isn't hard to master;
> so many things seem filled with the intent
> to be lost that their loss is no disaster.

At first, I was so nervous. But while I was reading, I started listening, and I just understood it.

> Lose something every day. Accept the fluster
> of lost door keys, the hour badly spent.
> The art of losing isn't hard to master.
>
> Then practice losing farther, losing faster:
> places, and names, and where it was you meant
> to travel. None of these will bring disaster.
>
> I lost my mother's watch. And look! my last, or
> next-to-last, of three loved houses went.
> The art of losing isn't hard to master.
>
> I lost two cities, lovely ones. And, vaster,
> some realms I owned, two rivers, a continent.
> I miss them, but it wasn't a disaster.
>
> —Even losing you (the joking voice, a gesture
> I love) I shan't have lied. It's evident
> the art of losing's not too hard to master
> though it may look like (Write it!) like disaster.

I think my voice might have been shaking too much, like the poem earthquaked me. The room was dead quiet when I stopped.

Mrs. Buster did what she does, which is to stare at the class with her big bug eyes and say, "What do you think?"

Natalie glanced in my direction. I think she felt bad because everyone was looking not at Mrs. Buster, but at me. So she raised her hand and said, "Well, of course she's lying. It's not easy to lose things." Then everyone stopped looking at me and looked at Natalie.

Mrs. Buster said, "Why are some things harder to lose than others?"

Natalie had a no-duh sound in her voice when she answered. "Because of love, of course. The more you love something, the harder it is to lose."

I raised my hand before I could even think about it. "I think it's like when you lose something so close to you, it's like losing yourself. That's why at the end, it's hard for her to write even. She can hardly remember how. Because she barely knows what she is anymore."

The eyes all turned back to me, but after that, thank god, the bell rang.

I gathered up my stuff as quickly as I could. I looked over at Natalie, and she looked like maybe she was waiting for me. I thought this might be the day that she would ask if I wanted to eat lunch with her and I could stop sitting at the fence.

But Mrs. Buster said, "Laurel, can I talk to you a moment?" I hated her then, because Natalie left. I shifted in front of her desk. She said, "How are you doing?"

My palms were still sweaty from talking in class. "Um, fine."

"I noticed that you didn't turn in your first assignment. The letter?"

I stared down at the fluorescent light reflected in the floor and mumbled, "Oh, yeah. Sorry. I didn't finish it yet."

"All right. I'll give you an extension this time. But I'd like you to get it to me by next week."

I nodded.

Then she said, "Laurel, if you ever need anyone to talk to . . ."

I looked up at her blankly.

"I used to teach at Sandia," she said carefully. "May was in my English class her freshman year."

My breath caught in my chest. I started to feel dizzy. I had counted on no one here knowing, or at least no one talking about it. But now Mrs. Buster was staring at me like I could give her some kind of answer to an awful mystery. I couldn't.

Finally Mrs. Buster said, "She was a special girl."

I swallowed. "Yeah," I said. And I walked out the door.

The noise in the hallway changed into the loudest river I've ever heard. I thought maybe I could close my eyes and all of the voices would carry me away.

Yours,
Laurel

Dear River Phoenix,

May's room at my dad's house is just like it always was. Exactly the same, only the door stays closed and not a sound comes out. Sometimes I'll wake up from a dream and think I hear her footsteps, sneaking back home after a night out. My heart will beat with excitement and I'll sit up in bed, until I remember.

If I can't fall back asleep, I get up and tiptoe down the hall, turn the handle of the door so it doesn't creak, and walk into May's room. It's as if she never left. I notice everything, just the same as it was when we went to the movies that night. The two bobby pins in a cross on the dresser. I pick them up and put them in my hair. Then I put them back in the same exact cross, pointing toward an almost empty bottle of Sunflowers perfume and the tube of bright lipstick that was never on when she left the house, but always when she came back. The top of her bookshelf is lined with collections of heart-shaped sunglasses, half-burned candles, seashells, geodes split in their centers to show their crystals. I lie on her bed and look up at her things and try to imagine her there. I stare at the bulletin board covered with dried flowers pinned with tacks, little ripped-out horoscopes, and photographs. One of us when we were little, in a wagon next to Mom in the summer. One taken before prom where she wore a long lingerie dress she found at Thrift Town, the same rose in her hair that is now dried and pinned there.

I open May's closet and look at the sparkly shirts, the short skirts, the sweaters cut at the neck, the jeans ripped at the thighs. Her clothes are brave like she was.

On the wall above her bed hangs a Nirvana poster, and next to it, there's a picture of you from *Stand by Me*. You have a cigarette half in your mouth, cheekbones carved from stone, and baby blond hair. My sister loved you. I remember the first time we saw the movie. It was right before Mom and Dad split up, and right before May started high school. We were up late together, just the two of us, with a pile of blankets and a tin of Jiffy Pop that May made for us, and it came on TV. It was the first time either of us had seen you. You were so beautiful. But even more than that, you were somebody we felt like we recognized. In the movie, you were the one to take care of Gordie, who'd lost his older brother. You were his protector. But you had your own hurt, too. The parents and the teachers and everyone thought badly of you because of your family's reputation. When you said, "I just wish I could go someplace where no one knows me," May turned to me and said, "I wish I could pull him out of the screen and into our living room. He belongs with us, don't you think?" I nodded that I did.

By the end of the movie, May had declared that she was in love with you. She wanted to know what you were like now, so we went on Dad's computer and May looked you up. There were all of these pictures of you, some from *Stand by Me* and some from when you got older. In all of them, you were vulnerable and tough at once. And then we saw that you'd died. Of a drug overdose. You were only twenty-three. It was like the world stopped. You'd been just right there, almost in the room with us. But you were no longer on this earth.

When I think back to it, that night seems like the beginning of when everything changed. Maybe we didn't have the words for it then, but when we found out you'd died, it's like the first time that we saw what could happen to innocence. Finally May shut off the computer and wiped the tears from her eyes. She said you'd always be alive for her.

Whenever we saw *Stand by Me* after that (we got the DVD and watched it over and over that summer), we always muted the part at the end where Gordie said that your character, Chris, got killed. We didn't want that. The way you looked, with the light haloed around your head—you were a boy, a boy who would become a real man. We wanted to just see you there, perfect and eternal forever.

I know May's dead. I mean, I know it in my head, but it doesn't seem real. I still feel like she's here, with me somehow. Like one night she'll crawl in through her window, back from sneaking out, and tell me about her adventure. Maybe if I can learn to be more like her, I will know how to be better at living without her.

Yours,
Laurel

Dear Amelia Earhart,

I remember when I first learned about you in social studies in middle school, I was almost jealous. I know that's the wrong way to feel about someone who died tragically, but it wasn't so much the dying I was jealous of. It was the flying, and the disappearing. The way you saw the earth from the air. You weren't scared of getting lost. You just took off.

I decided this morning that I really need even the tiniest bit of the courage that you had because I started high school almost three weeks ago, and I can't keep sitting alone by the fence anymore. So after I looked through all of my old clothes, which are terrible no matter how much I try to pick the most inconspicuous ones, I went and opened May's closet and looked at it, full of bright, brave things. I remembered her body filling them. She would leave in the morning with her backpack slung over her shoulder, and it seemed that everything outside of our door must have rushed forward to greet her. I took her first day outfit—a pink cashmere sweater with a Nirvana patch on it and a short pleated skirt. I put it on. I didn't look in the mirror this time, because I knew it would scare me out of wearing it. I just paid attention to the swish of the skirt against my bare legs and thought of how May must have felt in it.

In the car with Dad on the way to school, I could feel his eyes on me. Finally, as he pulled up to the drop-off line, he said carefully, "You look nice today."

I knew that he recognized the outfit was May's. "Thanks, Dad," I said, and nothing more. I gave him a little smile and jumped out of the car.

Then at lunch, I walked through the cafeteria to the outdoor tables and watched everyone swirling together, looking happy, like they should all be part of the same movie. I saw Natalie from my English class with this blazing redheaded girl. They sat down at a table together in the middle of the crowd. They both had Capri Suns and no food. They looked like the sunlight had landed on purpose right in their hair. Natalie had her pigtail braids and drawn-on tattoos and wore a Batman tee shirt that was tight across her chest. The redhead had on a black ballerina skirt and a bright red scarf, with lipstick to match. They weren't dressed like the popular girls, who look clean and cut out of a magazine. But to me, they were beautiful, like their own constellation. Like one that maybe I could belong in. They looked like girls who would have been May's friends. They shooed off the soccer boys who swarmed around the redhead.

I wanted to sit by them so badly I could feel it in my whole body. I started to walk toward them, thinking maybe Natalie would notice me. But I got nervous and walked back to sit down by the fence. I stood up and sat down again.

I remembered what you said—*There's more to life than being a passenger.* I thought of you soaring through the sky. I thought of May rushing out in the morning. I ran my hands over her sweater I was wearing. And I walked over. When I got close to the table, I sort of just stood there, a few feet away. They were in the middle of leaning in and trading Capri Suns, so they each got a new flavor, when they felt a body and looked up. I think they thought it would be another soccer boy, and Natalie looked annoyed at first. But her face turned nice when she recognized me. I tried so hard to think of something to say, but I couldn't. The voices rushed around me, and I started to blank out.

But then I heard Natalie. "Hey. You're in my English class."

"Yeah." I took my chance and sat down at the end of the bench.

"I'm Natalie. This is Hannah."

"I'm Laurel."

Hannah looked up from her Capri Sun. "Laurel? That's the coolest name ever."

Natalie started talking about the "lame-os" in our class, and I was doing my best to follow along, but really, I was so happy to be there I couldn't focus on what she was saying.

By the end of lunch, they'd liked my skirt and my whole outfit and asked me if I wanted to go to the state fair after school. I couldn't believe it. I called Dad on my new cell phone that is supposed to be just for emergencies (although I can tell already that it won't be). I said that some girls asked me to hang out after school, so not to worry if I wasn't home yet when he got back from work, and that I'd take the bus afterward like usual. I talked fast so that he wouldn't have time to object. I'm in algebra now, and I can't wait for the bell to ring. The numbers on the board don't mean a thing, because for the first time in forever, I have somewhere to go.

Yours,
Laurel

Dear Amelia Earhart,

When we got to the fair, it was good like when I was a kid and sticky like it should be—full of stands selling cowboy hats and airbrushed tee shirts and the smell of state fair food. We were all starved, and the way Natalie and Hannah said it— "I'm starved"—it was easy to say it like them. To fit in.

When we got in line for frilly fries, Hannah started flirting with this guy in front of us. He had a white tank top, slicked-back hair, and a stare that made me think he wanted to bite her. Hannah's red hair is straight as a board, or so she told me, but she puts it into curlers every day. Her bouncy red curls fall around her face, and her big eyes look like she's always seeing something incredible. Her lips look like she's half smiling at something that no one else could get.

I was worried about not having any money and thinking I'd say I wasn't so hungry after all, but when we got to the front of the line, Hannah let the guy pay for us. He was making me nervous, leaning into Hannah like he was. I kept thinking that he was going to do something, but when we got our fries, she just said thanks and walked off, leaving him staring after her. I think she was showing off a little, but Natalie didn't act impressed. She just said, "Um, hair gel much?"

After we ate, we went over to the fence to smoke cigarettes. I'd never smoked, and I didn't know how. I'd seen May do it before, so I tried to copy her. But I guess it was obvious. Natalie laughed so loud that she started coughing. She said, "No, like this," and she showed me how to keep the smoke in and then suck it down my lungs. That is how you inhale. It made me really dizzy and sort of sick-feeling. By the time we were done, I was walking pretty much in zigzags.

So when Natalie and Hannah were ready for rides, I wasn't sure if I wanted to go. There was this one, a special ride that costs extra, where they put you in a harness and pull you up, higher than any building in the city. And then they drop you, and you go flying over the whole fair. I finally told them that I'd forgotten to bring money, but Hannah said that she had some from her job and explained that she works a few nights a week as a hostess at a restaurant called Japanese Kitchen.

"She's so pretty," Natalie said, smiling at her, "that they hired her even though she's only fifteen."

"Shut up," Hannah said. "It's because they could tell I would be an excellent employee!"

When she counted out her money, it wasn't quite enough, but she said that if we flirted with the guy who ran the ride, he'd let us go for less. When we got to the front of the line, my heart was pounding. Part of me hoped the guy would say no, because I was honestly terrified. But Hannah did her best smile, and he agreed to give us a discount. I thought of you and how brave you were in your plane. And how you made other people around you brave, too. And suddenly, all three of us were harnessed together, and he was hoisting us up. While we were waiting to be dropped, we could see all of the tiny people in the fairgrounds. I forgot to be scared. I was thinking about how each one of them, so small from high up, was like their own island, with secret forests and hidden thoughts.

And that's when he dropped us! With no warning. We were flying. I couldn't have felt more perfect. Sailing through the late afternoon sun and the smell of roasted corn and frilly fries and funnel cake, above all of the islands. So fast that when I opened my mouth, a whole world of air would come in. Next to the girls who could be my new friends.

I thought of you, watching the earth always changing from above. The tall grass swaying. The rivers like long fingers and the fog from the sea sucking up the shore. And how, when you disappeared down there, you must have become a part of it.

Yours,
Laurel

Dear Kurt Cobain,

All weekend I had been worried that Natalie and Hannah might forget about me in school on Monday, but today in English, Natalie passed me a note that said *lame-o!* with an arrow pointing toward the guy sitting next to me, who was drawing naked boobs on his poem handout. I looked over at her desk and smiled to show that I got the joke. And at lunch, I saw Natalie and Hannah wave to me from their table. My heart leapt. I threw away my lunch bag with its kaiser roll in a quick toss and went to sit by them. Hannah was licking Doritos cheese off her fingers and passed me the bag.

I tried not to look, but after a while, my eyes found Sky. I saw him see me with my new friends. I wondered if the sun landed right on me like it did on them. I imagined growing brighter and let myself look back at him a moment too long.

Hannah caught me. "Who are you looking at?"

I mumbled, "Nobody," but my cheeks got hot and probably red like an unfortunate truth meter.

Hannah insisted, "Who?! Tell me!"

I didn't want to risk losing my new friends, so I said, "Oh. Um, I think his name is Sky."

Hannah's eyes picked him out, and she said, "Ooooh. Sky. Yeah. Mr. Mystery."

"What do you mean?" I asked.

Hannah shrugged. "He's one of those guys everyone

knows of, except no one actually knows him. He somehow manages to seem popular without having, like, any actual friends yet. He transferred here this year. He's a junior. But he's totally hot. I'd do him."

Natalie hit her shoulder. "Hannah!"

"What?" she said. "I didn't mean I'm gonna. He's Laurel's."

I blushed again. I mumbled that he wasn't.

Hannah looked over her shoulder and said, "We'll make him yours. He's looking at you."

When I glanced back, he still was.

I realized then that this could be who I am. Right there, with the cement burning my legs under the middle school jeans I'd cut off this morning, short enough that they would pass the longer-than-your-fingertips test only if I shrugged up my shoulders, and May's silver-white shirt that shimmered in the light.

It was as if an invisible band started playing the sound track to a new life. I heard you. I wondered if this was how May felt when she was in high school. It must have been, because it was her music. All the songs we'd listened to together, playing at once. The world she'd disappeared into was here. I looked up from my blush, away from Sky, whose eyes were still on me, and turned to Natalie and Hannah. I laughed out loud, full of the secret someone I could become. *Hello, hello, hello.*

Yours,
Laurel

Dear Kurt,

May's clothes must have worked like magic, because since I started wearing them, things have been happening. I sat with Natalie and Hannah at lunch all week. Then today, Friday, I was walking down the hallway to Bio, just making my feet follow the lines of light on the floor. Suddenly I looked up, because I was about to bump into someone. It was him. Sky. I could have reached out and touched him.

He said, "Hey. What's up?" His voice sounded like gravel turning to grains of sugar.

I started thinking of how to answer. I know that "What's up?" is just something people say, but it's a very hard thing to say anything back to. It's like the only response is "nothing." I didn't want to say "nothing" because, actually, a lot was up.

Instead I said, "I saw you the other day." Each word felt like its own stone, falling to the bottom of a lake.

He nodded, his head tilted a little. Like he was trying to figure out what I was.

"I'm Laurel," I added.

"Sky." He smiled.

I was about to say *I know*, but thought better of it. When my eyes finally focused, I saw he was wearing a Nirvana tee shirt. This seemed perfect. So I said, "I love Kurt Cobain."

"Yeah? What's your favorite album?"

"*In Utero.*"

"Right on. Everyone says *Nevermind*. That is, everyone who doesn't really listen."

I smiled and scrambled in my head to keep the conversation going. "Yeah. I really like how he's . . . how Kurt sounds like, like he's exploding from inside." I couldn't actually believe I said that.

But Sky nodded, like he knew what I was talking about. And that's when I suddenly realized that he was looking at me like he wanted to touch me. I tugged on May's tight orange shirt. My skin was burning. I had to get away before I broke out in flame.

"I'm just going to Bio."

"'K," Sky said. "Maybe I'll see you around."

I nodded and walked away, my heart pounding. I told myself not to turn around. But I did. And his eyes were still on me. I felt something spark—the mystery of what he saw when he looked at me.

In class, while Mr. Smith was talking about covalent bonding, I kept replaying it and noticing new things each time. Like the way one of Sky's sleeves was a little bit turned up over his arm. How the hairs on his biceps were standing up. The freckle on his eyelid. I thought of what Hannah had said, about how he transferred here. I wondered from where, and I wondered if he'd ever been in love before.

Yours,
Laurel

Dear Amy Winehouse,

I remember one night after May got back from sneaking out, she came into my room and lay on my bed and whispered, "You have to hear this song!" She put her earbuds in my ear, and as she fell back against the pillow, I heard your voice for the first time. *I go back to black*, you sang. The swinging rhythms of the song sounded bright, but there was a hurt in your voice under its honey—although it's not as simple as that, really. You had a way of singing that could mix together so many feelings. And I could tell that the words you sang came out of the real you. That they were true.

It turns out my new friend Hannah loves you, too. Hannah and I have PE together eighth period, and she's always forgetting her gym clothes. Since we went to the fair together two weeks ago, a lot of times now I pretend I forgot mine even if I didn't so that we can walk around the track together and talk instead of playing kickball or badminton or whatever with everyone else. Hannah wants to be a singer, and sometimes when we are walking around the track, she sings your songs to me. Her favorites are "Stronger Than Me," "You Know I'm No Good," and, of course, "Rehab." She likes to shout *"No, no, no"* and shake her red hair back and forth. The way that you didn't want anyone controlling you, that's part of Hannah's spirit, too.

Hannah acts fearless, but you can tell that underneath, she keeps secrets.

She's the sort of girl who guys fall in love with, but she doesn't act like a pretty girl. She acts like she's trying to find a way out of herself. She always has at least one boyfriend, sometimes two at once.

Hannah told me her parents died when she was a baby, so she and her brother used to live with her aunt in Arizona. But her brother got in too many fights at his school, so the aunt sent them here to live with their grandparents.

When Hannah first moved here in seventh grade, she dated one of the most popular eighth-grade soccer boys. Then she dated another soccer boy and another, and then by the time she was in eighth grade she dated a couple of guys in high school. Even though Hannah could have hung out with anyone at her new middle school, even the popular girls, Hannah said that she picked Natalie because she could tell that Natalie "got it."

"What's 'it'?" I asked.

Hannah shrugged. "What it's like to be different, even if you don't want everyone to know it. Like, I knew that I could have Natalie spend the night, and she wouldn't be too weirded out by the fact that I love my horse and live with my grandparents who are going deaf and have a mean brother who likes to yell a lot."

Hannah also told me about this guy, Kasey, who she's "messing around with." That's what she says. She met him at her job at Japanese Kitchen when he was there with a bunch of his friends for someone's birthday. (It's a good place to go for birthdays, because the chefs cook in front of you and do fire tricks at the table.) He's in college, so honestly, it's really strange for him to want to date a girl so much younger. It makes me a little bit nervous for Hannah because of this older guy who May used to date, named Paul. When I asked Hannah why she was dating someone in college, she just laughed and said, "I'm precocious."

I guess Kasey actually likes Hannah more than just to mess around with, because he sends her flowers—red tulips, which are her favorite. She likes to show them off for everyone at school. Principal Weiner is getting tired of Hannah having deliveries in the office, but Hannah says that the flowers are from her uncle for her to bring to her grandma, who's sick at home. The principal asks why he doesn't just send them to the house, and Hannah says that it's because no one answers the door there, so they would just wilt in the sun. The principal knows Hannah's lying, but she can't say much, on account of Hannah's grandma being sick and her grandpa being too hard of hearing to understand the principal if she tries to complain, and probably too tired to care much, anyway. So as it is, Hannah carries Kasey's flowers from class to class, puts them on her desk, and slumps down behind them so that the teachers can hardly see her. And she leans over to Natalie's desk and makes silly faces.

I think Natalie sort of hates the flowers and hates that Hannah gets them. Because she's always saying how she doesn't believe in flowers or things like that. But I don't know if that's completely true, because she's making Hannah a painting of tulips in her art class. Natalie showed it to me after school the other day, but she told me not to tell Hannah about it. It's a surprise. Natalie is really a good painter. The first petal of the tulip already had more shades of color than you could count.

I am at Dad's this week, which means I usually take the city bus home, because he works too late to pick me up. But today, instead of going right home after school, I walked with Natalie and Hannah to get Dairy Queen. On the way there, Natalie and Hannah kept wanting to flash people. I was scared of doing it at first, but I tried to remind myself to swallow what scares me, the way I learned to do when I'd go out with May. And I ran really fast afterward. I outran Natalie and Hannah every time. They'd catch up to me a few blocks later, still screaming and giggling. And then I'd scream and giggle, too, and the worst part was over, and I was happy to be one of them.

Hannah bought us our ice cream (she looked proud to be able to do this), and then she had to leave to go to work. Even though she's late for class a lot, Hannah's always on time for her job. Before she went, she said she and Natalie are going to spend the night at Natalie's house tomorrow, which is Friday, and that I should come. I was so happy when she asked, because it means that we are becoming real friends.

Dad came back from work a few minutes after I got home from Dairy Queen. He works at Rhodes Construction, fixing the broken foundations of houses and things like that. When May and I were kids, Dad used to walk in the door in the evening and we'd run to hug him. I loved how he'd be covered with sweat and dirt, like he'd been on an adventure. Mom would be making dinner, the smell of fried meat and chili filling up the house. She cooked like a baker, Dad always said. She didn't throw in ingredients and taste later. Each was perfectly measured.

But life isn't like that. You can't be sure how it's going to come out, even if you do everything right. They turn around on you, lives do. Dad used to come home and look strong from the day of building. Now he looks tired, like a bulldozer ran him over. When May and I were kids, he used to be good to climb on. But now it's like I'm afraid if I get too close to him, I'll trip and spill out all the sadness he's keeping hidden.

He used to love to play jokes on all of us, like switching salt with sugar (he did this so much that we got used to shaking it out on our hands and licking it to determine which was which). Mom got annoyed by it, but May and I thought it was funny. He'd hide his alarm clock on the weekends, under a couch cushion or something, and we'd have to go running through the house to find it when the alarm went off. Or sometimes he'd poke holes in the apples in the fridge and stick gummy worms in. This was our favorite, because it meant candy. He doesn't do that sort of stuff anymore, but he still kisses my forehead when he walks in the door. Then he asks about my day, like he knows he should, and I do my best to make it sound good.

Tonight I made microwave mac and cheese with little mini hot dogs for us for dinner, which is our favorite. We still have food in the freezer from May's memorial nearly six months ago, but I don't think either of us wants to eat it.

"So you're making friends?" he asked over our mac and cheese.

"Yep." I smiled.

"That's great," Dad said.

"Actually, I was going to ask you, can I spend the night at my friend Natalie's tomorrow?"

Dad hesitated a moment, and I crossed my fingers under the table. Finally he said, "Sure, Laurel." He paused and added, "I don't want you cooped up with me."

Then he turned on the baseball game—he's a Cubs fan, because he grew up in Iowa near their farm team—and I watched with him while I did my homework. Dad used to give me "baseball is like life" lectures, but he doesn't do that anymore. Now we just watch in silence. I guess some things turned out too sad even to be explained with a bases-loaded strikeout.

Yours,
Laurel

Dear Kurt,

Last night, I got drunk for the first time. When I got to Natalie's for the sleepover, we walked to the grocery store, which felt too cold in that air conditioner way. We walked half shivering down the liquor aisle, and Natalie pulled a bottle of cinnamon After Shock off the shelf and into her halfway-on hoodie. Then we took it to the bathroom and peeled off the label so it wouldn't beep. I ignored my quick-beating heart and tried to act normal, like I'd done this sort of thing before. I didn't say anything about the woman's feet with mom sneakers and a little girl in the next stall. Then we just walked right out.

We went back to Natalie's house, where we were alone, because her mom was on a date that night. Natalie said that means she doesn't get back till morning. We climbed up onto her flat roof with the bottle. The After Shock had cinnamon-flavor crystals in the bottom, and when I first took a sip it burned like someone lit a sweet fire in my mouth. I swallowed fast and didn't make a face, and I didn't tell them that it was my first time ever drinking. I thought if May did it, I could, too. How bad could it be? So I let the liquor burn down my throat and into my stomach. It made me laugh and got my body loose, until I forgot to be afraid. We lay down on our backs to watch the planes pass overhead and made up a song about them. I don't remember the words, though I keep trying. I do remember that Hannah's voice sounded like the cinnamon crystals, sweet and full of fire. I think she really could be a singer.

I am not sure what happened next, but then we were down from the roof and Natalie and Hannah had gone into the backyard to jump on her old trampoline. I was in the front yard on a hammock swinging, and the stars were buzzing toward me.

I remembered how May would sneak out at night and I'd wait up in bed until I heard her come back in. Usually I'd just listen to her tiptoe down the hall and close her door, and then I'd know that I could sleep because she was safe. But once in a while, and this is what I loved the best, she'd come to my room instead and whisper, "Are you up?" My eyes would pop open, and I'd whisper that I was, and she'd come to lie on my bed. I remembered how her breath would smell sweet and hot, like alcohol, I guess. How a smile would spread slowly across her face and she'd laugh in a whisper and slur her words a little, like every sound led into another. As she'd tell me about her adventures—the boys and the kissing and the fast cars—I pictured it sort of like I did when we were little kids, when I believed that May had fairy wings and I'd imagine her on her flights through the night, swooping under the stars.

When I looked up from where I was on the hammock, all of a sudden the stars started buzzing too loudly, and I didn't feel right. I wondered if this was what it was really like for

May on those nights, if the stars spun around her until she was dizzy and she didn't know where she was anymore.

I was scared suddenly and I couldn't keep my head straight. I worried that bad things were coming into my mind, so I went to find Hannah and Natalie. When I walked through the wooden gate into the backyard, I saw them there on the trampoline. They were kissing. Real kissing. And jumping all at the same time. They looked up for an instant and saw me watching, and then they kind of fell. Natalie started screaming. She had chipped her tooth on Hannah's tooth. She started looking everywhere for the lost piece of her tooth. I tried to help find it, but it was nowhere on the smooth black surface of the trampoline, and it was nowhere in the dirt. She got worried that she swallowed it. And Hannah got worried that I would tell everyone at school what Natalie had been doing when she chipped her tooth, even though I swore I wouldn't. Hannah started telling me I had to kiss Natalie, too, or else I would tell. I couldn't be the only one who wasn't kissing, she said. But I didn't want to. They weren't listening. Natalie grabbed me and said she was going to kiss me to seal the secret. Suddenly it was hard for me to breathe. I gasped for air. I ran.

I ended up in the park near school. I sat down on the swing and started swinging as high as I could, higher and higher, until it felt like the night was rushing into me, until it felt like I would go all the way over the bar. And then I jumped, and flew, and landed in the sand. I climbed onto a jungle gym like the one that used to be our ship when I would go to the park with Mom and May. We had to sail through a sea full of sea monsters to rescue the mermaids. And I started to cry.

The air smelled like fire smoke and fall leaves. It smelled a way that makes you feel how the world is right up close, rubbing against you. My head was starting to really hurt. It was late, and I didn't know what to do, so I went back to Natalie's. She and Hannah were asleep on the trampoline. I crawled underneath and slept on the ground.

The next day when we woke up with dew on our clothes, Natalie's mom was making pancakes and bacon and called us in for breakfast. It smelled in the kitchen the way you want home to be. She said we were silly girls for sleeping outside. She was being nice, I think, because of her date. Natalie's mom doesn't look like other moms. Natalie said she works as a secretary in a law office, but for the weekend morning, she was wearing a shirt knotted above her belly button with cut-offs, and her dark hair up in a high ponytail. We all ate and were pretty quiet, just answering her mom's questions, which were too cheerful. When she asked Natalie, "What happened to your tooth?" Natalie looked nervous for a minute. I knew it was my chance to show her I would keep their secret, so I said, "We got burgers from McDonald's, and hers had a bone in it!" Hannah started laughing and said, "Sick, huh?!" I think since her mom felt guilty about sleeping over at her date's house, she didn't notice that we were guilty, too. Hannah picked a leaf out of my hair and handed it to me. Its veins threaded in tiny patterns through the yellow skin.

We never talked about the kissing, and at school on Monday, we acted normal. I made sure to have enough money for Nutter Butters at lunch, and I shared them with my friends. I looked at Sky and laughed when Hannah said he was undressing me in his mind. It was like nothing had happened. I tried not to, but I noticed the tiny piece of one of Natalie's perfect teeth missing.

Kurt, I have this feeling like you know May, and Hannah and Natalie, and me, too. Like you can see into us. You sang the fear, and the anger, and all of the feelings that people are afraid to admit to. Even me. But I know you didn't want to be our hero. You didn't want to be an idol. You just wanted to be yourself. You just wanted us to hear the music.

Yours,
Laurel

Dear Judy Garland,

When parents talk about their pasts, the stories start to stick in your head. But the memories that you inherit look different from the now-world, and different from your own memories, too. Like they have a color all their own. I don't mean sepia-toned or something. My parents aren't even that old. I just mean that there is something particular about their glow.

When I think of the stories that I know about your childhood and your family, I see them in almost the same color that

I see my parents' stories. I'm not sure why, but maybe it has to do with the happy-sad of it all. Or maybe it's because of how my mom used to say that your movies gave her hope when she was younger.

She loved to watch them with us, so I don't only know you from *The Wizard Of Oz*. We saw you in everything—*Easter Parade, Babes on Broadway, Meet Me in St. Louis*. On movie nights, May and I used to get up from the couch and sing along with you—*"Zing zing zing went my heartstrings,"* May would belt out as she pranced through the living room.

Mom said that when she was a little girl, she wanted to be like you. My dad came from a pretty perfect family, but Mom didn't, and maybe that was the biggest difference between them. Mom grew up here, in Albuquerque. She never told us specifics, but her own mom (who died when I was little) was more or less an alcoholic, and I think her dad was pretty hard on her and Aunt Amy before he got cancer. He died when she was eighteen and Aunt Amy was twenty-one. Afterward, Mom's mom kept drinking too much, Aunt Amy found God and got a job as a waitress, and Mom moved into a studio apartment and got a bartending job so she could start saving up money to go to California to follow her dream of becoming an actress.

In the meantime, she took acting classes and starred in shows at the local theater. Her best part came right after her twentieth birthday. She played Cosette in *Les Mis*, and the papers gave her rave reviews. She saved them in a scrapbook that she used to show to us when we were kids.

One night, Dad stopped into the bar where Mom worked. He was passing through town, back in what he called his "wild days," when he rode his motorcycle across the country. Based on the old pictures, May and I thought he was quite a stud. Mom must have thought he was, too, because when he came into the bar, she asked him to come and see her in *Les Mis* the next night.

Dad said it only took the length of the performance for him to fall in love. When it was over, he was waiting outside of Mom's dressing room with a bouquet of daisies. She invited him over to her apartment, and they stayed up late, stargazing on the roof of the building and talking. After that, Dad found a job in town working on a construction crew for a new hotel, and he saw Mom as much as he could. They rode the tramway to the top of the mountains, watched the watermelon-colored sunsets, and danced in Mom's little studio to Beatles songs. Four months later, Mom found out she was pregnant with May, and they decided to get married.

When Mom told the story, she said that she'd always wanted a home, but it wasn't until she had us that she knew what that meant. Now that I'm writing it down to tell you, it seems like a tragedy. But when we were growing up, we thought it was romantic. May would ask to hear the story over and over, and Mom loved to tell May how she was the spark that started it all. "You were ready to come into the world, and so you did. We have you to thank for us, baby girl."

When we were little, Mom still used to go to auditions

sometimes for theater productions or local commercials. Once she got a part in a commercial for the Rio Grande Credit Union. They shot her waking up on the steps of a new house in her pajamas, saying, "Am I dreaming?" Then a lady dressed as the credit union fairy drops keys into her hand. We'd squeal when the ad came on TV, saying, "Look, it's you, Mommy!"

But mostly the auditions didn't work out, and she'd come home like a balloon whose air had been let out. Eventually, she said that she'd missed her window, and that if you want to be a real actress, you have to live in California. She took up painting instead and got a job filing papers in a doctor's office. She said that she thought being a mom was her real job. She said that we were her greatest accomplishment.

Mom would say all the time how she wanted us to have happy childhoods, happier than her own. Sometimes she'd ask us if we were happy, and we'd always say yes. Still, she said that she wished she could give us more. She liked to talk about somedays. Someday we'll have a house with a pool. Someday we'll learn to ride horses. Someday we'll have beautiful dresses with sequins head to toe, like the ones on TV. Someday we'll go to California. We'll see the ocean together.

She and May and I used to talk about it, planning the perfect road trip. Mom would say that the waves sound better than trains at night and better than rain and better than a crackling fire. We used to plan how, when we had the money, we'd get on I–40 and just drive. We'd stop along the way at

Arby's for "roast beast" sandwiches (we called them that because of *How the Grinch Stole Christmas*). We'd get a hotel room and stay up all night watching movies and drinking sodas with ice from the ice maker, and the next day, we'd drive all the way to where the land meets the water.

But as it turned out, Mom went without us. She cried when she told me. "I have to go away for a while. I'm so sorry," she said. "I just can't be here right now." As she tried to hug me, I felt frozen in her arms. I wanted to tell her she was breaking the promise. We were all supposed to go together. Of course it was too late for that, but I wondered why she didn't at least offer to take me with her. She said she'd get her head back on and her heart sewn as best she could and come back soon. She never said when soon is.

Now she's just a voice on the phone. She called me at Aunt Amy's a couple of hours ago. "Hi, Laurel. How are you, sweetie?"

"Okay. How are you?" I tried to picture where she is, but all I could see in my mind was a faded postcard—skinny palm trees rising into a pale blue sky.

"I'm okay. I miss you, honey." She sniffled, and my body tensed up. I thought, *Don't cry don't cry*. I hate it when Mom cries. May knew how to make her stop, but I never did.

"Yeah, I miss you, too."

"How is school? What did you do today?"

"The usual. Went to classes."

"Are you making new friends?"

"Mmm-hmm."

"That's good. I'm happy for you."

And then there was a long silence. I didn't know what to say to her.

"Mom, I should go. I have homework."

"Okay. I love you."

"You too."

I hung up, and just like that, Mom vanished back into the land of washed-out palm trees.

Judy, I read that you said your first memory was music. Music that fills up a home. And one day, suddenly the music could escape through a window. For the rest of your life, you had to chase it.

Yours,
Laurel

Dear Janis Joplin,

I am writing to you for an important reason, which I will get to. When I walked up to our table at lunch yesterday, Hannah was talking to some of the soccer boys who'd made their way over, and Natalie was squeezing the last of her Capri Sun out of its package, not looking interested. I sat on the end of the bench and scanned the crowd for Sky. I finally spotted the back of his head at the edge of a crowd of juniors. He hadn't noticed me, so I turned back to the table and started contemplating whether or not to break out my kaiser roll in public. Then as Hannah laughed with the boys, I noticed her brush her hand against Natalie's arm, like it was meant to be an accident, but in slow motion. Natalie sucked in her breath and closed her eyes for a second. Suddenly, she interrupted Hannah's conversation and said, "Come on, let's go to the alley." I got worried that they were going to leave me alone and I would have to go back to sitting by the fence, but Natalie looked at me and said, "Come on!" So I followed them. The alley, everyone knows, is where you go to smoke cigarettes and things if you are either cool or a senior.

It turns out that Natalie met this senior, Tristan, in her art class. He told her that he'd buy her cloves and she could come and meet his girlfriend, Kristen. When you see them, you can tell right away that Tristan and Kristen are so in love. Kristen wears long flowy skirts, and she has long hair down to her butt that looks like it must never come untangled. Her face is soft and exotic-looking. She doesn't talk loudly. Her voice is a whispery rasp, but musical, too. Tristan also has long hair. But otherwise, they are opposites. Everything about him is pointy and buzzing with energy. Tristan wears ripped clothes with patches sewn on from bands like the Ramones and Guns N' Roses and the Killers. He's always talking talking talking, and after everything he says, he says, "Right, babe?" and Kristen nods without moving her eyes.

Tristan was easy to meet, because right away he tossed Natalie her pack of cloves and said, "Hola, chiquitita!" And then he kissed Hannah's hand and kissed my hand and said, "Who are these miniature beauties you offer up to the alley of smoke?" Before we could answer, he turned to Kristen and said, "Looks like we have found the lost children of the freshman class, right, babe? Are you ready to adopt?" Then he pulled a giant kitchen lighter out of his pants pocket and lit our cloves with a flame that almost reached the top of my head. He saw me looking at his patches, especially the one that said SLASH across his chest in bright red letters. I thought that I should say something, so I asked, "Is Slash a band?"

Tristan laughed. "He's the lead guitarist of *the* band. Guns N' Roses. Definition of rock. We've got a ways to go on your education, don't we?"

My face got hot.

But then Tristan said, "Don't worry, you're young. There's still hope. Ready? First lesson. 'Being a rock star is the intersection of who you are and who you want to be'—quote courtesy of Slash himself."

"Is that who you want to be?" I asked.

He looked at me, sort of confused.

So I added, "A rock star?"

Tristan laughed again, only this time a little differently. Like I'd asked him a hard question he didn't want to answer.

"Well, you look like one," I offered.

Kristen didn't seem mad that I'd said that, or that he'd kissed our hands. I think because they are so in love, she doesn't have anything to get jealous of. She didn't really even look at us. She just lit another cigarette. I tried to smile in a way that would make it so she'd like me, because I really wanted her to, so badly it kind of hurt behind my eyes. I wanted them both to.

"I'm Laurel," I offered in a squeaky voice.

Kristen's face stayed blank, but her eyes focused toward me in a way that made me know she was deep-down nice. She said, "Kristen. 'I'm one of those regular weird people.'"

Tristan explained, "Quote courtesy of Lady Joplin. She's obsessed." So then Kristen started talking about you, and I figured out that Kristen really loves you, pretty much as much as she loves Tristan.

When I got home today, I looked up about Slash, and I also looked up about your life, so that I can start my education, and so that I can be friends with Tristan and Kristen. I read that you grew up next to oil towers in Texas, and that when you were a teenager, everyone in high school was terrible to you. But that made you fearless. And then you became famous. When Kristen and I are better friends, I am going to ask her to play me some of your music. I know that I could find some online, but I sort of hope that the first time I hear it will be with her. Until then, though, I am writing because I wanted to thank you for saying that thing about regular weird people, because I thought about that a lot, and I am one of them, too. With all of us standing there together, Kristen, Tristan, Natalie, Hannah, and me, I realized that there is a reason that we were all there—we are each weird in a different way, but together, that's actually normal. And even if there's a lot that I can't say to them, it feels good to belong somewhere.

Yours,
Laurel

Dear Allan Lane,

I am at my aunt Amy's. It's her week. I like the weeks with my dad better, because Dad is my dad and he's part of my used-to-be-normal family. But I still love Aunt Amy, which is why I am writing to you. Since you are Mister Ed the talking horse's voice, I figured you'd be the closest thing to Mister Ed himself. My aunt Amy *loves* Mister Ed. Really loves him. She also really loves Jesus.

When we were little, Dad didn't used to like us to spend time with her, because he thought that she was unstable. But Mom would cry and say, "Jim, they're all she has." Since Aunt Amy never had kids of her own, she's always thought of May and me as her daughters, too, I guess.

Even though she's only forty now, Aunt Amy's hair is silver already and long, and she wears flower-print dresses. You can tell that she was pretty when she was young. But she's not like Mom, who seems just as pretty now. Mom looks soft, like an out-of-focus picture that blurs her hair and her face a little bit into the landscape. Or maybe that's just how I see her now that she's gone. Aunt Amy is skinny and bony and you don't want her to stroke your head or hug you. She holds too tight.

Aunt Amy had a few boyfriends a long time ago, but they were all bad ones. I probably shouldn't know about that, except I heard Mom talking about it once when she and Dad were fighting. Aunt Amy hadn't dated anyone since I've known her until last year, when she fell for this guy who was walking across the country for Jesus. She found out about him on the news, and she decided she really admired this man. She sent him letters and care packages to pit stops along his route. And then she decided to fly out to Florida so she could join the end of his pilgrimage. She walked the last one hundred miles with him, and they struck up a romance on the road. I think Aunt Amy imagined she'd finally found her mate. Afterward, she called him a lot and left him messages, where she did impressions of Mister Ed or of the Jamaican bobsledders from the movie *Cool Runnings*. (That is her next favorite thing after Mister Ed.) At first, he called back a little bit. She'd ask him when she could see him again, but he'd never say exactly when. And soon the calls stopped coming. She's always checking the answering machine, though she tries to act like she doesn't care. I think she doesn't want me to see her being hopeful. (I don't know if being super into Jesus makes you against things like modern technology, but Aunt Amy still hasn't figured out cell phones.)

At the beginning of the summer, after Mom had told me

she was going to go to California for a while, she decided she needed to call some kind of family meeting. It was there that Aunt Amy asked if I wanted to spend Mom's weeks with her. Clearly the two of them had planned this. Mom and Dad and Aunt Amy and I were sitting in the house May and I grew up in, on the sofa that had been worn in by years of our bodies. Aunt Amy turned to me and asked, "What do you think, Laurel?" She looked so hopeful about it.

Dad didn't look so sure, but I knew that if I said no to Aunt Amy, she would start talking about how they let May go too far down a path of sin and how I needed God or something.

I shrugged. "I don't know."

Then Aunt Amy pointed out that if I stayed with her, I could go to the high school in her district. I had barely considered the fact that I'd have to go to high school at the end of the summer, but if I did have to go, it seemed like a good idea to go somewhere else. So I agreed.

Now Aunt Amy hardly wants me to do anything. Go out, or see anyone, or talk to boys, or anything. The only thing she really lets me do is go on "study dates," which is how I get to hang out with Natalie and Hannah when I'm at her house. Tonight Aunt Amy and I went to dinner at Furr's Cafeteria, like we've done ever since May and I were kids. I got what I always get at Furr's—Salisbury steak, mashed potatoes with no gravy, and red Jell-O. Aunt Amy always makes the two of us pray before dinner, even when it's only an iceberg lettuce and mayonnaise sandwich and I'm watching TV, and even though my dad and I never pray at our real house. Now the prayer is always for May.

Afterward, Aunt Amy asks if I have been saved or not and if I've accepted Jesus into my heart. And I always say yes, because I want to get it over with. And I don't want her to worry. May used to say no. Then she would ask, "What about a baby? What if a baby was just born, and didn't have time yet to accept Jesus, and the baby died? Would they still go to hell? Or what about a grown-up person, who wasn't a bad person, but just didn't know about Jesus because he never learned? Would they go to hell?" Aunt Amy never really answered. She'd just get sad and say that she wanted us to know Jesus' love. She'd say see no evil, hear no evil, speak no evil. She'd try to make it like a game, with us covering our eyes and ears and mouths. May hated that. Now Aunt Amy is scared, I guess, that May never got saved. She wants to make sure that doesn't happen to me. But she doesn't know how guilty I am. I can't ever tell.

We were sitting in the Furr's dining room in the dark red vinyl booth under the ceiling that is too high even for a high ceiling, and I was on to the red Jell-O, cutting every cube into a quarter. Aunt Amy was asking for more ice for her iced tea. And then she started doing her Mister Ed impression and asking me, "How does Mister Ed go? Show me." She wanted me to make my hands like horse hoofs on the table and a horse noise with my lips. Like we did when I was a kid. I've seen how her face falls when I say no, or how she keeps on insisting. So I swallowed and did the horse lips. Just then I looked across the room and I saw this guy Teddy from my history class with his parents, I guess. He's one of the popular soccer boys. My face turned hot, and I prayed he hadn't seen me pretending to clip-clop on the table.

I'm nervous, because I am going to sneak out for the first time tonight. Tristan and Kristen are coming to pick me up at midnight. Tristan nicknamed me Buttercup. They adopted me and Natalie and Hannah, and they are especially nice to me, because I am the quietest and I love to listen to their education. When they asked us what we were going to do this weekend, Natalie and Hannah said they were going to spend the night at Hannah's outside of town. I told them how I couldn't go because I am kinda trapped at my aunt's house. So Kristen and Tristan offered to break me out to hang out with them.

I explained living with Aunt Amy part-time by saying that my mom is on some sort of big retreat-type thing. I know that it's strange that I haven't talked to any of them about May, but it's like I have a chance now to forget the bad stuff. To be someone else, someone like her. If I'd gone to Sandia, everyone would be watching me, wanting an answer. But at West Mesa, her identity is my secret. Besides Mrs. Buster, if anyone happened to read the story in the paper all those months ago, or heard of it, they don't say anything about it. More likely, they didn't pay attention, or forgot.

Yours,
Laurel

Dear Janis Joplin,

I just got home from my first night sneaking out. The window was stuck, but I got it open. Luckily for me, it's the old push-up kind that's easy to get in and out of. I can hear Aunt Amy snoring a little, so I'm safe. There were no parties tonight, so we went to Garcia's Drive-In, which is open all night, and I ordered cherry limeade, and Tristan ordered ten taquitos, and they smoked pot in the car, and Kristen put you on the stereo.

This was the first time that I'd seen people smoke pot, and also the first time I'd heard you sing. Your voice whispered into me, exploding slowly. And Kristen sang along, her eyes closed and the neon lights broken by the window on her cheeks.

I got nervous that she or Tristan would pass me the pipe, and I wasn't sure what I would do. I was studying them in case I needed to know the right way to use it.

But when Tristan leaned into the backseat, Kristen took it out of his hand and said, "Don't corrupt her."

Tristan said, "What? It's part of her education, right, babe?"

Kristen hit him on the shoulder and said, "Let's keep it musical."

Tristan looked at me and shrugged and said, "Sorry, Buttercup. Can't cross the missus."

But I think that I might have gotten kind of high from

them smoking it in the car, anyway. Because the way you and Kristen sang "Summertime," it felt like I was so far inside of the song. There was nothing else around. You made me feel what summertime really is. Underneath what's bright, you knew the hot dark rasp of it. The other thing is, it was like a goodbye, and I could feel that, too. It's fall now. September's nearly over.

And then what happened is this. I asked them, trying to sound real casual about it, if they knew Sky. Since I ran into him in the hallway that day, I've been hoping for it to happen again, but it hasn't yet. He did wave to me at lunch the other day, when he caught me looking at him. I thought Kristen and Tristan might know something about him. I tried to sound like I was asking for no reason. But of course my cheeks burned and a giggle burst out of me, and they guessed immediately. Tristan started sing-songing, "Buttercup's in love!"

Kristen told me that the rumor is Sky transferred because he got kicked out of his old school. She said that he doesn't talk to anyone about that stuff, so no one knows for sure what happened. She also said that he stands around with the stoners, as if he was one, except he doesn't even smoke cigarettes. "But," she said, "he's cool, definitely. Capital C. I mean, everyone agrees on that."

Tristan decided we should drive by his house so I could see it. He looked up Sky's last name—Sheppard—on Kristen's phone and found a listing. Kristen said we were being creepy, but Tristan laughed and said it was fun. And secretly,

I was really excited to see it. We were out of the high school area, in a neighborhood where the houses are smaller and either adobe or tin-sided. Most of the yards were messy, full of sunflowers whose stems were scrambled together, parts of old cars, or trees that somebody cut at the trunk and never hauled away. But at Sky's address, everything was perfect. The tin siding on the house looked shinier than the rest, as if someone had polished it. And there were rows and rows of perfect marigolds in the front yard in two long flower beds. A welcome mat and a fall wreath on the door, and two same-sized pumpkins on either side, though they were early for Halloween. I saw there was someone outside. A woman, in her bathrobe, watering the flowers with a bright green watering can. It was two a.m. Just as we were driving away, I saw someone else open the door, and when I turned back, it looked like Sky.

Yours,
Laurel

Dear Judy Garland,

I'm in English right now, not paying attention in class and writing this letter instead, which is sort of ironic because technically this whole thing started as an assignment for English that I never turned in.

After I got off the phone with Mom last night, I went on

Google Earth and tried to see if I could find where she is. California was colored in blocky splotches of gray and brown and green, like all the other states. I knew the ranch is close to Los Angeles, but I didn't know where exactly. I scanned around, hovering above the city, trying to find some context. When I would start to zoom in, the picture plummeted toward the ground, until it would land in a street view of a road leading nowhere in particular.

Finally, instead I typed in the address of where you used to live in the desert town of Lancaster, California. It looked like a normal neighborhood, one that I could imagine walking in. My mom told us how before you were Judy Garland, you were Frances Ethel Gumm, "Baby" they called you, from Grand Rapids, Minnesota. Your family moved to Lancaster when you were four. It was dry and dusty, but after the winter rains, miles of red poppies would spring up everywhere. I found a photo of the Lancaster poppies online, and it made me think of you falling to sleep in the field of them in *The Wizard of Oz* after the Wicked Witch cast a spell. Mom didn't ever tell us this part, but I read that your family moved because of rumors that your dad hit on male ushers at this theater in Grand Rapids. Your parents used to fight so much it scared you, but you kept singing. Your mom put all of her energy into trying to make you a star. You traveled on the vaudeville circuit with your two older sisters—first the Gumm Sisters, then the Garland Sisters, and then it was you who got signed by MGM.

My sister was a bit like you were as a little girl. She was the bright spark of the family, the one who everyone relied on to shine, the one who tried to keep everyone from fighting. I think because of Mom's story about how May brought our family together, she felt like it was her job to keep it that way.

When we'd be at the dinner table, if Mom and Dad were fighting, I would sit there silently, trying not to cry. But May would disappear and come back wearing her leotard. She'd go into the living room, where we could all see her, and she'd start doing back walkovers and pirouettes. The way May was, it was impossible not to look at her. She'd do cartwheels and long leaps, and if they hadn't stopped fighting yet, she'd do handsprings down the runner of the rug. She'd say, "Look!" and flip right there. We'd clap for May, and when she had finished her show, she'd say, "Can we have ice cream for dessert?" So Mom would get the bowls, and everything bad was gone for the moment.

But once in a while, there were times when Mom was having a "bad night," and no matter how many handsprings May did, or songs she sang, or jokes she told, she couldn't make Mom snap out of it. Mom would put her hand on May's forehead and say, "I'm sorry, honey, but I'm having a bad night." Mom would say she was too tired for a bedtime story. She'd tuck us in early and disappear into her room. Dad would follow her in and try to calm her down. Sometimes, if it didn't work, we'd hear him leave the house.

We'd be in bed, May and I, both of us pretending to be

asleep but still wide awake, and we'd hear Mom cry through the wall. I didn't realize it then, but maybe she was thinking of her own mom who drank too much, or her dad who died, or the life she thought she'd have when she wanted to move to California to be an actress, and everything that didn't come true. Those were the nights when May and I weren't enough. And even though we couldn't say it, or even think it, somehow I think we both knew it.

It was one of those nights, one of Mom's bad nights, when May taught me magic. I guess I was maybe five. I whispered from the bottom bunk of the bed we used to share, before we got our own rooms as teenagers, "May? I'm scared."

She climbed down her ladder and lay next to me. "What are you scared of?" she asked.

"I don't know."

"I know what it is," May said. "You're scared of the witches. The bad witches are here, but it's okay, we can beat them. We have magic."

"We do?" I asked.

"I've been waiting to tell you until you were old enough. But I think you're ready."

The sound of Mom crying had faded away with the rest of the world. All that mattered was May and the secret that she was about to tell me. I leaned in, waiting. "What?" I asked eagerly.

May whispered, "We're fairies."

She explained that every seventh generation of children in

our family inherits the magic. It's in our genes, she said. And she said that because we were fairies, we had the power to fight the invisible evil witches.

"Come on!" she said, pulling me out of bed. "Are you ready to learn your first spell?" We snuck through the dark house and out the back door to gather up the ingredients. The moonlit yard was a world all our own. I followed her onto the grass, the feet of my pajamas wet with the dew, the cicadas making a strange sort of music. We needed three empty snail shells, the soft kind of sand, a bundle of berries, and the bark of one of the baby elms that sprang up at the edge of the garden. When we'd gathered all of our ingredients into a pail, we carried them back into our bedroom, and May stirred it up and said the spell in a whisper.

"Beem-am-boom-am-bomb-am-witches-be-gone!" She thrust her hands like she was throwing tiny stars from her fingers.

"See?" She turned to me, grinning. "They're gone."

And they were.

We put the potion under the bed, and May said that as long as we kept it there, the witches couldn't get us. In that moment, I knew that as long as I had May, everything would be okay.

Now that May isn't here, I have to find another way to make magic. And it feels like she's sending me a spell that might help. This is what happened. At the beginning of class, I asked Mrs. Buster for a pass. Instead of going to the bathroom, I walked up and down the empty hallways, peeking into the tiny windows of the classroom doors, as if I could find something that I was looking for.

Then I passed by one of the cases they use to display trophies for sports and debate and science fairs, and I noticed my reflection swimming in the blurry glass. Everything about me looked wrong. I couldn't very well try to rearrange my face then and there, so I started with my hair. I was smoothing my ponytail for the third time when Sky turned the corner.

"Do you want to go on a drive or something?" he just asked me right then. The second time we'd ever talked.

"Um, I'm in English."

He laughed. "No you're not. You're standing here. Right in front of me, in fact."

I smiled back. I wanted to ask him about his house and the woman who must have been his mother tending the garden in the middle of the night. But of course I couldn't. So I was quiet for a long moment, noticing things. Like the eyelash on his cheek. And the way his chest looked underneath his sweatshirt. And I forgot I was supposed to be saying something.

"So do you want to go for a drive or what?"

"After school?"

"Yeah. I'll meet you in the alley." And with that, he turned around and walked down the hallway.

I glanced back at myself in the murky glass and caught the edge of my grin. My face didn't look so wrong anymore, and before I turned to go, I noticed the way my eyes are shaped like May's.

My stomach is flipping all around. I wonder if Sky swerves and runs red lights and stuff like May did. I used to get scared in the car with her and grip on to the handle over the door and hold my breath, but I loved it. I loved the feeling of being alone together in the car, like we could go anywhere we wanted. Just us.

Luckily for me I'm with Dad this week and I take the bus home, so I won't have to think about what to tell Aunt Amy. I have to go now. The bell is ringing. Wish me luck and bravery.

Yours,
Laurel

Dear Jim Morrison,

I waited at the edge of the alley after school, and Sky pulled up in his truck. A Chevy. Kristen was there, smoking, and she gave me a quiet wink. I got in and looked at Sky. I wondered if he could hear how hard my heart was hitting my chest. Like my ribs really were a cage, and my heart wanted out. When the ignition turned, the music came on loud. I asked Sky who was singing, and he said it was the Doors, and the song was called "Light My Fire." He said, "If you love

Kurt, you'll love Jim Morrison, too." He was right—I do love you.

All of a sudden we were out of the lot and on the highway next to the mountains, flying. I put my hand out the window, and then I put my head out. I felt my hair blow behind me and the air rush into me, and I forgot for a moment to worry about how I was supposed to be. Because I was perfect right then. Everything was. And Sky was a perfect driver. Not scary. Just steady. And fast. I wanted the music to last forever.

When I brought my head back in, Sky looked at me and kind of smiled. "Sit closer," he said. So I moved to the middle of the bench seat, and everything slowed down except the car. The song and its drums were going. He put his hand on my thigh. High up. Right on the skin where my skirt ended. His fingers moved, just the littlest bit. Such a little bit that if I looked down, I probably couldn't even have seen them moving. But I felt them, just enough that I knew he knew what he was doing. He'd done this before.

For a moment, I went somewhere else. I remembered how it felt, those nights with May, when we were supposed to be at the movies. I got scared suddenly, and I tried not to let Sky know that I was breathing too fast. I stared straight ahead at the road and imagined I was above the earth, looking down through the window of a plane. The road would look like a streak of lightning laid across the land. Sky's truck would be a tiny toy car.

"What are you thinking?" he asked.

"Nothing . . ."

"Do you want to go somewhere?"

"No, I like driving."

And then he took his hand off of my leg, and his hand found mine, and he held on to it, and he seemed like an anchor to the earth. I was back in the car with him, and he kept driving, fast but never faster, and never slower. He stayed just right the whole time.

Yours,
Laurel

Dear Amy Winehouse,

In a way you were like the singers from the sixties, like Janis and Jim, and from the nineties, like Kurt, because your fearlessness seemed like it came from a different time. When your first album was released, you still looked innocent, a pretty girl who said she thought she was ugly. But by the time your second album came out, it's like you'd invented a new person to be. You would step onstage in your little dress, sipping a drink, with your big beehive hairdo and Cleopatra eyeliner, and sing with a voice that poured out of your tiny body. You wore your clothes like armor, but in your songs you opened all the way up. You were willing to expose yourself without caring what anyone thought. I wish I was more like that.

You were always wild, even as a kid. You got kicked out of your theater school in London when you were sixteen because you pierced your nose and because you didn't "apply yourself." Hannah told me this. She doesn't really apply herself, either, even though the teachers are always telling her how she's so bright.

Today, instead of forgetting our gym clothes, Hannah suggested ditching PE altogether. She said that Natalie would ditch her last class, too, and Natalie's mom would be at work until late, so we could go get some booze and drink it at her house. I was worried about getting drunk in the daytime, but I called Dad anyway and said, "I'm going to Natalie's house to study after school, so I might be home a little late, okay?"

"Okay," he said, and then he paused. "I'm proud of you, Laurel. It's not easy, what you've been through, and you're out there living your life."

He sounded like he meant it, and it was more than he'd said about anything in a long time. My stomach sank with guilt. I wondered what he would think if he knew what we were really doing.

I swallowed. "Thanks, Dad," I said, and hung up as quickly as I could.

On our way to the store, Hannah sang "Valerie," because that's Natalie's favorite of your songs. Hannah said that you had the best style of anyone, and then Natalie said that you had tattoos of pin-up girls, and Hannah said that she thought you even had affairs with a few, but she added, "Amy wasn't a lesbian, she said, at least not without a little Sambuca." Then she laughed. I wondered if this is what Hannah thought about herself.

When we got to Safeway, the pounding rain was sticking the bright leaves to the sidewalk. The way to do it, Hannah explained, is you just stand outside the door, trying to look pretty. And when a guy walks by, you stare at him in that way. You give him the money, and when he comes out and asks what you are up to, you take the bottle and run. You feel the whole rush of it. Natalie said Hannah is best at this, and that the guys always come when she looks. But Hannah made me try. Eventually a guy with a black ponytail and jeans with a patch that said XTC came over. He looked like a rocker left over from twenty years ago. I got my eyes ready, and he noticed me and said hi. I guess the key is to act like maybe he'll get something in return for the favor. That's what Hannah told me. It made me nervous, but I tried not to show it.

Then, when we were standing outside the door waiting for him to come back, I saw Janey, my old friend from elementary and middle school, walk up. *Oh no*, I thought. My heart started racing. She was holding hands with this cute soccer boy wearing a Sandia uniform. Her hair was perfect and pushed back by a headband, her skirt just the right amount of short with matching tights and rain boots. I wondered what she was doing here. Janey isn't the type for ditching, I thought, but then I realized that by now the school day must have been over. I tried to turn away so she wouldn't see me, but unfortunately it was too late. Janey's eyes fell on me and froze.

"Hey," I mumbled.

She glanced back at the guy she was with, and I wondered if she was embarrassed to be talking to me. "Hey, Laurel." She paused for a moment, and I hoped that she would just go inside. But she walked up closer and touched my arm, the way you would if you were a doctor who had to tell someone they were dying. "How are you?"

"Um, I'm fine."

She pursed her lips into a sad smile. "I miss you," she said.

"Yeah, you too."

I was about to ask her what she was doing when the XTC guy came out of the store with a bottle of Jim Beam. I knew I had to grab the bottle and run. So just as Janey gave me a freaked-out look, I said to her and the XTC guy both, "We gotta go," and I grabbed the bottle and ran as hard as I could, Natalie and Hannah chasing behind me.

When we got far enough away that we slowed down to catch our breath, Hannah asked, "Who was that?"

"Oh," I said, "just a girl I used to know. From middle school."

I didn't tell them that Janey and I had spent the night at each other's houses every weekend when we were kids, or that we used to put on *Wizard of Oz* performances with May and charge our parents quarters to see them. I didn't tell them that the last time I'd seen Janey was at May's memorial six months ago, or that over the summer she'd called and left messages a couple of times to see if I wanted to spend the night. I didn't tell them that I never called back. Because I didn't know how to explain that after May died, all I wanted was to disappear. That my sister was the only person I could disappear into.

Suddenly I wanted to let it all come spilling out, but when I thought of saying May's name, I froze up. If I tried to tell them, they'd want to know what happened, and I wouldn't know what to say. They'd feel bad for me, and when you are guilty, there is nothing worse than pity. It just makes you feel guiltier.

There was something between me and the world right then. I saw it like a big sheet of glass, too thick to break through. I could make new friends, but they could never know me, not really, because they could never know my sister, the person I loved most in the world. And they could never know what I'd done. I would have to be okay standing on the other side of something too big to break through.

So I did my best to forget about Janey and to laugh with Natalie and Hannah when we got back to Natalie's and opened our bottle of Jim Beam. In all of the excitement, I forgot to specify that we wanted something with fruit flavor in it. Straight whiskey, it turns out, is not so good, so we had to mix it up with apple cider.

Apple cider reminds me of when we would go apple picking in the fall with Mom and Dad. May and I always wanted to get to the apples we couldn't reach. High up, they were shiny and spotless and best. We would run ahead of Mom and Dad, and when no one was looking, we'd hide in between the rows of trees and climb up. Once I fell and skinned my knee. But I didn't cry. I let it bleed under my leggings so no one would know the secret and make us stop. After the apple picking, we'd get cinnamon doughnuts and apple cider, hot.

I wanted my whiskey cider hot, so I put it in the microwave. It smelled like memories mixed with fire. It didn't taste that good, but Natalie and Hannah and I drank it anyway, and took off our shirts and ran around the backyard twirling in the rain. We fell down laughing.

I ended up lying there a long time, just looking at the rain falling and trying to pick out each separate drop. They started coming so fast. I thought of Janey and how during sleepovers at my house we'd stay up late and eat root beer float bars and ask May to paint our nails. I looked down at my hands, the purple polish now chipped down to the shapes of foreign continents. I thought about how in middle school, after I started going out with May, Janey and I had fewer and fewer sleepovers. It got harder to be around her, because I didn't know how to tell her about the nights at the movies, and the guys, and how it made me want to slip out of my skin.

All of a sudden, I didn't want to be alone. The rain was blurry, and I was scared of something I couldn't see, but it felt close enough to breathe on me. And I got worried that somehow the XTC guy at the store that we ran away from would come back and find me.

So I went inside and found Natalie and Hannah in the bedroom. They were kissing again. Or more like making out, really. Their shirts were still off and their wet hair was stuck to their heads. When I opened the door, they didn't notice for a minute. Hannah saw me first. She jumped off Natalie and started laughing.

Natalie said, "We were just cold. We were trying to get warm."

"Come on, you can, too," Hannah said.

"That's okay," I said, and closed the door.

I don't think they worried as much, because last time I didn't tell anyone. They probably kept kissing. I went to the den, and I found where the heat comes out of the floor and fell asleep next to it until it was time to go home.

Maybe Hannah wants to kiss Natalie even without any booze, but she can't admit it. Hannah says that Natalie knows her better than anyone in the world. She says they are soul mates. But I think maybe Natalie loves her as more than a soul mate. I wonder if Hannah loves her like that, too, and if there's a reason she's too scared to say.

Yours,
Laurel

Dear Kurt,

When I was in English today, I looked up from my test to see Mrs. Buster staring at me with her big eyes, bugged out like I make her sad. After the bell rang, she said, "Laurel, can I talk to you for a minute?"

I thought, *Oh no, not again.* I walked up to her desk and didn't look up and hoped she wouldn't pretend to know anything about my sister or ask what's wrong with me. She ran her fingers through her ironed-flat blond hair and paused for a moment. Then she said, "You never did turn in your letter assignment, even after I gave you an extension." It felt weird that Mrs. Buster was bringing this up. I mean, that was nearly a month and a half ago. Why did she care?

"I know," I said. I worried that somehow she could see through me. "I'm still working on it."

"I normally wouldn't accept something this late, but I'd like to see you finish it. I think that it's important for you . . ." And with that she trailed off. I guess she didn't want to say *since your sister died.* I wanted to tell her that she didn't understand. She wouldn't. This is our world. And she can't have it. But instead of saying any of that, I nodded and left.

Then I went to my locker, and I was looking at the picture of you I have hanging inside of it, when I noticed something else. A homecoming invitation. It was cut from red construction paper into the shape of a rough heart. Like a kindergartner had done it for a valentine. For one hopeful moment, I thought that it could have been from Sky. But it wasn't. *Will you go to homecoming with me?* it said. *Evan F.* I felt queasy.

I've only talked to Evan Friedman once before. He's a popular boy, one of the most popular in the freshman class. His face is very pale, and honestly, it kind of looks like an albino monkey. But that makes him sound ugly, and he's not. Also, he's very good at sports and skateboarding and school, like everything in the world is easy for him. We are in algebra together. A couple of weeks ago, I turned around to ask him to borrow a pencil, because my lead had broken off. His hand was sort of down his pants. My eyes went there, and then darted back up. My throat got dry, but I had to say something so he didn't think I was just looking. So I just stuttered out my original question. "Do you have an extra pencil?" He took the one off his desk and put it in my hand. After that, I caught him looking at me more than once.

Why was he asking me? I am nothing like his ex-girlfriend, Britt, who is blond with cherry-kissed lips and bubbly like cream soda. I wondered if it was just because I looked at his crotch that time or what.

Secretly I had been hoping that Sky would ask me. I've been looking for him since we went on our drive, one week and a day ago. But he hasn't been at lunch. I saw him only once, walking in the hall with some other junior guys and a girl who had dyed-black hair that matched her tall black boots. She was laughing and touching his arm. Sky looked up as he passed by and saw my eyes on him. He held them for just a moment before tilting his head up in greeting. I must have pretty much seemed like a freak, just staring.

At lunch today, Kristen and Tristan came to sit with me and Natalie and Hannah at our table, and I told them about Evan's invitation.

Hannah exclaimed, "Mr. Popular is totally trying to get in your pants."

"Well, I know he gets in his own pants," I said.

This made everyone laugh, because I never say things like that. Hannah almost spit out her Capri Sun.

"Are you going to say yes?" Natalie asked.

"I don't know," I said. Then I asked Tristan and Kristen, "Are you guys going?"

"We're over school dances, right, babe?" Tristan answered. Kristen nodded.

"Do you think Sky's over school dances, too?" I asked.

"Unfortunately, I'd have to answer that in the affirmative," Tristan said.

Hannah said, "My analysis is that it appears that he'd like to spend as little time at school as possible, since he's been ditching lunch. And although he has license to stand with the cool kids, he still doesn't fully belong anywhere and hasn't relinquished his title of Mr. Mystery. Hence the throng of girls who are always leaning in and touching his arm. But of course, my money's on you."

Kristen added, "Mine, too, but I know his type, Laurel. He's not a girlfriend kind of guy. He's the type that just, like, has girls sometimes."

"Is Tristan the girlfriend kind of guy?" I asked, because I was trying to figure out what this meant.

Kristen laughed. "He wasn't before I met him," she admitted.

"But she converted me!" Tristan said. "I'm living proof it's possible."

"Maybe you'll convert Sky," Kristen offered.

"We haven't even talked since last week. I don't know if he actually likes me."

"I hypothesize that Sky *does* like you," Tristan said. "He asked you to ride in his Chevy lovemobile after all—and the fact that he hasn't spoken to you since is evidence that you make him nervous. Which is evidence that he likes you. Guys get shy, too, you know."

It's hard for me to imagine that I make Sky nervous, but I hope Tristan is right.

When lunch was finished, I still wasn't sure what to do about Evan. In Algebra, I sat on the other side of the room from him and tried not to look over. After class, I took a long time placing my notepaper in my binder and snapping and resnapping the rings, hoping he'd leave. But when I looked up, he was there.

"Did you get my note?"

I looked at him blankly for a moment. "Yeah."

"Does that mean yeah you'll go with me or yeah you got it?"

After what Hannah and Kristen said, I figured my chances of Sky asking were pretty much none, especially since there's only a week and a half left before the dance. And it seemed hard to say no to Evan and his paper heart. So I said, "Oh. Uh. Yeah, I'll go." Then I added, "But I kind of have plans beforehand. So, can we meet there?"

I've seen plenty of versions of homecoming dates on TV— the girls in their satin dresses cutting tiny pieces off of rib eyes they won't finish at somewhere like Outback Steakhouse, drinking Shirley Temples and virgin piña coladas, while the guys scarf their whole plates and then tackle the girls'. And I know that Evan probably has popular friends who do this kind of thing. But what would I say to them?

Honestly, I don't want him to pick me up, because I couldn't stand him coming to our quiet house. I don't want him to see inside it. And I don't want Dad feeling like he should have to pretend and pull out the camera. We don't take pictures anymore.

Evan was still looking at me.

I tried to give him a way out. "You know, if you want to ask someone else who can go to dinner first, I totally get it. It's totally okay."

Evan just said, "No, it's cool. You can come out after, right?"

I guess this was the part that really mattered. If he thought we would make out or not.

"Yeah, sure," I mumbled.

So now, this is going to be my first dance. With Evan Friedman and his jagged red heart. It was supposed to be Sky.

At May's first dance her freshman year, I watched her get ready in her red dress, not satin, but silk. She was so perfectly alive. Her date, Justin Alvarez, a senior boy, rang the doorbell like he should and pinned on a corsage. I stayed hidden in the door frame, watching. Even though they'd already split up by then, Mom and Dad both wanted to be the ones to see her off to her first dance, so Mom came over that night. She took pictures of May being beautiful. Dad shook Justin's hand and said, "Be home by twelve." I had this feeling that the boy dressed in a suit was carrying her away, into her new life that I couldn't see. I wished I could go.

When she got back that night at two a.m., she tiptoed into her room. She'd called Dad and told him what a great time she was having and begged for a couple extra hours. He'd finally agreed and gone to sleep, but I had been in bed waiting up, my eyes open to the moonlight. I heard her and pushed open her door. She said, "You have to hear this." She put on a CD and played "The Lady in Red." Over and over and over. I lay on her bed and watched her unpin her hair, placing freed bobby pins on the dresser, and wiping off the lipstick. When her curls were a mess over her shoulders, she lay in the bed next to me, starting the song over again and closing her eyes. She fell asleep in her red dress. I saw the hem of it with its sequins crumple between her thigh and the sheet. I thought she was the most beautiful thing I'd ever seen. I wondered if anyone could ever think that about me.

Yours,
Laurel

Dear Allan "Rocky" Lane,

I wanted to know who you were, besides the voice of Mister Ed, so I looked you up online. I found a picture of you, and I was surprised to see you were really very handsome. A

Western man. Rough and kind at once. Up until then, I had only seen the face of Mister Ed when I pictured you in my mind. But I discovered you were a boy who grew up in Indiana and left school because you dreamed of becoming a Hollywood star. Before you were Mister Ed, you were Harry Leonard Albershart from Indiana, and then Allan Lane the actor, nicknamed Rocky. The article said you made thirty B Westerns—the low-budget kind—riding a horse called Black Jack through movie sets. It's strange the way even dreams turn into jobs.

When you were on set shooting all of those B movies with titles like *Desperadoes' Outpost* and *Frontier Investigator*, I wonder if in your head you were riding a real horse across the desert, galloping off to somewhere else. It might not be what you'd imagined when you wanted to become a star, but when you were Mister Ed, you galloped yourself into the living rooms of so many people who loved you. I know that.

Aunt Amy has watched your show since she and Mom were kids. I think it reminds her of when the world seemed safe. The way you make us laugh, it's clean—a talking horse goes to a dentist, makes phone calls to movie stars, watches too much TV. Nothing really bad ever happens.

I wish that Aunt Amy could meet somebody like you. Someone who could make her laugh and look good in his cowboy hat as he tipped it toward her. If you were here, you could do your Mister Ed voice and make her crack up. Instead, Aunt Amy just has the Jesus Man, who never calls back.

When I see her putting on her apron in the morning to go to work, I can see the days stretch ahead of her like a desert. Even if it didn't come perfectly true, you got to live close to your dream. But she works at the Casa Grande diner, where people go for lunch, people who seem like they wish they were meant to go to lunch somewhere else. The cooks put too much chicken salad on the sandwiches. A huge ice cream scoop of it, over a slippery tomato. They don't bother spreading it out. And the whole thing slides off.

Last weekend, she asked me to come and visit her there. It was near the end of her shift, and I was one of only four tables. Across the room, there was a man wearing a tee shirt that said ABSTINENCE: 99.9% EFFECTIVE, with a picture of Jesus and the Virgin Mary. When his iced tea was empty, he sucked at the crushed ice through a straw. He sucked out all the liquid the ice was willing to give up. When no refill came, he snapped his fingers. Aunt Amy probably didn't like him on account of his shirt, and she walked over without her iced tea pitcher and told him that was rude. They got in an argument, and the manager ended up giving him his glass of tea for free. Another table sitting next to me sent back their fries because they were too crispy. I watched Aunt Amy behind the counter. She sneezed into her hand, and then when she thought no one was looking, she subtly touched the new plate of fries. It surprised me that someone who believes in Jesus would do this. But it's a hard job.

Homecoming is this weekend (thank god I'll be with Dad), but Aunt Amy saw it marked on the school calendar, so she knew it was coming up. After her lunch shift she wanted to give me a little pep talk. She said that if I was going to be attending the school dance, she wanted to remind me to use good judgment. Then she started on a lecture about not dancing too close. "Make sure you leave some room for the Holy Ghost." You might be laughing at that, but although she tried to smile at me when she said it, I don't think it was meant to be a joke. She reminded me of the pitfalls of sin, and then asked me if I wanted to go shopping. Even though I need a dress, I didn't want to go with her, because she disapproves of spaghetti straps, and all good homecoming dresses have them. I knew I'd end up with a church dress that I would feel guilty for not wearing. So I told her I had homework. Then she gave me $20 to shop with, but I didn't want to tell her that you can't buy a dress with that much. So I took the $20, and even though I felt bad, I figured I could get Nutter Butters for pretty much the rest of the year with it.

Today at lunch before I went to buy one, I looked for Natalie and Hannah. When I saw them, Natalie was giving Hannah a single tulip. Hannah took the tulip and put it to her face as if to smell it, even though tulips don't smell. Natalie giggled and said, "Will you go to homecoming with me, dah-ling?"

Hannah dropped the tulip on her tray. She looked at Natalie. "What do you mean?" she asked with an edge in her voice.

Natalie said, "I just think the whole thing of dances is so stupid. I thought we should have fun with it, you know, not worry about boys or anything. We can wear flapper dresses and eat at the fondue place first." Her voice went up at the end, in a sort of hopeful way. Then she turned to me quickly and said, "Laurel will go with us, too. Sorry I didn't bring you a flower, Laurel. I didn't know what kind you like. I stole the tulip from my neighbor's yard. Mr. Dickie came out and started yelling, so I had to run. He chased me down half a block before his asthma kicked in."

I tried to laugh.

Hannah said, "Laurel is going with Evan Friedman. Remember? Anyway, Kasey's going to take me. I talked him into it. He's borrowing his dad's convertible. But I guess you can come with us if you want."

Natalie looked annoyed. "Why would he want to go to a high school dance? He's, like, nineteen."

Hannah gave a sly smile and said, "I told him if he came, afterward I'd give him an extra good surprise."

I could see then that something in Natalie got crushed. The look on her face was like when you just finished making a waffle in the morning, and you got it out of the toaster, and you put on the butter and the syrup and had it cut along the lines into square inches, and you were carrying it into your room, so excited, but then you dropped it facedown on the floor. And you felt so sad about the whole thing, you didn't even want to make another.

Natalie just said, "Okay, that's cool. Actually, someone asked me, anyway."

Hannah looked at her and said, "Who?"

Natalie looked down at the floor, and then back up at Hannah. Her cheeks were red. If she was angry or embarrassed, I don't know. But it was their moment. So I mumbled something about Nutter Butters and went away.

As I was going up to get in the lunch line, I saw Sky standing there. I started to walk the other way. But I turned back and stood in line behind him. I stared at the back of his head and didn't say anything for a while. I kept opening my mouth, but nothing came out. Finally, I said, "Hey."

He turned around, surprised to see me. "Oh. Hi."

"Hey," I said again, stupidly.

"What's up?"

I was trying to think of how to answer that question again, such a terrible question. Instead I said, "So, are you going to the dance this weekend?"

"I don't know. Are you?"

"Going to the dance?"

He looked at me like, *Yes, obviously*.

"I don't know, either." Then I said, "Well, yeah, I guess I am. Someone asked me."

Sky tensed up, I swear the muscles in his arm got the teensiest bit harder, and he said, "Who?"

"Just this guy." It was too quiet. So I continued. "But I don't even know if I want to go anyway. I mean, it's like that kind of thing that's never what it's supposed to be, you know?"

Suddenly, out of nowhere, Sky said, "Your sister was May, huh?"

I felt frozen. How did he know that? No one here has asked me about May, except Mrs. Buster. Maybe Sky had friends who went to May's old school. He's a junior, the same age as her. Or maybe he went there before he transferred. It wouldn't be impossible.

"Yeah," I finally replied.

"You look like her."

"Really?" I felt like someone was waving sparklers inside my chest. I could feel hot stars jumping off of them. He thought I looked like her.

I never want to talk about May with any of my friends. But now, with Sky, it felt good almost, like he was part of her secret world. And he didn't ask any questions he shouldn't. He just said, "Yeah. You have her eyes."

Then we were quiet again, until he said, "I don't know if I'll show up."

"At the dance?"

"Yeah."

"You should."

"Why?"

"Just 'cause. What if it does actually turn out like it's supposed to? You know, like Christmas when you were little and it didn't make you sad."

Sky laughed a little and said, "You think a lot about that, don't you? How it's supposed to be."

Before I could answer, Sky was at the front of the line. He ordered his pizza, which came in a tinfoil triangle. When it was my turn, Sky looked like he didn't know if he should wait for me or carry his shiny pizza away. I looked at him as the lunch lady tapped her fingers impatiently on the counter. I was holding up the line. I knew there was something to say. But he just smiled, a smile that seemed to understand, before he walked away.

Yours,
Laurel

Dear Kurt,

The night of the dance, I ate cold potato pancakes with Dad. That sounds sort of depressing, but I didn't mind really. The only thing is I didn't have a dress. I tried on a few old ones, but they were all stupid and frilly and didn't fit right anymore. I wanted to look pretty, in case Sky came and saw me. So I went into May's room. I opened the closet, which has her cut-off-at-the-neck sweaters folded on the shelves with the arms behind them and her stuffed animals stuffed into the back, and I found the dress, the red silk one. I tried it on. It fit almost right. It was longer on me, and the open top hung lower on my chest (because I don't have that much of one), but I felt almost beautiful. The hem was cut in flowy spikes with sequins on them. I turned around and around until I was dizzy, in a good way. I put on eye shadow until my eyes seemed to smolder.

The bad part was I had to ask Dad to drive me. I think he thought I was lying when I said my date was waiting for me at the dance. I think he felt sorry for me, because he thought I was going alone. I told him that I'd get a ride home later, since I know he likes to go to bed early, but he made sure to say that I could call him if I needed to be picked up. Then he said, "Sweetie, you look beautiful," the way a dad does. I wondered if he remembered it was May's dress.

When I got there, I stood in front of the double doors of the gym, waiting for Evan. He'd texted me that we were supposed to meet at eight thirty. It was 8:43 when he finally came up behind me and grabbed my sides. I let out a little yelp, pretending to be surprised. He was wearing a black shirt and a purple tie.

"Hey. Did I scare you?" he asked. His eyes were red, like he was stoned. I realized that our clothes didn't match at all.

"Yeah. A little."

He looked like he already regretted asking me to the dance, but he tried to cover for it. "Are you ready?" He linked his arm in mine and we walked in. I felt bad for him, having to go with someone who is so not good at this stuff, and I thought I'd try to make the best of it for us both. But I just couldn't make myself say the right things. When he said, "You look pretty," I mumbled, "No, I don't." What I meant, I guess, was that he didn't understand. It was my sister's dress.

We got inside and I wasn't sure exactly what to do. Finally Evan asked if I wanted some punch.

"Sure," I said. He said he'd get some and left me standing alone in the middle of the bright room with the entryway and the picture booth.

I am usually good at finding things to look busy with, but there was nothing. I unstuck a bobby pin from my hair and stuck it back. I could hear a muffled version of "Bad Romance" coming from inside the gym.

Finally, I saw Natalie walk in with this boy Brian, who sits alone at the double lab table in Bio and raises his hand all the time. She had on a floor-length black dress that fit perfectly on her body. Her skin was smooth like usual, with no makeup. Brian trailed behind, wearing a bow tie and too much hair gel. She looked as relieved to see me as I was to see her, and we rushed over to each other.

"Why do people do this?" I asked.

Natalie laughed. "No idea. But I guess we're as stupid as the rest." She pulled out a little flask from her purse and handed it to me. "Schnapps?"

I took a swig. And another. Natalie loved May's dress, and I spun in it for her, and spun again and again. I spun until I was almost happy.

Natalie did a bang-up job of more or less ignoring Brian until Hannah came in. She was wearing satin like most of the girls there, but it looked beautiful on her. Her pale freckled shoulders stood out against the straps of the midnight blue dress. She was holding on to Kasey's arm. It was the first time I'd seen him. He's short, and even without heels on, Hannah must be taller than him. But he's made of big stocky muscles, the kind that you only get if you work really hard on them. As she maneuvered him over to say hi to us, all of a sudden Natalie pulled Brian closer. Clearly Hannah didn't feel the way we did about the dance, or she didn't let it show, or her piña coladas weren't virgin, or all of the above. Because she was a perfect girl on a college boy's arm, chatting and giggling at a private triumph, and finally dragging Kasey off to the photo booth.

When Evan finally returned and handed me a half-drunk glass of punch, I didn't ask what had taken so long. He shifted from foot to foot, looking unhappy about the company. Finally he said, "We're here to dance, yeah?" Then he reached his hand out to me. "Shall we?" I tried to be a good date and followed him into the gym. I was high enough on the swigs of Schnapps that I had stopped caring that this was not the way my first dance was supposed to be. They were playing a Jay-Z song. Evan was mouthing along, except he sang the real "Can I get a fuck-you" lyrics over the bleeped-out "Can I get a what-what" version they had on. He thrust around from foot to foot and put his hands halfway into his pants.

I tried to go with Evan's rhythm, but when it came down to it, he had none, and when he put his hands on me and tried to move me around, all I wanted was to wriggle away. Evan kept thrusting his hips, and the more I danced away from him, the more he tried to grab me, and the harder I danced away. As the song was ending, I saw him watching Britt, his ex, across the room. She was blowing pink bubble gum that matched her pink satin dress and shifting from foot to foot. He wanted her satin and watermelon. Evan probably asked me to the dance 'cause he thought I'd say yes, and then he'd have someone to make Britt jealous with. I should have been mad, I guess, but it didn't matter.

I said, "You should go ask Britt to dance."

He looked at me, caught off guard.

"Look," I said, "she's staring at you, too."

"Are you sure?" Evan asked.

"Yeah," I said. "She totally is. Go for it. Anyway, I'm kind of thirsty." And I walked off.

I went to the punch table and took a long time choosing one of the identical glasses. I put the pink stuff to my lips and let the ice clink on my teeth before I chewed it. And do you know what happened then? They started playing "The Lady in Red." I saw Evan across the room, dancing with Britt now. I must have been a good ruse, because they looked like they couldn't get close enough. Her watermelon gum had probably made its way into his mouth. I saw Hannah, dancing with Kasey. She looked over his shoulder at Natalie, who was dancing with Brian. Natalie was looking back. Hannah blew her a kiss. Natalie turned her face away. But then she changed her mind and reached her hand and caught the kiss from the air behind her. She put it softly to her lips. But Hannah's face, by then, was hidden in Kasey's shoulder.

I couldn't watch them anymore. I stared into my punch

glass. I picked a sequin off the hem of my dress and folded it between my fingers. I licked my lips and tasted the crayon color of the lipstick I had on. I thought of May wearing this dress at her first dance, brown curls all falling around her face, gliding across the floor in someone's arms. I tried not to cry.

Then, out of nowhere, Sky came up beside me. "Hi," he said.

I turned. He still smelled of the clean cold of the night outside. He was wearing his leather jacket over suit pants and a button-up shirt.

"Hi."

"You're wearing red," he said. "Like the song."

"It's my sister's dress."

Sky smiled a little half smile that made me feel like he understood what this meant. He held out his hand to me.

The touch of his fingers sent everything that was electrical in us toward each other. And then we were dancing. The bleachers with their wood smell, the perfume of everyone, the twinkle of the white Christmas lights, all of it came together to build a place that was just for us. Somewhere I'd never been before.

I wished I could stay forever inside of the song with him, but it was over too fast. Sky whispered, "Thank you for the dance," and I watched him start to disappear into the crowd.

But then he turned back. "I'm going to get out of here," he said. "Do you want a ride?"

"Sure." I could hardly hide the excitement in my voice. I

felt giddy as I followed him out of the gym, just as they started playing the electric slide song. I caught Natalie's eye as I was leaving and waved bye. She grinned back at me, because she could see I was with Sky. As we walked through the parking lot, I quickly texted Dad that I was getting a ride home. I told him good night and sweet dreams, and that I wouldn't be late.

When we got in his truck, Sky turned on the stereo, and "About a Girl" came on. It was the beginning of your *MTV Unplugged* album. A little part of me thought that maybe Sky had planned that on purpose, because he knows that we both love you. Maybe he cared that much.

We sat there in silence for a moment, listening to the song. I wanted to think of something to say out loud. Finally I said, "It's like part of what's so great is he's not afraid of his voice."

"You mean Kurt?"

"Mmm-hmm."

Sky turned to look at me, his eyes amused. "Are you?"

"Afraid of my voice?" I laughed, nervous. "Yeah, I guess."

Then Sky tilted his head to the side a little and got more serious. "I think we all are. With Kurt, it's more like he just faces the fear, you know?"

"Yeah," I said. "You're right."

"I think that's why he's so *loud*. I mean, he has to be. Because he's staring the monster in the face, and the only thing to do is fight back."

"Do you think," I asked, "do you think he won?"

"The obvious answer is no, 'cause he died. But I think he did in a way. I mean, listen." Sky turned up the stereo. "We have *this* now. And we'll always have it."

I knew then that I was right when I used to sit by the fence watching Sky and thinking that we were connected somehow.

I pointed ahead, to our exit off of the freeway. "You get off up there," I said. "Rio Grande."

"You live pretty far from school."

"Yeah. I was supposed to go to Sandia, but instead I go in my aunt's district. I live with her part-time." I paused a moment. "May went to Sandia . . ." I said, trailing off. I waited to see if Sky would say he went there, too. Did he? I wanted to ask him how he knew May, but I was afraid of breaking the spell.

He just said, "I transferred to West Mesa, too. Only two more years left, and then I'm free."

"What are you going to do after that?" I asked.

Sky shrugged. "I don't know. It's funny, if you'd asked me that at the beginning of high school, I'd have told you my whole plan of escape, all laid out." He paused. "Pre-law at Princeton or Brown. Amherst, maybe. Somewhere far away, with snow." I could tell by the tone of his voice that it was an ambition he'd created for himself, not one handed down by his parents. "But now," he said, "well, I don't exactly have the grades for that anymore, or the permanent record. I don't know . . . maybe it wasn't meant to be." He was quiet for another moment. "I guess I sort of want to be a writer now." He glanced at me.

"But it's not like I've ever written anything. And that's not something I tell most people."

"You'd be a really great writer," I said.

"Oh yeah? How do you know?"

"By the way you talk. Like when you said that Kurt is so loud because he's staring the monster in the face, and how you've got to fight back."

Sky smiled a little bit, like he was happy that I'd really been listening.

I pointed ahead. "Oh! Turn left up here." We'd almost missed my street.

When we parked outside of my house, we were quiet a moment, my breath clutched in my chest. I watched the sequins on my dress catch the glow from the street lamp. And then I looked up at Sky. He reached out and took my face in his hands. "You're beautiful," he whispered. I closed my eyes and let him pull me in. It was a perfect first kiss, like a gust of wind that swept through me, taking my breath away and letting me breathe again all at once. A kiss to come alive in.

When Sky finally got out of the car and opened my door, I was longing for more. He was so calm. In control. Unlike me, whose everything was shaking.

"So," Sky asked with a little smile, "did it turn out the way it was supposed to?"

"Yeah, it did," I whispered.

"Good," he said, and kissed me softly on the forehead.

As his truck pulled off, I went inside as quietly as I could, carrying the secret of the night as I tiptoed over the creaking wood floors, past the door of Dad's room that used to be Mom and Dad's. Past May's room. The house felt haunted, like only I understood the way all of our shadows, the ones we'd left, had seeped into the wood and stained it. How the floor and the walls were full of our bodies at certain moments. I went to my dresser and stood in front of the mirror. I unpinned my hair. I wiped away my lipstick onto the back of my hand. I looked at my face until it was only shapes. I kept looking, until something reformed. And I swear I saw May there. Looking back at me. Glowing from her first dance.

I got in bed and played "The Lady in Red" off of her CD. I thought of Sky's hands pulling me closer. How he had said that I was beautiful. And I knew that he had seen her in me. I skipped back the song again and again until my hand was too tired to move. Before I slept, I felt like I was breathing for both of us. My sister and me.

Yours,
Laurel

Dear Amelia,

I think I am going to be you for Halloween, which is coming up in a little less than two weeks. I'm excited about it, so I am getting my costume ready. I don't want to be a ghost or a stupid sexy cat. I want to be something that I really want to be, and you are like bravery to me.

Halloween is one of my favorite holidays. Christmas and the others can end up making you sad, because you know you should be happy. But on Halloween you get to become anything that you want to be.

I remember the first year Mom and Dad let us go trick or treating alone. I was still seven, and May had just turned ten. She convinced them that double digits meant she was grown-up enough to shepherd me along our block. We ran up to each house, the fairy wings we carried on our backs flapping behind us, ahead of the kids who had their parents in tow. Every time a front door would open, May would put her arm around me, and it felt like she would always protect me. When we got home, our noses were ice-cold, and our paper bags, decorated with cotton ghosts and tissue paper witches, were full. We emptied our candy onto the living room floor to count it up, and Mom brought us hot cider. I remember the feeling of that night so much, because it was like you could be free and safe at once.

I think that this year we are going to a party that Hannah's college boyfriend, Kasey, is having. I told Sky about it, and I hope he might go, too. It's been one week since homecoming. I don't think he wants to have a girlfriend, because of what Kristen said about how he just "has girls" sometimes. I try to remind myself of this so that I don't scare him off. But to tell the truth, I've never liked someone so much. Since the dance,

I've caught him watching me a few times at lunch. And I watch back. Then yesterday, when I was getting stuff from my locker, I closed the door, and there he was, out of nowhere. My body instantly remembered kissing him. The feeling almost knocked me over.

"What's up?" he said, just smoothly, the way he does.

"Um . . ." I was thinking fast. I was *not* going to say nothing. "It's almost Halloween."

"Indeed."

"What are you going to be?"

Sky laughed. "I usually just put on a white sheet and pass out candy to trick-or-treaters with my mom."

"Well, we're going to this one party, because Hannah's seeing this guy or whatever. It's a college party, and, I don't know, you should come . . ."

"You're going to a college party?" He sounded vaguely disapproving.

"Yeah."

"Well, I guess maybe I better. I don't want you getting into any trouble." Sky said it like he was mostly teasing, but meant it a tiny bit.

I tried to keep myself from giggling. "I'll send you the address, you know, in case."

When I told Natalie and Hannah about this at lunch, they were eating Halloween candy early, and Hannah said, in the middle of a handful of candy corn, "That means he wants to do you."

Natalie hit her shoulder and said, "Han-nah!"

"What? That doesn't mean she's gonna. Laurel's a good girl, can't you tell?"

My face got all hot.

Then Hannah said, "Sleepover at my house tomorrow, are you in?"

I was so happy, because the invitation meant that Hannah thinks I "get it," like she said Natalie does. That now we were real enough friends for me to go to her house. In my head, I started calculating how I'd get permission. I'd still be with Aunt Amy, before I switched to Dad's on Sunday.

Finally, as a last resort, I decided to call Mom and ask her to tell Aunt Amy that she should let me spend the night at my friend's house.

"What friend?" she asked.

"Hannah," I said. "I always hang out with her. My friend Natalie's going, too. Dad already lets me spend the night with them."

"What's Hannah like?" Mom asked.

She could probably hear the shrug in my voice. "I don't know. She's just normal."

"What does 'normal' mean?"

"She's cool and nice. What is this, twenty questions?"

"I just wanted to know a little bit about your life now," Mom said, sounding hurt. "Who your friends are."

I felt bad, but I couldn't help thinking that if she really wanted to know, she'd be here.

It was quiet for a moment, and then Mom laughed a little. "Do you remember when we used to play that game with your sister in the car on the way home from school?"

She meant twenty questions. "Yeah," I said. I couldn't help laughing a little, too. May was great at that game, like she was at everything. She always thought of something super specific. Instead of just a train whistle, it was the train whistle from the lullaby that Mom would sing us. And she added her own category, too—in addition to a person, place, or thing, you could also think of a feeling. Her feeling wouldn't just be something like "excited." It would be the exact feeling of waking up on your birthday.

"I'm thinking of a feeling right now," I said to Mom.

"A feeling that's more happy or more sad?" Mom asked.

"More sad," I said.

Mom asked a few more questions, but in the end she didn't guess, so I had to tell her that the feeling was missing her.

And of course, after all of that, she told Aunt Amy to let me go.

Hannah's house is outside of town, in the red dirt hills. Natalie's mom dropped me and Natalie off, and Hannah brought us upstairs to say hi to her grandpa. When she knocked on his bedroom door, he came out to the hallway. He smiled at us, but Hannah had to yell when she told him my name, because he doesn't hear very well. Her grandma was sleeping, and after we met him, her grandpa went back into his room to watch TV.

Then we went wandering in the forest behind the house, and Natalie and Hannah smoked cigarettes. You can walk to the river through the cottonwood trees covered in brambles and webs. The leaves have all turned yellow now, so the light looks golden even when the sun just leaks through the clouds. But when we started to get close to the sound of the river, it made me start to breathe too fast. I saw May that night in a flash, before my brain shut off and wanted to blank out. So while Natalie and Hannah walked to the riverbank, I hung back, pretending to get lost in looking at a spiderweb or something.

When we got back from our walk, we went to visit Hannah's horse named Buddy. Buddy was actually her grandma's horse, but since her grandma isn't doing well, Hannah takes care of him, and she says Buddy is more like hers now. She says that Buddy is her favorite one in the family. She also takes care of Earl, their donkey, since she doesn't trust her brother to be nice to the animals. To tell the truth, Hannah's brother, Jason, is scary. He's trying to train himself for the Marines, so he goes on obstacle courses he made for himself near the river, with old tires and ropes and things. He used to be a football player, but then he tore his shoulder, and he hasn't been able to play since. He should have gone to college this year, but he didn't. I don't know if it's because he couldn't get in now that he can't play football or because their grandparents are old and can't really watch after Hannah. I think her brother thinks he's supposed to be like her parent, but he's bad at it. For groceries he only buys Vienna sausages in a can and grocery store–brand sour cream and onion chips. Even though their family isn't poor or anything, maybe part of why Hannah wants to have a job is so that she can pick her own things to eat, without having to ask Jason. She likes to eat spinach out of the bag and Doritos (the real brand) and Luna Bars.

When Jason went for one of his workouts, which Hannah says take at least a couple hours, we decided to take Hannah's grandma's old van and practice driving. Natalie and Hannah both turned fifteen at the beginning of the year and have their learner's permits. Natalie went first. She rolled the van down the dirt road, and Hannah stood up and stuck her head out of the sunroof and screamed, "Woohoo!" which I guess made Natalie want to go faster, so she did. The thing is, she went off the road when she swerved to miss a bird. Probably the bird would have flown away at the last minute, but I guess Natalie got nervous. So the car wheels stuck in the soft sand. Natalie revved the gas harder, but the wheels just spun farther into the ground.

Hannah kept saying, "We have to get it out. My brother can't know." She sounded terrified. She yelled for Natalie to push the gas harder, and Natalie was all shaky because Hannah was so upset, and then Hannah made Natalie and me get out, and she went behind the wheel and tried to make the car go herself. Natalie and I pushed from outside, but it wouldn't move. It wouldn't move at all. Hannah started crying, and she

yelled at Natalie, "Why did you do that? Are you stupid?"
Natalie's cheeks and her chest turned red. I know it's because
she was trying not to cry, too. Eventually there was nothing
to do but to walk back and tell Jason, who by now would be
done with his workout.

Hannah told us to wait outside when she went into the
kitchen. But we followed her and watched from the hallway.
Jason wasn't just angry. He was really, truly mad. His face was
red, and he was screaming. He called Hannah a lot of bad
names. I've never seen Hannah like that before. She laughs at
everything and does whatever she wants, like she's not afraid
of anything. Like nothing can hurt her. But this was different.
She was crying and she kept saying, "Please, Jason."

I kept trying to think of a way to protect her, but I was
scared frozen. Natalie must have felt the same. She kept whispering that she hated him, and that she wished she could
punch him in the face, and those kinds of things. Finally
Natalie went into the kitchen and stood next to Hannah. Hannah looked at her like she wished she would disappear. But
Natalie said, in a very soft voice, "Please don't get mad at her,
it was my fault."

Jason glared, but his voice got a little calmer as he said,
"Like hell it was. That's her dying grandmother's car." Then
he threw his drink across the counter and he told Hannah,
"Clean it up," and he walked out. I guess he went to go get the
car out with the tractor hitch.

We didn't feel like staying in the house anymore after that, so what we did is we stayed in the barn that night. We got supplies while Jason was gone—flashlights and sleeping bags and Doritos and a bottle of this red wine that we took from her grandparents' cabinet, because Hannah said that it had been there for years. It tasted old, like shoe leather and fall leaves and dusty apples. Hannah sang songs, Patsy Cline and Reba McEntire and Amy Winehouse. Natalie and I closed our eyes and listened. Sometimes Natalie sang along. When we were falling asleep in the loft, I heard Natalie whisper, "I'm sorry." And she held Hannah, I think, all night. The hay in the barn smelled sweet, as if it were still growing in the rain.

I understood then, at least a little bit, why Hannah always has a boyfriend or sometimes more than one. I think she needs people to love her and give her attention. Her grandparents don't seem like they can be there for her, and her brother is terrible to her. I want her to see that Natalie could love her for real. I think that deep down, Hannah must know that, but I'm not sure if she can imagine what it would be like. Maybe part of her would rather have Natalie as a best friend, because best friends don't break up or anything like that. And even though it shouldn't be this way, a relationship like theirs still makes you different in some people's minds. Maybe Hannah isn't ready yet to stand up for it. Because once you're afraid of one thing, you can get scared of a lot of stuff. In school, the teachers tell Hannah, "Don't waste your talent." But she doesn't turn in her papers or anything. She acts annoyed that they care about her, like she doesn't trust it. Even if she can laugh at everything and have as many boyfriends as she wants, I think Hannah must be afraid like I get afraid, the way I did when I heard the river yesterday, the way I do when I don't even know what the shadow is, but I feel it breathing.

Yours,
Laurel

Dear Amelia,

I have to tell you about Halloween. My costume was a big hit! Everyone at the party truly loved it. I explained to all of them that I wasn't dead, only somewhere still circling in the air.

Natalie was Vincent van Gogh, which meant she taped a bandage over her ear to make it look like it was cut off and splattered paint all over her clothes. Hannah was Little Bo Peep, which meant she braided her hair in pigtails and wore a tight blue dress. Hannah's boyfriend, Kasey, was a sheep, because she made the costume for him. He looked pretty funny with his little fuzzy cotton ears and his neck and shoulders that are so big they blend into each other. When we walked in tonight, to the house that he shares with four other guys, Hannah jumped on him, and he picked her up. He called Hannah

"Jailbait" as a nickname, like "How's my little Jailbait?" which made his friends laugh. Hannah laughed, too, although Natalie did not.

Some other people at the party dressed up as characters from Candy Land—Queen Frostine, Princess Lolly, and Lord Licorice. I thought this was the coolest. Kasey and his friends knew how to throw a party right. Even though their house is pretty dirty, it wasn't just the typical college guy party with a keg of beer. For Halloween, they'd made it special. There were bowls of M&M's everywhere, and hot chocolate that was spiked. I kept looking around for Sky, wondering if he'd come, wondering if one of the people behind the masks across the room was him, but when I checked the way they walked, none of them were right. I decided I needed to distract myself from looking for him, so I went bobbing for apples. May and I used to fill up a washtub and put apples in it and practice, any time of year. I was always great at it, even when I still had my baby teeth.

I started bobbing, and the boy dressed as Lord Licorice bobbed down next to me. The top of his feathered hat kept bumping my aviator cap. And sometimes, when we'd look up at the same time, his dark eyes seemed like they were trying to make holes in me. I would let them burn until the holes got too deep, and then I'd put my head down again. When I finally got an apple and came up triumphantly, Lord Licorice was still bobbing, and I saw Sky standing there, right above me. I had the apple in my mouth when he said hi.

Normally I would have felt embarrassed or maybe guilty that I was bobbing for apples next to Lord Licorice, but I was feeling very brave dressed as you, and very cool. So I put down my pilot glasses as I took a bite out of the apple in my mouth.

I said, "Let's go flying." I guess at that point I might have been a little bit drunk, too.

Sky said, "The ceiling might get in our way."

So I took his hand and pulled him out the front door. And then I started running. Sky stopped following near the edge of the yard, but I ran down the street with my arms out like wings, laughing. I didn't care. I was happy. By the time I got to the end of the block and onto the next one, I was above the earth. I could see the treetops, I swear. I could see the streets crisscrossing. The houses were like toys, and pretty soon the whole earth had become a map.

When I finally landed, Sky was standing there, waiting for me at the edge of the yard, which just a moment ago was only a tiny square. I forgot to mention that Sky was dressed as a zombie rocker, which just meant he looked cool in his leather jacket, like he usually does, and had drawn some crisscrosses on his face with what looked like black marker.

"How was the flight?" he asked.

"You should have come," I said, out of breath. "I almost made it around the world."

"Who was that pirate boy in there?"

"He wasn't a pirate, he was Lord Licorice. Didn't you ever play Candy Land?"

"It looked like he thought you were the candy." His voice sounded disapproving, in a way that I liked. It meant that he was protective of me, or maybe that he wanted me to himself.

I could feel myself blush, and I hoped he couldn't see in the dark. I fidgeted with my aviator cap. "We were just bobbing for apples." I put my aviator glasses on over my eyes. "Anyway, you're the one who doesn't want to be my boyfriend."

"How do you know?"

I shrugged. "You're not like that."

"What if you're wrong? What if I am?"

"You are?"

There was a moment of quiet. "Well, I am now."

"So am I," I said softly, and I fell into him so he'd catch me, a swoony kind of fall where you don't hold your body up, and I laughed. He lifted the glasses back off my face, and we kissed, and I felt his cold hands slip under my shirt, onto my stomach. I felt his hands warmer on my back, and I felt his lips on my neck, and I felt like I'd landed in my body for the first time. Against his hands, it was something new to me. Sky made me feel clean, a first-snow kind of clean that covered everything. I remembered how it was being above the trees, which were making a good sound, a rustling sound, a leaves-turned-brown-and-ready-to-fall sound. "Listen," I said.

Yours,
Laurel

Dear River Phoenix,

Maybe this is weird to say, but when I was younger, before I'd ever kissed, sometimes I'd imagine kissing you. Now that I kiss in real life, I'm happy to say that it's a lot like I'd hoped it would be.

My boyfriend, Sky—my first boyfriend—he is perfect to me. It's been two weeks since the Halloween party where we got together. And now, we've gotten to kissing everywhere. Kissing in the alleyway between classes, when no one is there, and the sun makes spots in the bright middle of my eyelids. Kissing in his truck that smells like thousand-year-old leather. Kissing when it's dark and I crawl out of my window. (I've gotten good at it at both houses. At Aunt Amy's my window pushes up, but at Dad's I have to unhook my screen, the way that I used to see May do.) I love these middle-of-the-nights with Sky the best. Everything else is sleeping, and the whole world feels like our secret. It reminds me of the feeling I used to get when May and I would sneak into the yard to collect ingredients for fairy spells.

For the first time in forever, it feels like I have magical powers—the ones that May taught me about when we were little. With Sky, I can make the scary stuff disappear. We walk through the neighborhood after dark, and our shadows stand on top of each other, stretching across the whole street. We kiss, and I feel that if my shadow could stay inside of his, then he could eclipse everything that I don't want to remember. I can get lost in the things about him that are beautiful.

Sky reminds me of you a bit, honestly. How he's a boy, and strong, and the air makes way for him when he walks through it. But also how there is something fragile like moths inside of him, something fluttering. Something trying desperately to crowd toward a light. May was a real moon who everyone flocked to. But even if I am only Sky's street lamp, I don't mind. It's enough to be what he moves toward. I love to feel the wings beat.

Last night we walked to the park, and we kissed with my back pressed up against the cold bars of the jungle gym. We stopped for breath, and his bottom lip fell a little crooked to the left, like it does. I whispered, "Can we go to your house?"

He sounded uncertain. "I don't know if that's a good idea."

"We don't have to go in. I just want to see it." I didn't tell him that I already had, the night that I drove by with Tristan and Kristen at two a.m. I wanted to be there with him.

"I don't think you understand," he said finally. "My mom isn't really . . . like other moms."

"How do you mean?"

On the outside, Sky got tougher. "She just has her own way of doing things." Then he said, "Like, she sings lullabies to the flowers in the middle of the night."

"Oh. Well, that's okay."

"They're dead now," Sky added. "Her marigolds are. She sings to them anyway."

"Maybe we could plant some bulbs for her. Tulips, or something that will grow in the spring."

Sky wasn't so sure about it, but I promised him we could just stay in the front yard and we wouldn't have to go inside, and he finally agreed. So tonight, I snuck out again to meet him, and we drove to his house to pull up the dried-out marigolds and put in tulip bulbs. Earlier today I'd gone into our shed, where Mom used to keep her gardening stuff, and found some stacked in a box with newspaper between them. It was a new moon night, and we worked in the dark, wearing our jackets. As we were patting down the last ones, our nails with dirt under them, we looked up at each other, and our eyes touched, closer than you can get even with skin.

That's when the front door opened. It was his mother, standing there in her bathrobe, holding a watering can.

"Mom?" Sky asked wearily. "What are you doing?" I think he'd been hoping that she would stay asleep and he wouldn't have to introduce us yet.

"I wanted to help," she said innocently.

Then she turned to me and looked me in the face, as if she'd just noticed that I was there. Her expression was warm. "And who is this?" she asked Sky.

"This is Laurel," Sky said.

"We, um, we planted tulip bulbs," I said, "so they'll grow in the spring."

Sky's mom smiled and nodded, as if planting flowers in the middle of the night were normal. "Thank you, dear."

She started to walk up and down the rows, sprinkling the dirt. She sang softly as she went, something about horses in the sun.

"It's important to sing to them," she said when she was done. "So that they know you are there." Then she took her watering can and set it near the front door and just walked back inside.

"So that was my mom," Sky said.

"She . . . she seems really nice."

"You mean crazy."

"Well, no. But what's, um, what—"

Sky's voice turned hard. "That's just the way she is."

"Oh."

I reached out and put my arms around his body. It was then that I could feel that the moths in him, with their wings so paper-thin, will never be near enough to the light. They will always want to be nearer—to be inside of it. It was then that I could feel the lost thing in him. I wanted to put my hand on his chest, against his heart, and touch all the way inside his beating. I wanted to find him. But he stepped back, and his bottom lip, crooked just a little to the left, straightened out.

I felt like there were a million questions and answers and questions all stuck in the back of my throat. But I couldn't speak from everything being stuck there. I stopped.

"Sky?"

"What?"

I looked at him. And I meant everything. "Nothing," I said, and then I paused. "Those flowers are going to be really pretty." The cold night sent a shiver up my spine, and we kissed again.

Yours,
Laurel

Dear John Keats,

Today we got our report cards from first quarter. I had all As, except in two classes. In PE, I had a C-, not because I can't run fast, but because Hannah and I pretended to forget our gym clothes so many times. And in English I had a B, even though I've gotten As on all of my essays. The reason for this is that I don't talk in class, because I hate the way Mrs. Buster looks at me, so my participation grade was low. And also that I had a missing assignment—a letter to a dead person. It's one little assignment, and I wish I had just made myself fake it, but I couldn't. I mean, my letters are actual letters to the people I am writing to. Not to Mrs. Buster. But there is one way to make Dad happy, and also for Aunt Amy to feel sure that I am free of sin, and that's to get all As. I tried to make sure that my grades were good so that no one would have any reason to worry or ask questions. I hope this is close enough.

Mrs. Buster called me over to her desk after class today and asked why I hadn't done the letter assignment, even after she gave me two extensions. She said I should be an A student. And I tried to explain that I did do it, I just couldn't show her. But she said the point of an assignment is to turn it in. I tried to explain that I thought that letters were actually very private.

She looked at me funny. Then she said, "Laurel, you are a very talented girl," but she said it like it was not a good thing.

I shrugged.

Then she said, "I notice that you don't speak up in class much."

I haven't really talked at all, actually, since the second week of class when I said something about Elizabeth Bishop. I just pass notes now with Natalie, or look out the window. I pay attention only when we are reading poems.

I shrugged again.

"Laurel, I just want to encourage you . . ." She paused, like she wasn't quite sure what she wanted to encourage me to do.

Then she said, "May was special, too, like you."

I almost smiled at her. She said that I was like May.

But her big bug eyes started bugging out at me, like what she saw when she saw us was a tragedy. "I just don't want you to waste your talent." She paused again. "I don't want you to go down the same road that May did."

And then I was so angry that everything in my body clenched together. I didn't know what "road" she thought May went down, or if she was trying to say that's why she died. She wouldn't know. No one did. She wasn't there. No one was, no one but me. I was so angry that if my throat hadn't been clenched too tight, I might have screamed at her. If she felt so bad about it and all, why didn't she just give me an A? *Grown-ups can be such fakes*, I thought. They are always acting like they are trying to help you, and like they want to take care of you, but really they just want something from you. I wondered what exactly Mrs. Buster wanted. Finally I just nodded and forced myself to mumble something about I'm fine, just that one assignment was really hard.

The thing is, I can't hate Mrs. Buster entirely, because she gives us things like your poems to read. Yesterday we read "Ode on a Grecian Urn." The poem is about an ancient urn with pictures on it. It sounds like it would be boring, but really it's not. I like this part, where you are talking about two lovers, trapped in the instant just before they kiss:

> *Fair youth, beneath the trees, thou canst not leave*
> *Thy song, nor ever can those trees be bare;*
> *Bold Lover, never, never canst thou kiss,*
> *Though winning near the goal—yet, do not grieve;*
> *She cannot fade, though thou hast not thy bliss,*
> *For ever wilt thou love, and she be fair!*

The boy and the girl beneath the trees, they will forever be frozen into exactly what they are just then—they will never touch lips, but they will never lose each other, either. They will be full of possibility, immune to whatever sorrow might follow.

It's like that, almost, when you look at any picture. Like this picture framed on my desk in my room, of May and me as kids in our yard in the summertime. We are swinging on the swing set. I'm just starting to pump, still near the ground, watching her. She's high up, right in the moment before she jumps. But she'll never fall off. It's just after sunset, so the air is still warm. We will stay where the sky is deep electric blue, never turning to night—a place beyond time that can't be touched. When I sit at my desk and see the November sky purring with snow, it doesn't matter. I am seven years old in the summer dusk.

But what I love most is the end of your poem, when the urn talks to us. It says this: *"Beauty is truth, truth beauty,—that is all / Ye know on earth, and all ye need to know."* I keep trying to figure out exactly what you mean, but that sentence is like a circle. If beauty is truth, and if truth is beauty, they are defined by each other, so how do we know the meaning of either? I think that we make our own meanings, by putting ourselves into them. I put the moon over the street lamp into the idea of beauty, and I put the feeling of Sky's heartbeat like moths wings, and I put Hannah's singing voice, and I put the sound of my footsteps running after May along the trail by the river, chasing the sky. And then I start to circle back to the idea of truth. I put how May said her first memory was of holding me after I was born, and how she said she was proud when Mom trusted her to take me in her arms. I put the way Sky's voice sounded when he said he wanted to be a writer, and that he'd never told anyone before. I put Natalie holding Hannah the night we slept in the barn. And I put when May whispered in my ear, "The universe is bigger than anything that can fit into your mind."

Then I just go around and around. And I still don't know how to make sense of the world. But maybe it's okay that it's bigger than what we can hold on to. Because I think that by beauty, you don't just mean something that's pretty. You mean something that makes us human. The urn, you say, is a "friend to man." It will live beyond its generation, and the next ones. And your poem is like that, too. You died almost two hundred years ago, when you were only twenty-five. But the words that you left are still alive.

Yours,
Laurel

Dear Kurt,

I was reading about you tonight, because I wondered what your life was like when you were a kid. You were the center of attention in your family, but after your parents divorced when you were eight, you were orphaned in a way. You were angry.

You wrote on your wall: *I hate Mom, I hate Dad, Dad hates Mom, Mom hates Dad, it simply makes you want to be sad.* You said the pain of their split stayed with you for years. They passed you from one of them to the other. Your dad remarried, and your mom had a boyfriend who was bad to her. By the time you were a teenager, your dad had custody of you, but he passed you off to live with the family of your friend. Then you moved back to live with your mom. When you didn't graduate high school or get a job, she packed your stuff into boxes and kicked you out. You were homeless then. You stayed on other people's couches, or sometimes you slept under a bridge, or in the waiting room of the Grays Harbor Community Hospital—a teenager just becoming a man, sleeping alone in the hospital where you were born eighteen years before.

For me, it's not as bad as it was for you. But I understand how it is when a family falls apart. Tonight is Sunday, the house-switching night. It makes the gloominess of the end of the weekend even worse, putting my things in the little Tinker Bell suitcase that I've had since I was eleven. Mom and Dad bought it for me as a consolation prize when they split up.

It was the summer before May started high school. She would turn fifteen at the beginning of the school year. I was going into seventh grade, about to turn twelve that summer. May and I had just finished the waffles that Mom had made us, and then she and Dad said that we had to have a family meeting. We went to sit outside, and although it was morning, it was already hot. The elm trees were raining their twirling airplane seeds. It was Mom who said it. "Your father and I don't think we can be together any longer. We are going to take some time apart."

It was hard for me to understand at first what this meant. What I remember most is how hard May cried. She cried like someone had died. Dad kept trying to put his hand on her back, and Mom tried to hug her, but she didn't want anyone to touch her. She walked away, into a corner of the yard, and curled up. I pulled out one of my eyelashes and hoped that it would count. I didn't even wish for Mom and Dad to get back together. I wished for May to be okay.

Later that night she said to me, in a voice that was flatter than anything, "I failed."

"What do you mean?"

"I wasn't good enough to keep them together."

I wished I knew what to say back, but I didn't. "You're good enough for me," I said meekly.

May smiled at me, although it was a sad smile. "Thanks, Laurel." And then she added, "At least we always have each other."

I made a decision right then that I would love her even more than I already did—enough to make up for everything else.

After that day our lives turned different. Dad stayed in the house, and Mom moved into an apartment, which sort of made it seem obvious that the split was her idea, although they never explained that part of it. The next month May went to high school, and she started to act happy again, but it wasn't the same. Now she had a new world to be in, and it didn't include any of us. Something invisible took her. She was there, but gone.

We still did one thing together, all four of us, because Mom and Dad said it was important, which was to have family dinners at the Village Inn like we'd done every Friday since we were kids. It was always strained, Mom and Dad talking mostly to us and not to each other. I was quiet, but May told stories, pretending like everything was normal. The waiters would stare at her. Bucky, the Village Inn bear (i.e., the owner dressed in costume), would come over to our table, even though we weren't little kids anymore. May played along and flirted with him. She didn't give Mom and Dad anything to complain about. She was beautiful and smart and she had good grades and talked about lots of friends. But we never saw the girls she used to hang out with in middle school anymore. She was always going out, no one was ever coming over, to either of the houses.

When we were with Dad, he'd let us order stuffed-crust pizza or Chinese takeout, and then he'd retreat to his bedroom. I think he didn't want us to see him being sad. He still tried to have rules, so May had to sneak out when she wanted to stay out late, but it didn't seem difficult for her to get away with it.

Mom tried hard during our weeks with her, almost too

hard. She got strawberry kiwi tea (May's favorite and mine, too), and hung prisms in the windows over the dingy brown carpets in her new apartment, and set up her easels, and took us out to dinner at the 66 Diner, which we probably couldn't afford. Mom would stare at May over milk shakes, her eyes welling with tears, and ask, "Are you mad at me?" May would push her hair back and say, "No," the crack in her voice barely hidden. May couldn't just scream *I hate you* at our parents, the way that some kids can, and know that everything would be okay later. With Mom, it's like if May did that, she would have crumbled. Whenever May wanted to go out with friends, Mom looked sad, like she felt abandoned or something. But she let her go. She gave her a key and didn't say when to be home. She wanted to be the cool parent, I guess, or to make up for things.

At first I'd asked to go with May, but May would say I was still too young. So I'd be left in the apartment. Mom would ask, "How do you think your sister is doing?" Or, "Who's she going out with? There must be a boy, right? Do you think she likes him?" Mom was testing to see if I had the answers. And for a while, I just pretended. I answered the questions as if I knew, even though I didn't.

But the worst was when I'd hear Mom cry herself to sleep. I'd lie awake and stare up at the blank white wall and remember how May used to cast fairy spells when we were little to make it better.

When Aunt Amy dropped me off at Dad's tonight, I thought

about how he's the only one from our used-to-be-normal family who hasn't left me. I wanted to do something nice for him, so I went into his bedroom and brought him some apples. I'd cut them up and spread cream cheese and cinnamon on them. This is something Mom would do, and I thought he'd like it. He was listening to baseball. The season is over, so he plays CDs with broadcasts of the greatest Cubs games that he orders online. This is what he does basically always now, when he's not at work. Maybe it takes him back to the days when he used to play himself. He was really good at it in high school, and then he used to play on a team here just for fun. We loved to go and watch him when we were kids. I remember the smell of the first sweet summer grass, and the big lights that would come on when it started to turn to dusk. If Dad got a hit, we'd jump up in the stands and scream for him.

When I gave him the plate of apples, he smiled. I couldn't tell if his eyes were teary or if it was just the light. Sometimes the light is like that. He turned the game to half volume and said, "You doing okay?"

He was wearing his nightshirt, the one that May and I made him for Father's Day one year. It says *We love you, Dad* in puff paint, with a small and an even smaller handprint, side by side, on the front of it.

"Yeah, Dad."

Then he said, "Who is it that you're always talking to on the phone? Is it a boy?"

"Yeah. Don't worry. He's nice."

"Is he your boyfriend?" Dad asked.

I shrugged. "Yeah," I said. I would never have told Aunt Amy. But I figured there was no point in lying to Dad about it. Maybe he'd think it was a sign that I was well adjusted or something.

"What's his name?" Dad asked.

"Sky."

"What kind of a name is Sky? That's like naming your kid Grass," he teased.

"No it's not. The sky is not at all like the grass!" I laughed.

Then Dad got more serious. "Well, the point is, you know what boys your age are after, don't you? One thing. That's all they think of, night and day."

"Dad, it's not like that."

"It's always like that," he said, only half kidding.

I tried to tell him that he doesn't know and that boys are different now, different from when he was a boy, but in my heart, I didn't mind if Sky was thinking about having sex with me.

Finally Dad said, "Laurel, I understand why you haven't brought your new friends over here. I know that it's hard, and I know your old man isn't much to brag about, either, these days. But if you are going to be hanging out with a boy, I'd like to meet him."

I didn't want to bring Sky to our house, but it made me sad to hear Dad say that he thought he wasn't much to brag about, so I said, "All right."

"And how about those girlfriends you're always with? They're not a bunch of rabble-rousers, are they?" He raised his eyebrows, trying to make a joke of it.

"No, Dad." I tried to laugh. Then I took a deep breath and asked, "When do you think Mom is going to come back?"

He sighed and looked at me. "I don't know, Laurel."

"I wish she hadn't left," I blurted out.

"I know." He frowned. "I know there are things you need a woman to talk about. But at least you have your aunt for now."

"Aunt Amy doesn't know those things, I don't think. I think you should tell Mom she should come home." I looked at him, waiting.

I wondered if he was mad at her still, for moving into that stupid apartment when she did, and then for leaving us again. I saw him start to tip over with pain, and I regretted saying anything. He sighed the kind of sigh that makes you wonder how he ever got that much air into his lungs to let out, and I understood that he couldn't help Mom being gone any more than I could.

Where Dad grew up, life made sense. His parents still live on their same farm in Iowa where he used to wake up at the crack of dawn to do the chores. He always said he loved the smell of alfalfa in the morning. When he was twenty-one, he rode away on his motorcycle, stopping in different towns and picking up odd jobs, mostly in construction, then moving on when he was ready. He said that he thought that the world might have more in store, and he'd gone out to find it. But mostly he had loved to tell how it all changed the day he met Mom. How he'd met her and understood, suddenly, why loving somebody and building a family could be enough.

I think I might have been starting to show tears without meaning to, because Dad leaned over and gave me a knuckle-rub on the head, which meant the conversation was over. It's more talking than we ever do these days, anyway.

I remembered then how Dad would sing me and May a lullaby at night, after he'd cleaned himself up from work, and I could smell the spicy cologne still on his cheeks. He'd sing:

> *"This land is your land, this land is my land*
> *From California, to the New York Island*
> *From the redwood forest, to the Gulf Stream waters*
> *This land was made for you and me."*

When he'd sing that song, each place was like a mystery that I would one day discover. It made me feel the world was huge and sparkling and full of things to explore. And I belonged in it, with him and Mom and May. And now, Mom is actually all the way in California. And May is nowhere.

Yours,
Laurel

Dear Jim Morrison,

At Fallfest, there is a band that plays your songs. Everyone crowds into a park near the foot of the mountains the weekend right after Thanksgiving. When May and I were kids, we would get excited for it every year. There are tents with crafts, and booths with Indian fry bread and roasted chiles, and booths with ladies selling dried red corn for decoration and pies. But once it gets dark and colder, all anyone wants is the music. Moms and dads and kids and teenagers, too, all head for the stage. Everyone puts on their jackets and dances.

Mom and Dad used to swing dance on the dirt dance floor. They were the best. Everyone would watch them, spinning and lifting. May and I would be on the side, with the Thanksgiving wreaths we made at the craft booth, licking the powdered sugar from the fry bread off our fingers. Mom laughed like a little girl as Dad threw her in the air. It was almost time for the winter to come, but we forgot about our cold toes and our frozen fingers, because we could see what it looked like when they looked like love. We could imagine the story of them, how it was when they met, how it had happened that they made our family. We were proud that they were our parents.

Last year May really wanted to go to Fallfest again, so just the two of us went together. It was the second fall after Mom and Dad had split up. We walked around and ate fry bread, and when the dancing time of night came, we went over to the stage. I stood on the side and watched as May danced with everything in her body, twirling alone in the middle of the floor. It reminded me of when we were kids and how if there was a fight, she'd dance around the living room, using all of the power she had in her to make things better.

But after the first song was over, she said, "Let's get out of here."

We were about to leave, and that's when he walked up. He was wearing a heavy flannel shirt, and he had a cigarette in his mouth and dark hair that hung over his forehead. He looked old to me. May told me later that he was twenty-four.

"I'm Paul," he said. "You looked amazing out there." He held out his hand to May, and I saw the dirt under his nails.

May's cheeks flushed, and the sadness that had been coming off of her was replaced by a smolder. "Thanks," she said with a slow smile.

Paul flicked his cigarette out and asked her for the next dance. May let him take her hand, and I stood there, watching the two of them together. As he spun her across the dirt stage, May giggled.

When it was over, he asked for her number. She said, "You'll have to give me yours. I don't have a cell yet, and you can't call me at either of my parents'." So he gave it to her, and he kissed her hand and made her promise not to lose it.

After that night, May started coming into my room when she got home from sneaking out and telling me things about

Paul, who she had started seeing in secret. I remember once she lay down on my bed and whispered excitedly, "You wouldn't believe the stuff he says to me, Laurel."

"What does he say?"

She grinned and said, "I'll tell you when you're older."

"Do you kiss him?" I asked.

"Yeah."

"What's it like?"

"Like being above the earth." She smiled like the secrets she had were enough to live off of. "He got me this." She pulled a thin gold chain out from underneath her shirt. It had a charm that said *May* in cursive writing. A heart dangled beneath the *Y.* I thought that it was funny that Paul with his rugged boots and his calloused hands had picked out a necklace like that.

I wasn't sure how I felt about her kissing Paul. I always imagined that May would have a boyfriend who looked like River Phoenix, but Paul didn't look anything like that. It scared me a little bit to think of them together, but I'd been there when they met, and the secret of him tied May and me together. She was opening the door to her new world, just a crack, and I wanted to be in it with her. So when she started to take me with her soon after that, to the movie nights where she'd meet him, it didn't matter if deep down there was something wrong. I would have followed her anywhere.

This year I went to Fallfest with Sky and my friends. I kept seeing May dancing alone in the middle of the floor, and then giggling with Paul, and for a while I couldn't shake the anxious sinking feeling I had. But then, when the country swing music was over, the band that covers you came on, last in the night. When they started playing "Light My Fire," it made me feel like the world wasn't tired. Like it was just starting to spin, faster and faster. Like there was a new beginning. We all danced like we were trying to get our feet to float off the earth. Tristan bounced up and down and shouted with the lyrics, and Kristen shook her long hair. Natalie and Hannah held hands and spun until they fell down on top of each other laughing. When I turned to Sky and kissed him in the middle of the music, I felt like I was holding a match. And I could strike it. Strike it on the trees holding on to their shining brown leaves. Strike it on a star.

After Fallfest, Sky drove me home. As we were sitting in his truck outside, I remembered Dad telling me he wanted to meet Sky. I thought maybe I could get it out of the way, so I asked Sky if he wanted to come in. "Sure," he said, and followed me up to the front door. My heart started beating fast. It would be the first time that he'd been in my house. It would be the first time that anyone had been in our house in a while, except for me and Dad and once in a while Aunt Amy.

I opened the front door, and we stood there, in the half-dark living room. I realized it was pretty late. Almost ten o'clock. Maybe Dad was already asleep. "Well, this is it," I said, and flipped on a light. "My house." Sky standing there made me notice everything again. The dried wildflowers in the ceramic vase. Mom's painting of the sunset over the mesa that Dad had never taken down. The family picture on the out-of-tune piano. I wondered how it all looked through Sky's eyes. I wondered if he noticed May in the photo. Even though we've been together for a month now, I still don't know where he went to school before West Mesa, or what happened there, or how he knew my sister. I guess I'm scared to ask.

Just then, Dad came out of his room in his red bathrobe. "Hi, Daddy," I said. "This is Sky."

Sky shook his hand and said, "Hello, sir."

Dad looked at Sky suspiciously and nodded. "How was Fallfest?" he asked.

"It was good," I said. "We danced."

Dad smiled a small smile. "That's nice," he said.

It seemed too much suddenly, standing there in the quiet house. So I said, "Dad, we're going to go on a walk."

Dad frowned, but he nodded. "Get your coat." Then he kissed my head good night.

When we went out, I was happy to be with Sky in the night air. It was cold in the clean way, in the making-stars-clear way. It smelled like burning leaves. There were pumpkins that never got carved sitting quietly under people's porch lights. Sky took my fingers and blew hot breath on them, and then wrapped them up in his hands. He said, "Your dad seems nice."

"Yeah, but I think he's really sad. He and my mom split up a couple years ago. And then after, you know, May . . . my mom left for a ranch in California." I paused. "I guess I'm kind of mad at her, you know? It's like, it's not truly fair. Why should she be the only one to get to go away? As if taking care of horses could change anything. It's supposed to be clearing her head. But I wish she would come home."

I missed her a lot right then. For some reason, I thought of her in her teddy bear pajamas, making Eggos for May and me in the morning. How she put a drop of syrup in each square. It felt funny to say it out loud—*I'm mad at Mom*. But I am.

Sky nodded. "My dad left us, too, a few years ago. Just walked out. I was so mad at him, I didn't know what to do. It's like he left me alone to take care of my mom. And after he went, she got worse. Things were always a little bit hard for her. But now, sometimes it's like she's not living in the same reality as everyone else. It's not her fault she's like that . . . I just wish I could make it better. But I can't."

It was a big deal that Sky was talking to me about this. I wanted to think of something to help. "Have you . . . Has she seen a doctor or anything? Maybe there's medicine that could help?" I suggested.

"I've tried. Every time I bring it up, she says that there's nothing wrong with her."

I could feel him getting tougher on the outside. I took his other hand so that he'd know I was there, which made it hard to walk. He seemed like he wasn't sure if he wanted to take the hands away from me or not.

We walked in quiet for a while, until we got into a nearby neighborhood where the houses start to get bigger. We passed by the golf course, and Sky asked, "Do you ever jump the fence?"

I hadn't yet, but it seemed like a good time to start. I smiled and looked at him over my shoulder and started climbing up. My tights got stuck on the wire at the top, the part above my thigh, and Sky had to pry them loose. He followed me over the fence onto the damp brown November grass. The fall geese that had settled there for the night just kept standing about, seeming not to mind us.

I had taken Sky's hands again, and since I had them, I said, "Spin with me." I think that's the kind of thing that boys like to do but won't do unless a girl asks them to. We spun and spun and spun until we fell down in a heap, laughing. But for some reason, on the perfect cold night grass next to the geese, my laugh just turned to crying.

"What's wrong?" Sky asked. I didn't know how to explain it. I didn't know where to start. Sky held me against his chest, which made me push harder away from him into whatever the crying was for. But when I got quiet, I was glad to be with him. I didn't say anything for a while. Neither did he, but it was like we both knew what it meant to be there.

When we got back to my house, Sky tiptoed into my room with me. We sat on my half of the disassembled bunk bed that got split apart when May started high school and moved into her own room. I'd never really put up posters or pictures on the wall the way May had done in her new room, so it looked pretty much the same as it had when we were kids. Pink walls, gauzy curtains, dried flower crowns draped over dusty stuffed animals that looked out from a hammock in the corner, wands made of ribbons peeking out from the top of a pencil holder. I felt self-conscious and flipped off the lights, and plastic glow-in-the-dark stars shone down on us.

Sky and I started kissing. We kept kissing, and kissing, and his hands were everywhere on me, and everything inside of me was hot, like pavement on a summer night. A burning you can't stop. When Sky paused and asked, "Are you okay?" I noticed how fast I was breathing. I remembered, in a flash, what it was like those nights at the movies, and I thought for a moment that he could see it. That he knew, somehow, all of the things that I'd let happen. That he could tell. But then I saw him just staring at me, worried. "Laurel?"

"Yeah. Yeah, I'm good. It's just . . . intense."

He'd never have to know, I thought. I could be new. I would be May, the May who was brave and magical. I wouldn't be me, the one who let everything go wrong. I focused so hard, until Sky was all that I could see. And then I got this feeling that I needed to be so much closer to his body. I wanted our skin to stop keeping us apart. So I kissed him harder, and he kissed me harder, and my clothes came partway off, and he touched me everywhere. It was then that all of the sad things inside of me turned into hungry things.

Finally, after we'd made out and gotten quiet and made out

again, when the littlest bit of gray light started to leak in through the curtains, Sky tucked me under the blankets and started to sneak out of the house through the window, so Dad wouldn't hear him.

"Sky?" I said as he was leaving. I was half-asleep, but I didn't want him to go. As the night air rushed into the room, it seemed like it could swallow him up and take him from me.

He turned back. "Yeah?"

"You'll still be here, right? Tomorrow?"

He smiled and kissed my forehead. "No," he said, "I'll be at home."

"But, I mean, you won't leave me, right?"

"Right."

When I woke up today to the memory of Sky's body, all of the sad things in me were still hungry. They started to take everything in—the rain streaking in the sky, the spill of light on the table, the tiniest drops of water clinging to a pine needle on a tree outside my window. Maybe that's what being in love is. You just keep filling up, never getting fuller, only brighter.

I looked you up, and I found out where the name of your band came from—from this quote, written by a poet named Blake: "If the doors of perception were cleansed everything would appear to man as it is, infinite." I've been thinking about that. About what it means to see the endlessness of each moment, of each piece of it. I want to be cleansed—I want to burn away all of the bad memories and everything bad inside of me. And maybe that's what being in love does. So that a life, a person, a moment you need to keep, stays with you into infinity. May smiling back at me. The two of us as little girls at Fallfest, with parents who danced. Your song playing into eternity. The night leaves on the cottonwood trees catching the white lights. And every little star that burns hotter than we could know.

Yours,
Laurel

Dear Janis Joplin,

Kristen's parents have money, but she drives a super old Volvo anyway, because she thinks it's cool. She has a bumper sticker on the back of it that says I'M NOT TALKING TO MYSELF . . . I'M TALKING TO JANIS JOPLIN. When she and Natalie and I were driving to Garcia's Drive-In during lunch on Friday (Kristen never ditches classes, only lunch, because she's a good student and keeping her grades up for college applications), of course we were listening to you. Since Kristen loves you so much, she knows all of your songs, not just the most popular ones. You were singing "Half Moon," and Kristen turned to Natalie and said, "Did you know that Janis had women lovers, too?" Natalie shook her head no. Kristen continued, saying, "She could have been singing about a woman when she sang this," as you crooned, *Your love brings life to me*.

Natalie looked off and said, "That's cool," trying to sound like she didn't care. But by the way her face spread with a little smile, I could tell she did think it was really cool. I think Kristen was trying to make Natalie feel like she knew about her and Hannah. Like it was okay.

Hannah got another boyfriend. She has two right now, counting Kasey and the new one, whose name is Neung. She met Neung at Japanese Kitchen, where he's a busboy and she's a hostess. Yesterday, we went to his house, Hannah and Natalie and me. It was Sunday, and after we opened the fourth day of Aunt Amy's advent calendar, I'd asked her if I could go to Dad's early in the day, so that really I could go and hang out with Natalie and Hannah.

Before we left Natalie's, Hannah kept trying on new shirts and asking Natalie if she looked fat, and Natalie was getting mad and saying, "Of course you don't." Hannah put on a lot of makeup, so she had these crimson lips, darker than bloodred against her pale freckled skin. She looked like someone who was beautiful but trying to show how she hurt.

We walked to Neung's from Natalie's, and it was really far. It's getting cold now even when it's still sunny, but Hannah didn't wear enough clothes, so the whole way there she was shivering. Natalie was putting her arms around her to keep her warm, and Hannah was talking about Neung and how his skin is so smooth that when she touches it, she feels like the world will never end. And how he used to be a gangster. Natalie said she didn't want Hannah going over there alone, which is why we went along. I was glad, too, because I didn't want her going alone, either. I didn't know what might happen to her.

Neung lives in this tiny house with his whole family, his mother and his father and his uncle and his grandfather and his brother and his sister and his sister's son. Before we got there, all the way down the block, we could smell the hot peppers cooking. His mom and sister were cooking them on the grill outside. They must have been the hottest peppers in the world. As we got closer and closer, our eyes started to burn so badly from the smoke that by the time we made it to Neung's, our faces were covered in tears, and Hannah's mascara had streamed down her cheeks.

We played outside with Neung's little nephew, wiping away pepper tears the whole time. Neung was nice around us, and he picked up his little nephew and spun him like an airplane. He laughed at our chile tears and called us *güeras*, which means "white girls" in Spanish. He did this even though he's Vietnamese and Natalie's Mexican, so it didn't make that much sense.

Then Neung drove us to the 7-Eleven to get Slurpees and cigarettes. Once we were away from his family, Neung started touching Hannah a lot, and calling her baby girl and putting his hand in the back pocket of her jeans when they were walking, which made Natalie roll her eyes at me. When we got back to Neung's, we sat on the sidewalk and drank the Slurpees, and they all smoked the cigarettes. (I didn't smoke any, because I don't actually like them that much. I thought I'd get used to the taste, but I haven't.) We all laughed about our chattering blue lips. Then it was getting to be nighttime, and Neung said he wanted to be alone with Hannah. So they went inside, and Natalie and I sat on the steps, waiting.

I kept looking up at the moon. It was so bright. Not yet a whole circle, but trying to be. Like it wished so much to be round and full and perfect. I thought about the nights when May would leave to go away with Paul, and I started to worry for Hannah. Natalie was quiet, building a little house out of twigs and smoking a lot of cigarettes. Everything I said seemed to come out of my mouth and fall to the ground in slow motion. When I ran out of things to say, I said, "You love her, huh?" And Natalie kind of nodded, and then she started crying. Really, really crying. I put my arms around her.

She said, "You know when you think you know someone? More than anyone in the world? You know you know them, because you've seen them, like, for real. And then you reach out, and suddenly they are just . . . gone. You thought you belonged together. You thought they were yours, but they're not. You want to protect them, but you can't."

I told her I did know. And in that moment, Hannah came running out. She was giggling too loudly, in a weird way, like she was trying to cover up some big cry. And then she saw Natalie's face. She said, "I'm sorry. I'm sorry." She just kept saying it. And stroking her hair. "It was terrible. I hated it. All I could think of was you. All I could think of was you. I only love you."

I tried to look away, and the only other thing to see was the moon.

Yours,
Laurel

Dear River Phoenix,

I read that when you were little, before you were famous, your family moved around a lot. You lived in communes, and then you guys joined a cult for a while called the Children of God. Your family did missionary work for them in Texas, Mexico, Puerto Rico, and finally Venezuela. The cult called your father the Archbishop of Venezuela and the Caribbean, but they didn't give your family any money to live on, so you and your next-oldest sister, Rain, used to sing in the streets for change. People would gather around to hear the two of you.

Your family quit the cult when your parents heard about what the leader was asking the women to do, "flirty fishing," they called it, which was to have sex with men to recruit them. When you left Venezuela, your family got back to Florida by being stowaways on a ship carrying Tonka toys. The crew discovered your family, but they were nice to you and gave you some damaged toys for presents.

After the cult, your parents changed your family's last name from Bottom to Phoenix—to symbolize the mythical bird that rises from the ashes. Then your family moved to Hollywood when you were nine so that you and Rain would have a chance to become stars. You loved to sing together, and you decided you wanted to be an actor, too.

At first, it was hard. Your family had no money, and you got kicked out of your apartments every few months, and you and your sister kept singing on street corners. But your mom got a job working for a casting agency, and then a famous talent agent signed you and Rain and your other two sisters and brother, too. Soon she started getting you small jobs, and then the jobs got bigger and bigger.

When you became an actor, you had the ability to dissolve your own personality and inhabit any character. You were brilliant at it. We can lose ourselves, I guess. And you used that. You found the magic in it.

You and your siblings always supported each other. You loved your family so much and talked about your childhood as being happy. But I wonder if there was something that happened to you when you were little that you couldn't talk to them about. People have said that a lot of bad things went on in that cult, like the cult leader said it was okay to do sexual stuff with kids. When I read that, it made me so angry. I wondered if there was someone who hurt you. You said once in an interview that you lost your virginity when you were four. But then you took it back and said that it was just a joke. So I don't know. But maybe there was a time that you needed someone to protect you and they couldn't.

I am writing to you now because there is something that I can't talk about, too. Something that I wonder if you would understand. I keep trying to get rid of it, to push it out of my head, but it keeps coming back in. I am worried, because I am falling in love with Sky, but I feel like one day, he'll find out everything and leave me.

Last night, I snuck out to meet him. Since it was a cold night, instead of walking through the neighborhood, he picked me up and we decided to drive in his truck. We blasted the heater and rolled the windows down and listened to music, and finally we pulled over on a dark street and made out in the car. We made out so much, my whole body was burning up, and the windows were frosted with breath. I finally pulled away from him and sat up a moment. I was trying to remind myself of where I was, and I turned to the glass and drew a heart in it with my finger. That's when he asked, "Do you want to come over?"

His mom was sleeping when we got there. In the low light I could see that the house, which looked so perfect on the outside, was different indoors. Every surface was piled high with fading housekeeping magazines, abandoned library books, scattered crafts. A half-finished needlepoint sampler with a scene from summer. A pile of cutout snowflakes and their paper scraps for the winter. Sky wanted to go quickly to his bedroom, but I lingered. I wanted to see everything, as if the house were full of clues to him. Then, in a cabinet crowded with delicate china, I saw that there were soccer trophies and a framed photo of Sky. He was younger, maybe twelve. He was in his uniform, grinning with a ball in his hands. There was something about seeing him like that—the same boy I loved looking out at me as a kid who smiled for the camera. I wanted to pull him out of the picture and protect him from everything between then and now.

"I didn't know you played soccer," I whispered. "Are all of those trophies yours?"

"Yeah," he said, shifting, like he didn't want to be there. "That was my past life."

Then he took my hand and pulled me through the maze back to his bedroom. I wanted to know more, but he started kissing me. He started kissing me hard, and hungry, and for some reason it scared me. But I tried to go with it. Because I was in his house. Because I could feel the moths that needed a light beating hard, and I wanted to keep glowing for him.

Soon he had my shirt off, and he had his hands up my skirt, and everything felt confusing. I wanted him to love me. I wanted to be a light. So I told my brain to be quiet. I told my brain to just go somewhere else. And I went. I went somewhere I didn't mean to go. I went back to May, when we were kids.

I remembered the night I asked her, "If we are fairies, why can't we fly?"

I was scared that somehow the seventh generation inheritance missed me. That I wasn't a real fairy and she'd find out. More than anything, I didn't want her to be disappointed in me.

"Only the oldest child inherits the flight gene," she told me. "But that doesn't mean you aren't a fairy."

"But you can fly?" I asked hopefully.

"Yeah," she said.

I was so excited. "Can I see you?"

"No one can see my wings, or it breaks them."

"Oh," I said, trying not to show her I was devastated. "When do you use them then?"

"At night. When I know everyone is sleeping and no one can see me."

"Can I just see you once?"

"You don't want my wings to break, do you?"

"No," I said.

But still, I couldn't help it. I couldn't help how badly I wanted to see her wings. If I saw them, I would know for sure I was part of the magic.

Some nights, I used to beg her to let me sleep in the top bunk with her. I'd climb up the ladder and curl in next to her. After she fell asleep, I'd stare up at the ceiling, looking for patterns in the splotches of paint—a dragon, and the cave he'd set fire to by accident, trapped in his own flames. The princess who would come to rescue him. I'd tell myself stories and try to keep my eyes open all night, so that if May went out on a flight, I wouldn't miss it. I thought that maybe if I just saw by accident, it wouldn't count. But eventually, sleep would take over. I'd open my eyes again at dawn, and she would be turning under the blankets.

"Did you fly tonight?" I'd whisper.

"Mmm-hmm," she'd murmur.

And I'd imagine her adventures.

I was staring up at Sky's ceiling now, trying to find pictures in the walls the way I used to do, when he asked me, "Laurel?"

I tried to shake myself out of it. "Yeah?"

"Where did you go?"

"Nowhere. I'm here."

"You left me."

"No, I . . . I didn't mean to . . ." I started crying. I couldn't help it.

"Laurel, what's wrong?"

"I don't know," I said, trying to wipe the tears away.

I had that same feeling that I did when I was a kid. She was a real fairy, and I was faking it. I knew that eventually, Sky would find out.

"You can't always do this," he said. "You can't just disappear on me."

"I'm sorry."

I pulled him closer and tried to keep kissing. Sky's hands were hot on me. I wanted to like it, but the world was spinning. I tried to focus on his face, but I couldn't. I was going backward through a tunnel. I was seeing magic carpets, riding on one with Aladdin. I was seeing May, her lips turning dark with lipstick. May leaving the movie theater in Paul's car. I saw her look back at me, and all of a sudden her smile that had looked so bright seemed scared.

"We don't have to have sex if you don't want to," Sky said.

"Okay."

"But you have to talk to me."

"I—I don't know what to say." I wondered again how he knew May. I couldn't help it anymore. After a moment, I asked, "Sky? What was your old school?"

"Sandia."

My heart stopped for a beat, or maybe three. It was true. "So you went with May."

"Yeah," he said.

I imagined him seeing her, turning a corner in the hallway. She would be wearing her pink sweater, cut to show her collarbone, her hair flowing behind her. She would have taken his breath away. I wonder if when he sees me coming around a corner, sometimes he thinks for a moment he sees her there.

"I bet everyone loved her," I said.

Sky was quiet.

"Right?" I asked softly.

"Yeah," he said. "Do you want me to take you home?"

"All right," I said. "I guess."

So we drove in his truck, the quiet of the night stifling us. I wished that I wouldn't have been weird. I wished that I hadn't broken the spell. I was scared, and there was nothing to stop it.

We pulled up in front of my house.

"Good night," Sky said. "Get some sleep."

And I snuck back into our house full of shadows.

Yours,
Laurel

Dear Kurt,

I have this picture of you in my locker, with Courtney and baby Frances. You are holding her in your arms, peering down at her. Courtney is leaning over your shoulder, looking, too. Her shirt is cut to show her stomach, which has FAMILY VALUES written on it in black scratchy letters. It would almost be ironic, but it's real at the same time, because you are there, Kurt and Courtney, with your baby girl. Your family got broken when you were a kid, but then you made your own. And at the same time, you became a father, in a way, to all of us. I know you didn't want that. But you couldn't help it. You didn't want to be the spokesperson of a generation. But you couldn't help singing.

I don't know anyone who has a perfect family to start with.

And I think that's why we make up our own. Regular weirdos together. I feel that way about my friends.

Yesterday was the last day of school before Christmas break. We all met in the alley after school to celebrate. I made everyone clove oranges, which are oranges with cloves pressed into the skin and ribbons attached to make them into ornaments. I felt like making them because May and I always did at Christmastime. I put Kristen's cloves in so that they spelled *NYC*, which is where she wants to go to college. Tristan's said *Slash*.

For vacation, Tristan and Kristen are going to Hawaii with her family. They've been dating since the beginning of high school, so I guess her family lets him go along to stuff like that. It's funny to me, because when I think of Hawaii I think of hula, and neither of them seems like the type for leis or swimsuits with birds-of-paradise. Tristan says that he's going to stay in the hotel room and order piña coladas and watch *Oprah* reruns all day, but Kristen has to finish her college applications. She says he better watch on mute.

Tristan smokes pot a lot and didn't take the right tests, and he likes shop and art the most of his classes. But more than that, even, he likes rock music and playing guitar. I think he really wants to be a musician, but not just because he wants to be famous. He wants to be one because of what Slash said, about how being a rock star is the intersection between who you are and who you want to be. He plays guitar so well, you wouldn't believe it. But he doesn't have a band. And he doesn't try really hard to get one. He mostly plays alone in his room instead. That's what Kristen says. I think he does this for the same reason Hannah doesn't turn in her work when her teachers say she is smart. I think a lot of people want to be someone, but we are scared that if we try, we won't be as good as everyone imagines we could be.

Kristen is different. She studies all the time, and she got a 2180 on her SAT. She's always talking about going to Columbia. She flips through magazines and cuts out pictures of people who look like they'd live in New York or other cities where things happen. She lets me and Natalie and Hannah come over to her house after school sometimes, and we always just get a snack then sit in her room and actually do homework. Her bedroom walls are covered with the magazine pictures, so that the walls don't end at the walls. They go outward, to a dream of somewhere else.

I think that it makes Tristan feel like she doesn't want to be here, with him. But the thing is, even though Kristen wants to go, I think she wishes he would come, too. See, last month she gave Tristan this stack of college applications in the cafeteria at lunchtime. She smiled a little smile and said, "Hey, baby. I got you something." Like it was a good surprise. Then she pulled them out from behind her back and handed them to him.

He took the stack of papers. He said, "What's this?" already with an edge in his voice. He flipped through them and then he said, "Ladies and gentlemen, I can see the headlines now! Tristan Ayers attends backwater bumfuck college in the city of Poughkeepsie." He said it like he was joking, but his voice had a razor in it. Then his eyes got really angry, and he turned to Kristen and said, "That shit's not even in New York City." Like, *Who do you think I am?*

Her eyes were still as usual. She said, really quietly, "It's close."

"It's not close. It's a fuckin' world away."

She told him he could transfer after a year if he got his grades up. Tristan just looked at her and said, "I'm not good enough for you. We both know it." He tore the stack of applications in half. And threw them on the table and walked out.

Kristen turned her head and watched him go. Finally she said, so close to her breath you could barely hear it, "You're wrong."

I'd never seen her cry or get emotional in front of people. Her face always looks the same. But when she swept the torn papers into a neat pile and then off the table, she wiped her eyes with the long sleeve of her gypsy shirt. She walked through the cafeteria and threw out the applications in the trash by the door.

Now they both act around each other like you do when you know something is going to end and you've decided not to know. But for today, they are still here. We were happy, smoking cigarettes and laughing in the alley under the December sky, bright with possible snow. Everyone liked their oranges. Hannah laughed at hers, which I had decorated with a stick horse made of cloves.

When Natalie walked up, she was carrying a painting-sized package, wrapped in a sheet with orange paisleys on it and tied with an orange cloth bow. She giggled and pushed it toward Hannah and said, "Open it."

Hannah looked suspicious, like she was worried that suddenly everyone could see through her. Even with our friends, Hannah still likes to pretend that she and Natalie aren't in love like that. Finally she untied the bow and pulled off the sheet and screamed, "Oh my god!" like she didn't know how to take it. Maybe no one had given her something that good before. It was the tulip painting Natalie had made her in art class.

Natalie shifted back and forth between her feet. "You don't like it."

But Hannah kept looking at it, like she didn't want to take her eyes away. The way there were so many shades of color in the tulip petals, opening and closing at once, it reminded me of the feeling of watching a sunset—you are in awe of something so beautiful, and at the same time, you know that particular sunset will only be there for a moment.

Hannah said, "Thank you." She meant it. She could have cried, I could see, but she was in front of everybody, so she shook herself out of it.

When we were walking to the parking lot, Natalie said to Hannah, "I made the tulip that way, I made it a painting, because now you'll always have it. It can't wilt or die." Natalie had taken what's ephemeral and turned it into something that Hannah can keep. Hannah looked at Natalie like she was trying to make herself understand what it means to have someone love you like that.

At least that's what I imagined, because I know that it can be hard to believe that someone loves you if you are afraid of being yourself, or if you are not exactly sure who you are. It can be hard to believe that someone won't leave. Since that night at his house a week ago, things have been strange between me and Sky. He's trying to act like they're not, and when I asked him if he was mad at me, he said, "No. Forget about it, all right?" So I am trying my best.

Yours,
Laurel

Dear River,

I watched *My Own Private Idaho* last night. In the movie, you'd changed, like I have. You weren't the kid from *Stand by Me* anymore. You'd grown up, and I could see that it hurt. You play Mike, a narcoleptic who lives on the streets as a hustler. The movie opens on an empty open road. You are stuck there, alone, waiting for sleep to take you over. The clouds roll away, so fast through the wide-open sky.

When you fall to sleep by the side of the road, you dream of your mom rubbing your head, telling you everything will be okay. "I know you're sorry," she says. In the movie, your mom abandoned you when you were little, and you want more than anything to find her.

My mom went away, too. I know how it feels to be sorry for something you can't say. If I could have walked through the screen, I would have taken you in my arms. And I knew what you meant when you said, "The road never ends." I know a road like that. It's the last road I drove on with May.

It stretches past the cottonwood trees lining the river and the railroad tracks and the bridge. It stretches past when me and May were kids making spells, past climbing trees and picking apples and past the first time I saw her wearing lipstick, past the look on her face when she met Paul, past the movies that we never saw. It goes into a place where none of it ever existed, where it always did, where there is no such thing as time, but just a feeling that goes on forever. A feeling I can't escape from. *I'm sorry. I made her leave me.*

It's the feeling that I am afraid will make Sky go, too, eventually. And it's the feeling that was with me all night when Tristan and Kristen took us to a senior's party before they left for their trip. They said it's a big holiday party that happens every year, where they like to go to watch the straight-edge kids cut lose. It was at a huge house with a Christmas tree and parents who were out of town and spiked eggnog and lots of kids I'd never seen before, some of them from other schools, I guess. Kristen wore a necklace that lit up with mini Christmas lights. She's the kind of girl who can do stuff like that and make it seem cool, paired with her long tangled hair and her broomstick skirt.

Kristen had hijacked the iPod, and she and Natalie were dancing together and singing *"Freedom's just another word . . ."* at the tops of their lungs. Hannah had brought Kasey along, and the two of them were sitting at the dining room table nearby, doing shots with some other guys. Natalie kept glancing over her shoulder at Hannah as she danced.

I was standing off to the side, thinking of calling Sky. He'd said he was tired and didn't feel like coming out tonight. I wished I were somewhere with him, instead of there. I was feeling like some kind of strangely shaped balloon whose string he was holding, and if he let go, I'd float off into the ether.

I was thinking about that, how high a balloon could fly before it popped, and what the world would look like from there, when out of the corner of my eye, I saw Janey, my old friend from elementary and middle school. She was with that soccer player she'd been with when I saw her outside the supermarket. I tried to look for somewhere to hide, but it was too late. She'd let go of his hand and was walking over. Her already rosy cheeks were a few shades brighter than usual, and I guessed she'd been drinking.

"Laurel!" she shouted, throwing her arms around me. I looked around to see if anyone had noticed, but Natalie and

Kristen were now dancing to "This Is What Makes Us Girls," and Hannah was licking salt off Kasey's wrist.

"Hey," I said, and smiled weakly. "What are you doing here?"

"Same thing you are, I guess," she replied, her voice turning suddenly curt. Then she added, "Landon's older brother is friends with the guy who lives here."

"Is Landon your boyfriend?" I asked, gesturing to the guy I'd seen her with.

"Yeah," she said.

"That's cool. He's cute."

"It's so weird," she said, "that I haven't even seen you since . . . I mean, where have you been?"

"I'm sorry. It's just, you know. I've been busy, I guess. With the new school and stuff."

"So, you're here with those girls?" she asked, pointing toward Natalie and Hannah, who she'd seen outside the supermarket.

"Yeah."

"They seem sort of weird."

"No, they're actually, I mean, they're really nice."

Natalie and Hannah are obviously different from Janey, who now looked like a popular girl through and through, in her red-for-the-holidays minidress and matching headband. Janey stared at them for a minute. Natalie had stopped dancing and walked over to Hannah and Kasey at the table. She took the shot out of Hannah's hand. *Hey!* Hannah mouthed.

Natalie threw it down and then left and went back to dancing, dancing like if she stopped, she would collapse.

Janey leaned in and said, real soft, "Are they, like, in love or something?"

"Who?" I thought she meant Hannah and Kasey. "Oh, no. He just—I think he makes her feel safe or something."

"No, *them*. The girls."

I was really surprised that Janey had noticed this. I was impressed. They did a good job of covering it up. I think what Janey must have recognized is the look of hurt in Natalie's eyes when she took the shot. I nodded, slightly. I made a *shh* finger over my lips. Janey nodded back, like, *I get it.*

Then she said, "Well, are you going to introduce me?"

"Yeah. Just don't, um, don't say anything about my sister or whatever, okay?"

Janey looked back at me, her face falling into a worried frown. Before she could say anything else, I led her over to the table where Hannah was.

"Hey, Hannah," I said, "this is my friend Janey, from—"

Janey broke in. "From forever. Only she doesn't talk to me anymore."

Hannah nodded, studying Janey. "You're pretty," she said. "You look like a Disney princess or something."

I think Hannah meant that as a compliment, but it didn't quite come out that way. Janey let it roll off. "Thanks," she replied. "I like your dress."

Then Janey looked at Kasey next to Hannah, and she

looked back at Natalie dancing, and she did something pretty great. She grabbed Hannah's hand and said, "So, do you want to go dance or what?" and she pulled her away from Kasey and onto the dance floor.

I watched them, Hannah dancing with Natalie and Kristen now, and Janey doing more conservative moves on the edge of the circle. I remembered how actually wonderful Janey is. I felt a pang, watching her bobbing her blond head and remembering how there was a time when there was no secret I couldn't tell her.

I needed some air, so I went out to the balcony. I was standing there, looking at the tangled fingers of the tree branches reaching for the winter-clear sky, when Tristan came out and lit a cigarette with his giant kitchen lighter.

"Laurel. What are you doing alone out here? Wait, let me guess. You are 'thinking about things,'" he teased.

"Shut up." I smiled.

With Tristan around, the sad I felt changed from sad like watching a balloon drift out of sight to sad in an it's-good-to-know-your-soul-works way.

"How are you doing, Buttercup?" he asked.

"All right." I shrugged. "I guess." And then I asked him, because for some reason it's easy to talk to him, "When you first thought you were falling in love with Kristen, did you ever get scared? Because I get that way with Sky, and I think that I might have sort of screwed stuff up."

Tristan looked at me, and he said something I'll always

remember. "Let me tell you something, Buttercup," he said. "There are two most important things in the world—being in danger, and being saved."

I thought for a moment of May. I asked him, "Do you think we go into danger on purpose, so we can get saved?"

"Yes, sometimes. But sometimes the wolf comes down out of the mountains, and you didn't ask for it. You were just trying to take a nap in the foothills."

Then I asked him, "But if those are the two most important things, what about being in love?"

"Why do you think that's the most profound thing for a person? It's both at once. When we are in love, we are both completely in danger and completely saved."

When he said that, it made sudden sense. "Thank you," I said.

He stomped out his cigarette and ruffled my hair before he went back inside.

I took out my phone and dialed Sky's number. His voice was soft with the edges of sleep creeping around it.

"Sky?" I asked.

"Yeah? Where are you?"

"I'm at this party. Could you come and take me home? I really want to see you."

He agreed, so I said bye to my friends and blew a kiss to Janey, who was sitting on Landon's lap by then. I waited outside until Sky's truck pulled up. When I got in, I put my hands against the heater. He took them in his and rubbed them to warm them up. I leaned over and kissed the part of his shoulder that pushed against the threads of his sweatshirt.

When we pulled up outside my house, I asked, "Do you think I'm too messed up?"

"For what?" Sky replied.

"For you."

"No."

He said it so plainly that a flood of relief rushed into me. All I wanted was to lose myself in his body. I crawled onto him across the seat and felt his hands on me. I don't mean we had sex, but we got closer than we have yet. As the neighborhood Christmas lights on their timers started to shut off, one by one the houses went quiet. The windows in the truck turned foggy, with patterns like icy feathers cracking across them. I let him keep me warm, and I promised myself I would be brave this time.

Yours,
Laurel

Dear Judy Garland,

Today is the second day of break, and tomorrow is Christmas Eve. Luckily I got permission from Aunt Amy to stay with Dad the whole vacation. I know how much she'll be all about Christ's birth and salvation and stuff this time of year, and I'm not really up for it at the moment. It's depressing at Dad's, but the ghosts in the house are ours, and I just want to be with them. Even though Aunt Amy and Dad are not exactly best friends, Aunt Amy will still come over on Christmas, because I don't want her to be alone. I got her a super fancy advent calendar that you can use every year, all with Jesus-type pictures in it. Dad was harder, but I got him a basket of joke things to remind him of how he used to like that kind of stuff—whoopee cushions and plastic spiders and chewing gum that turns your mouth blue.

I watched *Meet Me in St. Louis* twice already this morning. I cried both times when you sang "Have Yourself a Merry Little Christmas" with your voice full of longing. I wonder if when you had to sing the song for the movie you were remembering how Christmas was when you were little, singing "Jingle Bells" on the stage in your daddy's theater. He died when you were only thirteen, just after you signed with MGM. He was so proud of you, driving you to the studio every morning, walking you into its one-room schoolhouse. While he was dying in the hospital, you were on the radio, singing to him. You never got to say goodbye. This will be my first Christmas without May.

After the credits rolled for the second time, I figured that at some point I should get out of my pajamas. Since Dad's been too depressed, I think, to do anything Christmassy so far, I decided to try to cheer him up. I pulled the Christmas box out of the attic, and then I pulled Dad's ladder out of the shed, and

I was going to put the lights up outside the house so they could be glowing for Dad when he came home from work.

I was topsy-turvy on the ladder, trying to carry the bundle of lights up to the rooftop, when Mark, the neighbor boy, walked up.

I've known him and his twin brother, Carl, since I was born, because our parents would trade us for babysitting. When they were younger, their mom dressed them in different colors of plaid and kept their sandy hair swept across their foreheads. They smelled of chlorine from their pool, where we would all swim every summer, even after we got old enough not to need babysitting anymore. While they called "Marco Polo" or tried to dunk May under, I would tread water and try not to notice Mark in his swimsuit. I knew they were twins and supposed to look the same, but to me, Mark looked like nobody I'd ever seen. He was my first crush. But he and Carl were both in love with May. I was too young for him. Kid, they called me.

Carl and Mark went away to college this year, and I hadn't seen them since May's memorial. I remember them both dressed in suits, standing around our house with their parents. I kept staring, because for the first time I couldn't tell them apart.

But now, I knew it was Mark. He called up, "Hey! Do you need some help?"

I climbed off the ladder. I could see his house down the street, where his parents were out with Carl, putting the final touches on their usual winner-of-the-block decorations, complete with a blow-up Santa Claus. Next to them, our old man neighbor, Mr. Lopez, was fiddling with his glow-in-the-dark manger scene, behind the bars of his wrought iron fence. "Jesus in jail," May used to joke.

I wondered if I still had a crush on Mark, but I guessed that I didn't anymore, now that there's Sky. Still, it was comforting to see him, as if he were proof of a life that used to exist.

When he offered help, I said, "Sure," laughing. "It's sorta harder than it looks."

So together, we strung up the lights, not having to talk about much other than how to get them in place on the hooks and where to run the extension cord.

When we finally climbed down from the roof, it was starting to get dark out.

"So," I asked, "how's college?"

"It's good." He smiled. "Harder than I thought. But no parents, so that's nice. You'll like it." He looked me up and down. "Crazy," he said. "You're all grown-up."

"Yeah," I said with a smile. "I guess."

I was really hoping that he wouldn't say anything about May and how he was sorry, and, thank goodness, he didn't. Instead, he said, "How's your dad?"

"He's all right. At work." I gestured to the lights. "I'm going to surprise him with this. Thanks for the help."

"Well," he said, "come by if you want some cookies. Mom's got the oven running twenty-four/seven."

I nodded, although I knew I wouldn't.

When Dad came home and saw the lights, he said that I'd

put him in the Christmas spirit, so we went out and got a tree from the lot where we always go, in a rural neighborhood in the middle of the South Valley. The thing about traditions is that they hold up the shape of your memory. I saw May and me running up and down the aisles with our hands in our mittens, looking for the sort of tree that we thought would be left behind if we didn't take it. I picked out the scrawniest tree again, and Dad and I laughed about it.

Then we took it home and started to decorate it. Dad put on Bing Crosby's Christmas record—the one with "Mele Kalikimaka" on it—but as he sat down on the couch and watched me put up the ornaments, it might as well have been silent. Each one seemed to carry the whole weight of our family and what had become of it. The bells I made in first grade, with glittered foil over egg cartons and unraveling red yarn to hang them by. The Play-Doh stars, the animals, the pinecones. My favorite, which is a glass angel with May's name etched on it. I hung that in front.

When I was putting the tinsel on, Mom called. I heard Dad's voice strained as he carried the phone into the other room to talk to her. Then he brought it to me.

Mom said it's strange to see it sunny and still warm at Christmastime. She said the light is bright and clear in California. I tried to picture where she was at the ranch and imagined horses with sleigh bells running around a field of palm trees. It didn't make any sense. I told her I thought maybe I'd bake moon cookies. I thought that might make her wish she was home, because she always baked them every Christmas. The powdered sugar sounds like pushing clouds through the sifter and sticks to the cookies when they're hot. I remember stealing them off the cooling rack with May.

"That's great, honey. The recipe is in the brown box."

"I know." Then I blurted out, "When are you coming home?"

"I don't know, sweetie." She sounded tense. "This is good for me, okay?"

I was just quiet. I guess Mom decided to change the subject. "Dad says that you have a boyfriend now?"

"Yeah."

Her voice turned excited, like a gossipy girlfriend. "So, tell me! What's his name?"

"Sky."

"Is he cute?"

"Yeah."

"Are you being careful, Laurel?"

"Yep."

Mom sighed a long sigh. "I mailed some presents. They should get there tomorrow."

"Okay, thanks." Then I asked, "Have you been to the ocean?"

"Not yet," Mom said. And then, "Merry Christmas, Laurel."

"Merry Christmas, Mom," I said, and I hung up the phone.

Yours,
Laurel

Dear River Phoenix,

Have you ever heard of luminarias? They are a tradition in New Mexico for Christmas Eve. You fill lunch-size paper bags with sand from the sandbox, or if you don't have a sandbox, you get some from one of the sand banks that are in parking lots around town for the holidays. You set up the bags outside your house, put candles in, and pull the wicks up to a flame.

I think they are most beautiful at the cemetery, where people leave them on graves. I went there alone tonight to see the ocean of light, which makes the quiet so much quieter. Each bag in the night was made by someone's hands. Left for someone that they loved.

I brought a luminaria for May and found a place to leave it under a tree. I wanted to do something to show that she's still glowing. We cremated her body. That feels so strange to say. We haven't scattered the ash. I don't want to see it. Honestly, it still feels sometimes like I'll wake up one day and there she'll be. That night plays in the back of my head like a movie where everything is out of focus on the screen so you can't see what's happening. The road races by. The river rushes on. I try to turn down the volume and just focus on the ocean of light.

Above me, the stars twinkle like they want to be as bright as the candles, but distance dims them. I bet your brother and sisters miss you tonight. I guess I just wanted to write to say hi. Or Merry Christmas. Or maybe to see if you are up there, in the sky with the stars, and if from where you are, they look brighter than a flame or a bonfire or the dawn.

Yours,
Laurel

Dear E. E. Cummings,

Christmas night is practically the most silent time that could exist. Like the whole world is made up of memory. After Dad went to bed with the tree lights still on, Sky came and I crawled out my window. We opened the presents we got each other in the dark of my driveway.

The newspaper he wrapped my present with was fragile, so I opened it carefully, not wanting to tear. What I uncovered was a heart that he had carved out of driftwood. It had my name on the back. It was perfect. He had sanded the wood down so it was smooth, but the grains don't go away. I told him it was my favorite present I'd ever gotten. He looked proud.

I'd gotten him a book of your poetry. I made a bookmark from pretty paper with geese on it and put it in to hold the poem "somewhere I have never travelled,gladly beyond." We read it in English class, and I loved it. When Sky unwrapped the book, I read the poem out loud to him.

The line at the end that says, "Nobody, not even the rain, has such small hands" makes perfect sense to me. It means they can go anywhere inside of you, because like the rain, like water, they find places that nothing solid could pass through. It explains the way that Sky gets into me, into places that I never even knew were there. How he touches a part of me no one has ever touched. We both have secret places in us.

"Thank you," Sky said, like he meant it.

"I got you the book," I explained, "because the poem reminds me of you. And also because of how you said that you might want to be a writer, that time after homecoming. I know that you'd write something really different from that, but it made me think of how sometimes when you feel so much, you have to find a way to let it out."

Sky smiled. "I hope we'll both find the words for it."

I had taken off my gloves and was running my hands over the heart he made me. I looked at him, and then I said something I think all the time but always swallow back in. I said, "I love you." I could see my breath hanging on to the air. Or maybe the air was hanging on to my breath, for warmth.

Sky looked back at me, quiet. He took my hand and we started walking. All of the Christmas lights glowed softer and softer down the street, a path of light fading in front of us. We were halfway down the block when he said, "I don't think you would love me if you knew me."

I stopped. "I do know you."

"If you knew everything I've done."

"What do you mean?"

He was silent.

"Tell me. See if I still love you."

Then he said, "Well, to start with, I beat someone up. That's why I got kicked out of my old school."

"That's okay."

"I really hurt him. Really bad."

"Why?"

Sky stopped a moment. "I don't know . . . There was this girl, this girl I knew. I thought he took advantage of her. And once I hit him, it's like everything I was angry at just sorta came out."

I nodded. This is strange, but in a way, thinking of Sky getting in a fight like that made him seem fragile. "I love you more," I whispered, and then I was trying just to listen, to see if he wanted to say something else.

We kept walking through the night quiet. Through it and through it. But I couldn't stop the feeling that was suddenly splitting inside me.

I said, "I've done bad things, too."

"Like what? You forgot your homework?" he teased.

"No," I said. And I think I sounded suddenly angry then. Because he stopped.

"She's dead," I said.

"I know she is, Laurel," he said gently. "What happened?"

My chest got tight and heavy at once, and I started to feel spinny. I held on to his arm to stay up.

"I don't know."

"Yes you do. You can tell me."

But I couldn't. We were driving back from the movies. And we stopped by the tracks over the river, off the old highway. And there were flowers growing out of the cracks in it. And now that I was thinking about it, I really couldn't breathe. The river was very loud.

Sky was holding on to my shoulders. He was saying, "Laurel." I tried to suck in the air, tried hard to get it into my lungs. Sky told me to watch my breath. So I breathed and watched it hanging on to the air for a while and didn't think about anything.

"Laurel. Stay here with me."

His face was clear, and all of the houses with their Christmas lights faded behind him. With his smallest hands he had opened a door in me, and I cried and cried. He held me there until I laughed a little. Like the whole thing was a joke. I wanted to forget all of it. We kept walking. Along the path of light, I saw every bulb come into focus only as we got close to it. And finally he said, he said it to me, "I love you, too."

Yours,
Laurel

Dear John Keats,

I am looking out the window at the clouds cracking from cold, letting the silent sun in. Today it's a new year. I bet in California on New Year's Day, the air is velvet with warmth. I bet everything glows, and the palm trees stretch off the earth in a new morning yawn. Mom must be waking up there right now, in her new life. And I know I shouldn't feel this way, but I hope that you'll get it. I hate her for leaving me.

When we were younger, Mom used to have New Year's Day tea parties for me and May and May's friends. I never invited my own friends, because I loved belonging in May's world. I loved how May would smile at me and drop sugars into my tea. Mom made sandwiches cut into perfect triangles and scones that she served with miniature jellies, which she would take from diners and save up for us. There were always more jellies than we needed. We never ran out of any flavor, not even raspberry. I can't get those jellies out of my head today. Maybe my mind is holding on to them because I don't want to think about everything else.

Last night, we all went to Kristen's house for a New Year's Eve party. Not a big party. A just-for-us party. And it started off perfect. Kristen lives in the foothills, up by the road where Sky and I drove that first time. You can see the city lights from there, spreading out below you like stars on the ground. Her parents are still in Hawaii, so we had the house to ourselves. We made New Year's punch, with cinnamon After Shock and cinnamon sticks and apple juice and red food dye. It might sound gross, but it was delicious, and we all got blushed from it. Now that we'd done the rest of the break with families and all, New Year's felt like it was a holiday made just for us.

After a while, Kristen wanted everyone to sit in a circle and give our New Year's intentions. She knows about Eastern philosophy, and she said that when you set an intention, you can create transformation. Like the universe will listen. So we all got these papers she picked out especially for us. Mine had stars, Tristan's had music notes, Hannah's had horses, and Natalie's had a design that looked like brush strokes. Sky's had a design that looked kind of like fish and kind of like sperm, or at least that's what Tristan joked. Sky was not really keen on this whole part of the night, since he doesn't much like things that have to do with talking about feelings around other people. But when I watched him writing down his intention on his paper, he looked serious, like he meant what it said. The plan was we could read what we wrote out loud or not, and then we would burn our papers in the candles that were lit in the center of the circle.

Kristen went first. She said you can also set intentions for people you love. And hers was for Tristan, that he would recognize and use his true gifts and brilliance. That he would become who he was meant to be, even if it took him away from her. She said that he is a very talented musician.

Everyone, including Tristan, was quiet when she read this. She threw her paper into the flame.

And then it was Tristan's turn. He said, "My intention is to handcuff Kristen to the bed every night until I have to unlock her and put her on a plane to New York." We all cracked up. Kristen looked a little mad that he wasn't taking it seriously, and maybe also that he brought up handcuffs in front of everybody. But then he got more serious than he ever is about anything and said, "No, all right. This is what I really wrote." The first part he read is a quote from his second favorite band after Guns N' Roses, the Ramones. " 'Experiencing us is like having the fountain of youth.' My intention is that it will always be that way, as long as we live. We'll get old, but my intention is that we'll never sell out. That we'll never get too old to remember who we are right now, together."

What they read, I think, explains the difference between Kristen and Tristan, which is that Kristen wants to grow into something, and Tristan thinks that right now, being young, is the most real thing. As Tristan put his paper into the fire, he said, "And I might add, I am in love with a beautiful woman. I pray that I will be able to survive losing her. And that she will come back to me if she can."

Kristen tried to catch tears on her sleeve before anyone could see and said softly, "Your turn, Natalie."

Natalie didn't read her intention out loud, but she looked into Hannah's eyes for a moment as she burned her paper.

Hannah said, "Okay, these are my intentions. I have more

than one." She gazed down and read them off her paper. "For my grandma to get better. For the shadows to stop growing. For people to stop being angry. For the world to be safe for love, every kind of love. For me to be one day brave enough to sing in front of everybody. For Buddy, my beautiful horse and dear friend, to drink from an eternal spring and never die." Then Hannah kissed her paper before she burned it.

It was my turn next. I was a little drunk from the punch, I guess, but the intention seemed important, like a real intention. I wanted to read it out loud, but I couldn't do it. I opened my mouth, but my throat got dry, so I threw the paper into the candle and watched the flame grow with it.

It was Sky's turn last. He didn't read his out loud, either, of course. But when he put his paper in, instead of burning inside the candle like it was supposed to, part of the paper flamed up and flew right toward me! I scooted out of the way just in time, but everyone was screaming "Fire!" Tristan threw his cinnamon punch at the paper, which blazed brighter for a moment and then burned out, and the punch soaked my dress. Sky screamed, "Shit!" But after a second we started laughing hysterically, and Tristan said to Sky, "That's a pretty wild intention you had there, brother." I wondered what it might have been.

My favorite part of the night came next. We danced to "Sweet Child O' Mine" in the living room, which was full of windows that show the city star-lights. Natalie twirled Hannah, Tristan dipped Kristen, and even Sky danced with me, and although he's not a good dancer, it didn't matter. After a while, everyone let go of the person they were dancing with and we all just danced together. Spinning and dipping and singing like that night was all there was, all there needed to be. I'd have stayed in it forever if I could.

When the clock turned to midnight, we shouted and kissed, and do you know what? I saw Hannah throw up her hands and throw back her head, like she forgot that there was anything to be afraid of, and she pulled Natalie in and kissed her.

I kissed Sky, and he pushed my hair back from my face, which was a little sweaty from the cinnamon and the dancing. He said it in my ear, for the second time ever. "I love you." He said it hard, like he meant it, and like maybe it hurt. It made me want to stay right there, with his voice in my ear. I would have given him every part of me if he wanted it.

When the song ended, Tristan started it over, and Kristen set the clock back three minutes, and we had another midnight, all hugging and kissing each other, and then we had another and another, until we were so tired from dancing that everyone collapsed.

I'd kept drinking and drinking the punch, and I guess by this time I must have been pretty drunk, because when the music finally stopped, the world was spinning.

Natalie and Hannah fell asleep wrapped around each other on the couch, and Kristen and Tristan went to go to bed in her room, but I wasn't tired. I told Sky I needed some air, so we went out to the balcony and leaned over the city. "Sky," I asked him, "what was your intention?"

He looked at me for a moment, deciding. "If I tell you mine, will you tell me yours?"

I nodded that I would.

"My intention was to learn how to feel again like I felt when I was eleven and my dad took me to my first concert. The Stones. I wasn't even into music then. But something about that night, it got into me. My intention was not to hate him so much that I can't remember that feeling, and feel it again sometime."

"What was the feeling?" I asked.

"I don't know. Like loving something so much that you want to create it. I mean, not *it* exactly, but like you want to do something. I mean, I was eleven. I don't know if I knew that then. But I knew that it was the best night of my life."

I wanted to hold his heart in mine and to make a safe place for it. "You're going to create something great. You'll be an amazing writer."

Sky smiled at me. "Your turn," he said. "What was yours?"

"It was sort of long. It was about this John Keats poem that we read in English, the one that ends with 'Beauty is truth, truth beauty.' I've been thinking about what that means. And then, when we were writing stuff down, I thought I understood it all of a sudden. The intention said, 'Truth is beautiful, no matter what that truth is. Even if it's scary or bad. It is beauty simply because it's true. And truth is bright. Truth makes you more you. I want to be me.'"

When I finished, I was waiting for Sky to say something, but he just looked at me for a minute. "That's pretty," he finally answered, "but I don't really get it. I mean, what is the truth you're scared of?"

I shrugged. I thought somehow he'd understand. I thought somehow those words would have been enough to tell him everything I couldn't say. "I don't know," I replied.

"If you want to be you, you can tell me. I want to know you."

I wanted to tell him, but the story seemed to start such a long time ago. It didn't fit into my mouth. It didn't fit into my brain, even. It started when I figured out how things could get broken. When suddenly May couldn't protect me anymore. It started when knowing that was sadder than all of the things themselves. My thoughts were spinning away, and then it hit me. She's gone. I tried to push the reality away, but it was so heavy, I could barely breath.

"Laurel," Sky said, "talk to me. Stop disappearing. Tell me something. Anything."

I was spinning again. I started going backward, everything from the past blurring into the present, and through it all was the worst guilty feeling. I had to make it go away. I had to find May.

"Okay," I said. "I'll tell you a secret." I leaned into him and whispered, "I'm a fairy."

Sky looked at me and raised his eyebrows.

"You don't believe me, do you?" I said. "Watch, then, I'll

show you." I got up and climbed onto the low wall at the edge of the balcony. "Close your eyes, and I'm going to fly off of this." I ignored the voice in the back of my head that said, *Only your sister has wings.* It made me mad.

"Laurel, get down from there!" Sky said, from what felt like the distance.

"No. I want to fly. I want to fly like May," I said, and started crying.

Sky came over and grabbed me, pulling me off the edge. I tried to hit him. I tried to hit him and hit him, but he wouldn't let me. He held me tighter, so I couldn't move.

And when I stopped, when I went limp in his arms, he lifted my face and said, "Laurel, I can't do this. I can't be with you if you're going to be like this."

"Be like what?" I asked. "How am I?"

"Like your sister," he said.

"You don't know what she was like. You didn't really know her." I paused. And then I asked, more quietly, "How did you know her?"

Sky just shook his head. "Come on," he said. "You need to go to sleep."

I was so tired all of a sudden, and so scared, and so ashamed. I could feel everything that's bad about me and wrong and everything that I know I shouldn't feel, all of the ways that I am angry at her rushing toward the surface. I followed him inside and lay on the couch. He brought me some water, and then he told me, "I'm going to go home." I got the worst sinking feeling, like I'd ruined everything.

"Please don't leave me."

"I'm tired," he said.

"Sky," I said, "Sky, May wasn't like that. She didn't do it on purpose. She was good. She wasn't like me."

He just nodded. "All right, Laurel."

"You know how good she was, right?"

Sky squinted back at me, like he didn't know who he was looking at.

"Say yes," I said, frantic.

"Yes," he said. But then he added, "She wasn't perfect."

I wanted to scream that he was wrong, but I couldn't find my voice. I kept hearing his words echo in my head as I lay on the couch watching him walk away from me. I kept hearing it all night, until I finally fell asleep, and woke up from a dream where May came back, her fairy wings shimmering and intact. She said she hadn't died after all. She'd just flown away for a bit.

I called Sky this morning, but there was no answer.

Yours,
Laurel

Dear Kurt,

Today is a day when the world turns out to be flat. January fourth. It's a taking-down-the-Christmas-tree day. We waited too long this year, until all the pine needles were brittle and shedding so hard they fell past their snow-white sheet and onto the carpet, and finally started to show up in the kitchen. Neither Dad nor I had the heart to do it. Until I woke up this morning and I knew it couldn't go on any longer—Dad and I looking at each other over Rice Krispies and not saying anything about the dying tree or taking it down, not saying anything about anything, me just putting my ear to the cereal bowl like I used to and making some lame joke about snap crackle pop.

So today when I woke up early, I went in my pajamas and started unscrewing the base, and by the time Dad walked out I had the whole tree over my shoulder, and it was raining its needles all over the cream carpet as I carried it to the door.

Dad asked, "What are you doing?"

"Taking down the tree."

"Here, let me help."

"No," I snapped, without meaning to. "I can do it myself."

When I got outside, I didn't know what to do with it. So I went to the toolshed and looked around until I found a saw. I laid the tree down on the cement and started tearing through its trunk, until it was in jagged pieces. The smell of pine was overwhelming, like the tree's heart was leaking out. I piled the series of sawed-off limbs next to the trash.

When I went inside, Dad was vacuuming up the last of the needles on the floor. The sound covered my stomach's growl as I walked past him and into the kitchen to pour some Rice Krispies.

Dad came in and poured himself a bowl. He was wearing his work clothes, ready to go. "What do you have on the docket for your last day of vacation?" he asked, looking at me expectantly.

"Oh, just a little TV in my pajamas," I said, giving him a weak smile. I don't have to go back to school until tomorrow, thanks to teacher planning day.

"Where's that boyfriend of yours?" Dad asked. "You think you might want to bring him around in daylight hours one of these days?"

"Uh-huh," I said, my heart plunging into my stomach. I didn't want to tell Dad the truth, that Sky hadn't called me back in five days.

And then, as I picked up my spoon to try to force down some cereal, I saw it. One of the little plastic spiders I'd given Dad for Christmas, floating in my bowl. He must have snuck it into the cereal box. I did my best to laugh, and then I looked up at him. He was smiling so hopefully. "Gotcha," he said, before he left for work.

When he was gone, I put on *In Utero* and lay down and listened to "Heart-Shaped Box"—it must have been a thousand times—and felt sick. I thought about dialing Sky's number again, just to hear it ring. I've called over and over since New Year's, and when the voice mail picks up—not even Sky's own voice, but the generic woman's that comes with the phone—I hang up. I haven't left a message. I don't know what to say.

Earlier tonight when I was trying to fall asleep, I kept thinking of the tree going in the trash, and it just wasn't right. I couldn't stand it being there like that. So I snuck out, and I carried the limbs, two by two or three by three, all the way through the dark neighborhood where I would walk with Sky and back behind the golf course to the ditch, and I tossed them into the water so they might get to go to the river and then, who knows, maybe to the ocean. They could become driftwood on a beach in California.

I am back in bed now, but I still can't sleep. My hands have splinters. They smell like something stolen from the forest. I keep thinking about the day that May's wings broke.

We were fairies, and when we were together, the magic worked and I believed in it. Every time the shadows in our room seemed to come alive, I could wake May up, and we would sneak out into the yard with new lists of ingredients for a spell. They changed with the season. Six red berries. Seven yellow leaves. A drop of honey from the honeysuckle. A hard-searched-out feather. A melted icicle. We cast spells to keep the shadow people at bay, spells to preserve the fairy gene, spells to defeat the evil witches. When I found an injured bird one day, we cast a spell to help her heal, and sure enough, when I went back to her box the next day, she was gone. She'd flown away.

But there was this part of the fairy world that I could never share with May; I couldn't fly. I knew the rules. Only the oldest child had wings. But I kept thinking maybe there could be some exception. It was all I wanted. When Aunt Amy would take us to church, that's what I'd pray for. When May pulled an eyelash off my cheek, I'd squint my eyes shut and wish for wings with all my might.

But when they didn't come, I thought that if only I could see May fly, that would be the next best thing. If I saw her soaring into the sky, I would for sure be part of the magic. I would look at her naked back when we'd lie on the bed after a bath and Mom rubbed cold lotion on us. I would see her shoulder blades jutting out and imagine how she could unzip her smooth skin to reveal these transparent, magnificent, shimmering wings.

I would beg and beg to see. Just the tip of a wing. Just for a minute. But she always said she couldn't show me. I kept begging, and one day, I must have been about seven by then, I begged so hard that I started to cry. So finally she told me that she would fly to the top of the elm tree in our yard, and after she flew up there, I could come out and see her.

"But you can't look until I tell you. Until I've landed. Do you promise?"

I promised. I meant to keep the promise, too. I really meant to. But as I stood by the back door, waiting for her to call me, something so strong pulled at me. I thought maybe if I saw by accident, it wouldn't count. So I cracked the screen door and peeped out. And I let my eyes flash toward the tree, just for a second, just in time to see her falling from high up. She was screaming, "You broke them! You broke them!"

I ran over and started sobbing. "But I didn't even see. I didn't even see. I didn't look!"

"You broke them." May was crying, too.

"I can fix them! Can't I fix them? Isn't there a way?"

May looked into my face. I was crying harder than she was. She wiped the tears from my cheeks. She said, "Maybe I can find a way to sew them. They might be crooked, but maybe they could work again." And she gave me a list of things to find for sewing and said to go get started. She was going to take out the wings and have a look.

It was at that moment that I understood what the wings were. They would never work again. Because they were made up, and the magic spell that May had cast to make me believe, it was broken. But neither of us could admit it. Neither of us could stop pretending for the other. She had crutches after that for a month. As she'd hobble through our house, I kept telling her that I was sorry. But she'd tell me it was okay—her wings were working again, and by night she'd be soaring.

Yours,
Laurel

Dear Amy Winehouse,

Your parents got divorced when you were nine. Your dad had been seeing another woman for almost your whole life. He said later that it didn't even seem like the divorce affected you that much when you were a kid, but that somewhere deeper maybe it really did. You sang a song about it called "What Is It About Men." The song talks about your destructive side that comes from a past that's "shoved under" your bed. *"History repeats itself,"* you sang. I wonder if that's true. If there's a hurt that's buried in us, maybe it keeps finding its way through.

You said this thing once: "Often I don't know what I do, then the next day the memory returns, and I am engulfed in shame." I feel like that. I keep thinking about May, how she tried everything and how she was bright and beautiful. But then it keeps coming in, what happened to her that night. I keep seeing her falling. I keep feeling like I did that day when I was seven. She could fly, and I broke it.

I have a new favorite song of yours that I've been listening to over and over—"He Can Only Hold Her" *for so long.* The man in the song tries to love the girl, but she's not really there, not all the way. She's running from something inside of her that he can't see. I think that there's something like that inside of me.

On the first day back at school today, I wore my new sweater that Mom sent me for Christmas. I cut the neck off and pinned a patch to it, like May's first-day sweater, and I snuck into May's room, and for the first time I put on some of the lipstick she left on her dresser—Cover Girl Everlasting. I kept imagining what it would be like when I saw Sky. We'd kiss by his locker. He'd say I looked beautiful. I'd say I was sorry. That I didn't mean to scare him on New Year's. I'd had too much to drink. He'd say he was sorry for what he said about May. He'd say he meant to call. And we'd be able to forget about all of it. He loved me. He'd said so, after all.

But all morning he was nowhere. And all day, nothing made sense. At lunch, Hannah started flirting with one of the soccer boys, and a few of them, including Evan Friedman, came over to our table. I felt him looking at me and heard his friend whisper something and snicker. I just tried to avoid eye contact. Hannah was bragging about Neung, how he's a gangster and stole Christmas presents for his nephew and a gold necklace for her. (She hasn't been back to his house since that night they hooked up, but I guess she sees him at work, and she told me if it's slow sometimes they still make out a little in the back.) Everyone was impressed by this, except Natalie, who said that's not the Christmas spirit, and if it were her and she had no money for gifts, she would have made her nephew something instead. What Hannah didn't tell everyone was that on New Year's Eve, she and Natalie had kissed out in the open, like the promise of a world where Natalie was the only one.

I didn't say anything about Sky. When they asked where he was, I just shrugged. When they asked if I was okay, I just smiled. In spite of everything, I was still hoping that he'd come up and wrap his arms around me. I was trying to concentrate on specific things, like the thread unraveling on the seam of my new sweater, to remember that I was still there.

Finally, in eighth period, I went to chorus with Hannah. Last semester we had PE, which is over now. "Thank god we're done with that," Hannah said. She was excited for chorus since she loves singing, and she said what's great is that in a chorus full of other voices, you can sing without feeling self-conscious.

As we walked into the room, I saw him. Sky. I didn't expect it. The electives are shared between all of the grades, but I thought he'd take shop or art. Maybe those classes had filled up. He was all the way across the room, talking to a couple of other juniors. I kept waiting for our eyes to catch. But all class, he didn't look at me, not even once. Mr. Janoff and Mrs. Buster, who co-teach, grouped us into altos and sopranos and so on, and when we started to learn our first song, "A Whole New World" from *Aladdin*, that's when it got really bad. I felt like something was stuck in the back of my throat. I couldn't sing, or even breathe right. I was gasping and looking across the room at Sky, not looking at me. Like I didn't exist. I wondered if I wasn't really there. I kept telling myself to get on the magic carpet and fly above everything. I could feel the hot breath of a shadow on me as I closed my eyes and tried to concentrate on the voices, tried to pick out each voice from the whole chorus of them, blended together. I could hear Hannah near me, singing in her sweet soprano. I could hear the boy from Bio who sells fake acid. And I thought I could hear Sky. The lyrics to the song said not to close your eyes. But when I opened mine and looked at him, he was staring down at his sheet music, not even moving his lips. The song said that there was a whole new world to share. Sky looked blurry across the room. A fading photograph.

When the bell rang, Hannah grabbed my arm, asking, "What's wrong?" I pulled away. "I don't feel well," I said, and I rushed out. I walked down the hall like a ghost who could walk through anything. Anyone. I forgot to move when I saw a crowd of boys walking in my line. One of them said, "Watch where you're going!"

Sky's driftwood heart is still on my dresser. I run my fingers over it to make sure my hands are real. To know that his must have been, because he carved it.

Yours,
Laurel

Dear Kurt,

Have you seen the trees in the winter, when the branches are bare and covered with birds who have landed there? It was like that today. They kept perfectly still, shawling the tree in feathers. I was shaking. The wind was blowing hard, but the branches with their blackbirds didn't move at all.

But I'm not starting at the beginning. This was Sky and me breaking up. His voice kept getting carried off by the wind. I was looking at the birds in their trees, thinking of how fast their hearts beat and wondering if their fast-beating hearts keep them warm. I might sneak out right now just to get to cry out loud.

When I came home from school today, our second day back from break, there was a letter taped to the gate with my name on it. It was a strange thing to find, but I knew it would be from Sky. I sat down on the bench outside and tore it open. I think part of me was still hopeful, in spite of myself. And it started out like a love letter, too, the old-fashioned kind. All about how I am different from other girls. And so special, et cetera. And even about how he loves me. He said he decided to leave a letter like this because he hasn't been sure what to say to me in person. He said that all he's wanted is to know me, but on New Year's he realized that neither of us is ready. He said that I have to take care of myself, and he can't take care of me. He said, *You'll be much happier, without me.*

When I read that, it was like I landed with a slam in the world that I had been trying not to live in—the world where he was really leaving. It's a lot like something you said in your suicide note. You said that your daughter's life would be so much happier without you. I can tell you that you are wrong. It's a terrible excuse from someone who can't bear to be around. It's a bad way to make yourself feel better when you know you are leaving someone who doesn't want you to go. Someone who needs you.

After I read the letter, I lost all sense. I had to see his face. So I got up from the bench and started to walk to his house. I brought my phone and kept trying to call him. When no one answered, I walked the whole two and a half miles, crying all the way.

I knocked on the door. I wasn't seeing straight, until his mother answered, in her frayed satin bathrobe, a bun coming undone in whispers. Her face shocked me, and I stopped sobbing. It was so soft, the way she looked, and so kind. Her eyes said she understood everything. But before I could get a word out, Sky came. He said, "Mom, go inside. I'll be back in a little bit." He shut the door and stepped onto his porch, now decorated with sparkling plastic snowflakes.

I had had so much in my head, but suddenly, there was nothing to say. Sky's body was tense, and his eyes didn't want to look at me. Finally he said, "Come on, I'll drive you home." So I followed him, and on the way to the car, he said, "You understand, right? You can't come here anymore."

That's when I started crying again. I cried the whole way back in his truck that smelled like thousand-year-old leather. His truck where we first touched. Your voice was playing low on the stereo. *Aqua seafoam shame . . .*

When we got to the golf course near my house, I said, "Stop."

He glanced over at me like he didn't want to, but I said it again. "Sky, stop!" Then I said, more quietly, "I just want to go on one more walk. You can't just never talk to me again."

So he parked. And we got out. I remembered the golf course with the geese and the time we fell down laughing there. The geese were gone and the leaves were gone, and there were just the blackbirds now, shawling their trees. The tears wouldn't stop. I wanted to find him.

"You said you love me," I said.

"I know." I could see Sky's face start to freeze over.

"Then why would you leave me?" I shouted.

"I don't know. I can't watch you like this. Sometimes it's like you disappear. It's not just that you cry so much. It's that you cry and I don't know what you're crying about. And you won't tell me. I can't fix it."

I was sinking. All I could do was cry harder. The thing is, Sky was right. I wondered if I could have told him, if he would have stayed. But I knew it was too late. The damp was under my clothes. The moon in its almost circle shape was under the clouds. When I looked up at Sky, I couldn't see his face. Just a shadow.

There was something shattered in me, and now he saw it. No one could fix it. I had tried to be brave like May, to be bright and free and a bolt of stars, but I couldn't. I wasn't. He'd seen it. He had opened the door to the underneath part of it where I was just her little sister, who couldn't save her or anything. Bad and wrong and it was all my fault.

All at once, the blackbirds flew off the trees. Like there was a thing that told them when to go. To some secret place in the sky, before they would have to come back down and find new trees. I think I went with them, but I wasn't sure if I would ever land again.

Yours,
Laurel

Dear Kurt, Judy, Elizabeth, Amelia, River, Janis, Jim, Amy, Allan, E.E., and John,

I hope one of you hears me. Because the world seems like a tunnel of silence. I have found that sometimes, moments get stuck in your body. They are there, lodged under your skin like hard seed-stones of wonder or sadness or fear, everything else growing up around them. And if you turn a certain way, if you fall, one of them could get free. It might dissolve in your blood, or it might spring up a whole tree. Sometimes, once one of them gets out, they all start to go.

I feel like I am drowning in memories. Everything is too bright. Mom making tea for May and me. Walking home from the pool in a thunderstorm, with the mulberries stained red on our feet. Galloping our imaginary horses through the snowfall. Dad riding away on his motorcycle, with the elm trees raining seeds over him. Mom folding clean shirts into a suitcase. May walking toward the movie theater, her long hair swinging behind her. May's hand pressed against window glass. They don't stop.

What I remembered first from that night is the sound of river water. The sound kept moving, steadily, like it would never stop. I saw the bluebell-shaped flowers, popping up between the cracks in the pavement. Two of them trampled, one still cupping the moonlight. The river getting louder, drowning everything with its roar.

We were driving down the old highway, May and me. The night was filling with stars. We had the sunroof open and the music loud and she was singing "Everywhere I Go," in a voice that was sweet and slow. *"Tell me all that I should know . . ."* She knew every up and down and lilt and curl. May started singing so hard, I thought her voice would explode into millions of pieces. I kept my eyes glued upward, watching the stars start to eat the sky alive. I made a wish for her to be happy.

She pushed on the gas, and the car sped like a blast down old Highway 5, into the dark. The speed took all of the sound with it, until there was only the music left. We were alone on the road. She pulled over at our place, where the old train tracks cross over the river. In the springtime you can hear the rushing water. By the end of the summer, it dries up and moves so slowly, you can hardly hear a thing. In the winter, it nearly freezes over. But this was spring. Flowers, everything's-possible spring.

We first discovered our spot when we'd go on river walks with Mom and Dad as kids. And then May and I started coming here together again, on weekend afternoons when we were supposed to be at the library, or after movie nights like this one. We'd park by the tracks and crawl out on our hands and knees over the wood planks. We would sit there and feel like we were floating. We would play Poohsticks like we did when we were little, searching out the perfect fallen branches and dropping them over the edge of the tracks and into the river, then leaning over the other side to see whose would appear first. We'd say whoever's stick won would be the first to get to the ocean. We would collect piles of them and play forever. Imagining what great adventures they would have riding the river all the way to the sea. And then we would crawl back to land.

But something different happened that night. We were sitting in the middle of the bridge. I said something I never should have said. May stood up and started to cross back to land on the metal edge of the track, like a tightrope.

I could feel myself begging for her to balance. I wish I could have run out after her, to stop her, to do anything to undo it all. But I couldn't move. It's like I had left my body and I was in hers instead. I felt her waver. I kept feeling her fall. It's like everything that was going to happen had already happened, and I couldn't do anything but watch it.

And then she turned back to look at me, her dark eyes searching their way through the dark. Wisps of her hair coming loose from her ponytail. Her arms slender and white in the moonlight.

Our eyes met, and in that moment it was real again. I opened my mouth to call her name. But before a sound came, all of a sudden, it's like the wind just blew her over. Like her body was simply sailing over the blackness below her. She didn't trip. She didn't jump. It was as if she floated off. I could swear she stayed there, standing on air for a moment, before she fell.

I can't stop seeing her body floating there. And all I want to do is run out after her and pull her back. I didn't save her. My feet were frozen. My voice was broken. I wish I could tell you why.

Because now it's all I can see. May standing on the air, waiting for me to take her hand and pull her back onto the tracks. Crawl with her back to land. And go home together.

Yours,
Laurel

Dear Kurt,

In the second sentence of your suicide note you said it would be pretty easy to understand. It is and it isn't. I mean, I get how it goes, what the story is and how it ends. Becoming a star didn't make you happy. It didn't make you invincible. You were still vulnerable, furious at everything and in love with it at once. The world was too much for you. People were too close to you. You said it in one sentence I can't get out of my head: *I simply love people . . . so much that it makes me feel too fucking sad.* Yes, I understand.

I feel it, too, when I see Aunt Amy rewinding the answering machine, playing a Jesus-man message from months ago as if it were new. When I see Hannah running over in her new dress to meet Kasey, all the while looking over her shoulder at

Natalie. When I see Tristan, playing air guitar to one of your songs, when what he wants is to write his own. When I see Dad, coming over to kiss my head before bed, too tired to worry about where I go at night. When I see the boy in Bio who fills the always-empty seat beside him with a stack of books. Everything gets in. I can't stop them.

So yes, in a way, it's easy to understand. But on the other hand, it makes no fucking sense, as you would say. To kill yourself. No fucking sense at all. You didn't think about the rest of us. You didn't care about what would happen to us after you were gone.

It's been three days since Sky broke up with me. I couldn't bear to see him at school the next day, or the day after that, so I told Dad I wasn't feeling well and stayed in bed, burying myself under the blankets. When Natalie and Hannah called to check on me, I texted them back that I had the flu. I wasn't actually sick, but I drank some NyQuil from the medicine cabinet and slept away the days. Dad cooked me Lipton chicken noodle soup every night when he got back from work, which is what Mom used to make me when I was home sick. It was so sweet, him trying like that, but it only made me feel worse. Tonight, when I was still loopy from the cold medicine that I didn't really need, I asked him for a lullaby. He sang "This Land Is Your Land." I closed my eyes and tried to travel in my mind to the feeling that I'd had as a kid when he sang it.

But I couldn't go anywhere, except back to the night that

May died. And to the nights before that—what it was like waiting for her to come back. There's something wrong with me. I can't say what it is.

I was frozen still when May fell. The policeman found me there the next day, just looking down at the water—that's what they say. I don't remember. When they asked, "What happened to your sister?" I didn't answer. They found her body in the river.

Dad never pushed me, but Mom asked all the time, wanting to know what we'd been doing at the bridge, why we had gone there, why weren't we at the movies like we were supposed to be. I think Mom was mad at me for not being able to explain. I think that could be why she moved to California and stopped being my mother. I think she thought it was my fault. And I think she's right. If she knew the truth, she'd never come back.

One day just before she left, I remember Mom was wiping off the counter after breakfast. She looked up and said, "Laurel, did she jump?"

"No," I said. "The wind blew her off."

Mom just nodded back at me, her eyes teary, before she turned away.

After Dad went to bed tonight, I lay awake. I tiptoed down the hall and started to turn the handle of the door to May's room. But then I turned it back. I was afraid, suddenly, of how I knew she wouldn't be there. Of how quiet all of her things would seem, staring at me just as she'd left them.

Nirvana means freedom. Freedom from suffering. I guess some people would say that death is just that. So, congratulations on being free, I guess. The rest of us are still here, grappling with all that's been torn up.

Yours,
Laurel

Dear Amelia Earhart,

I keep thinking of you, having flashes of what it would have been like in your plane that morning before you disappeared. You'd already flown twenty-two thousand miles of your journey across the world, with only seven thousand to go over the nearly empty stretch of the Pacific. You'd meant to make it to a tiny island called Howland. From the air, its shape would be hard to tell apart from the clouds.

Your plane didn't have quite enough fuel, and your maps were off by a little bit. Radio communication was bad. When you sent a message to the Coast Guard on Howland—*We must be on you, but we cannot see you. Fuel is running low*—were you in a panic? They answered back twenty minutes later, but didn't know if you'd heard them. And then they got your last message, full of static, an hour after that. They sent up smoke signals to you, but we'll never know if you were close enough to see them. They sent out search parties, and we've been searching ever since. It's a testament to how much we loved you that we are still looking seventy-five years after your death. But sometimes I can't help wonder what would be different if we finally had an answer.

Today is Monday, my first day back at school after the breakup with Sky. Dad finally said that he thought that he should make an appointment with the doctor, and I knew I couldn't go on playing sick forever. So when it was time to switch to Aunt Amy's yesterday, I said I was feeling better. This morning I put on a sweatshirt that I hadn't worn since eighth grade and pulled my hair back. At lunch, I didn't feel like eating my kaiser roll or even a Nutter Butter. I went over to our table and sat down with Natalie and Hannah. Before they could start asking questions, I blurted it out. "He broke up with me."

They went into a chorus of *Oh my god, are you okay, how come?* After something really bad happens, the next worse thing is people feeling sorry for you about it. It's like confirmation that something is terribly wrong. I tried to hold back the tears that were burning behind my eyes, but they came out anyway. Natalie and Hannah rushed to put their arms around me, and Hannah pulled my head against her shoulder and started to stroke it. "He has no idea what he lost. You are the best, most beautiful girl ever. What a complete idiot asshole, Laurel."

"No," I said, my voice muffled by her shirt. "I think it's me."

"What? No it's not. It's not."

"I can't go to chorus today," I told Hannah. "I can't see him."

"Okay, it's all right," she said. "You don't have to go. We'll ditch."

So in eighth period we snuck off campus, walking through the little flecks of swirling snow that were melting against the blacktop, and went to the sketchy Safeway to get some liquor that we would drink at Natalie's house before her mom got back from work. We climbed up onto Natalie's roof, bundled up with blankets, and passed the bottle of cinnamon After Shock between us. Hannah was trying to make me laugh and trying to think of a new boyfriend for me, suggesting friends of Kasey's that made Natalie wince, and then Evan Friedman—"He and Britt are on the outs again, and I've seen the way he looks at you."

But I could hardly pay attention to what they were saying. There was only one thought that I could hear, that kept repeating itself in my head, over and over. *She's dead.* And then it happened. Maybe because I was grateful for Natalie and Hannah, or maybe because I was too tired and too sad to try to be like her anymore—I just said it out loud.

"My sister's dead."

It was silent for a moment. Finally, Hannah nodded. "I know," she said. "I'm so sorry."

It didn't make sense. "What do you mean you know?"

She hesitated, and then she said, "Tristan told us. He and Kristen used to hang out with some kids from Sandia, and they said that a girl from there died. It wasn't that hard to figure out that she was your sister."

"What?" I was suddenly angry, like when your parents yank the blankets off in the morning to make you get out of bed. In the cold January air, my skin felt so thin that it was almost transparent. "Why didn't you ever say anything?"

Natalie answered, "You never talked about it. We were just waiting until you were ready, I guess."

And then Hannah said, "I mean, you've never had us over to your house or anything like that. We just thought that you didn't want us to bring it up."

I stared at them. My body drained of everything, including the anger that had been so palpable only a moment ago. They'd known this whole time, and they hadn't treated me any differently than they did. I wondered what they saw when they looked at me.

Hannah passed me the bottle, and I took another sip. "What was she like?" Hannah asked.

"She was beautiful," I said. "She was . . . she was great. She was funny, and smart, and she was basically perfect." *And she left me*, a voice screamed from inside my head.

I looked at my phone. "Shit, it's three o'clock! My aunt!" Hannah passed me the mouthwash out of her purse, and I climbed topsy-turvy down the ladder in a rush and ran back to school, slip-sliding over the coating of snow on the sidewalks that was starting to stick. When I arrived, half an hour late, Aunt Amy's car was one of the few still in the parking lot.

"Where have you been?!" she asked.

"I was just—I—"

"Your cheeks are all red," she said, and put her hands against them. "You're freezing!"

"I'm sorry," I said. "I . . . this kid, he fell on the ice and I had to help him inside."

Aunt Amy gave me a look like she didn't know if she believed what I was saying. "Lying is a sin, Laurel."

I looked back at her. "Yeah, I know."

She was quiet for a moment, tucking her silver hair behind her ear as she tried to decide whether to trust me or not. My stomach knotted with guilt.

"Can we go?" I finally asked.

She nodded, and her old white Beetle pulled off through the parking lot.

When we got home, it was like I'd never been so tired. I told Aunt Amy I still wasn't feeling well and went to lie down. For some reason I started thinking of this game called the dead game that May and I used to play with Carl and Mark, the neighbor boys.

In the summer, after a day at their pool, we'd go home for dinner, and then afterward they'd ring the bell to ask us to come play basketball in their driveway. May would look beautiful, giggling and dribbling the ball, her bikini top still on and bleeding through her tee shirt. She liked to run across the court, but when she got to the basket she'd pause and laugh and never make the shot. But sometimes Mark would pass the ball to me. I would concentrate until I couldn't see anything else, and I loved the swish that meant he'd high-five me afterward. I loved his hand against mine, if just for a moment.

Then when it started to turn to dusk, before the street-lights came on and we'd have to go in, May would usually say it was time to play the dead game. It was the perfect time of night, when parents would be watching TV and the light was low and sticky. She loved the game because she always won.

She got the idea for it that summer before she started high school, just after Mom moved out. Once our basketball game was over, we'd started playing truth or dare. May thought that Carl's and Mark's dares—stuff like flashing the neighbors' houses—were boring, so she said she had a better dare, for all of us.

The dead game worked like this. You'd lie in the middle of the road on your back with a blindfold—it had to be the dead middle, we made an *X* with chalk—and wait for a car to come. Whoever could last the longest before they got up and ran out of the way won. The thing is, since you had the blindfold on, you could only know if a car was coming by the sound it made on the road.

Sometimes, the car's driver would see us in the street and screech the brakes. But lots of times, because it was dusk, the driver couldn't see. May would wait just a second too long before she rolled away. The first time we played, I thought the car would really hit her. I ran out into the street in front of it, waving my arms up and down, until it came to a screeching stop. An old woman got out and started yelling at us. When she was gone, May turned to me. "What's wrong with you? Don't you get it? That's not how the game works." The point was that when you were the dead one, you and only you knew exactly when to run. My cheeks turned hot with shame.

So after that, when it was May's turn, I would stand on the sidewalk, curling my bare toes into the cement, still warm from the day's sun. I would try not to look at the street. I would look instead at the coming stars and wish for May to be okay. But at the last minute, I couldn't help it. I always looked down and saw her body there, motionless. When she'd roll away in time, I would wipe the hot tears from my eyes. And then she would be so alive, grinning and panting in the summer night air, high on it.

Yours,
Laurel

Dear River,

In chorus today, Hannah held my hand almost the whole time. I kept thinking, *Don't look at Sky*. But I couldn't help lifting my eyes, just once, to where he was like a mirage across the room, and remembering how his chest felt rising up and down with breath. I would have given anything to go back to his arms around my body. I would have given anything to be someone different, someone he wouldn't have left.

After class, Hannah was waiting for me, but I told her I'd meet her in the alley. When the room cleared out, I sat down, putting my head against my knees and trying to stop breathing so fast.

Eventually I walked out to the alley and found Natalie and Hannah with Tristan and Kristen. When they saw me, they all got quiet and looked at me, in that way that makes you certain about why you never wanted to talk about anything in the first place. If it had just been about Sky, they would have found something to say. But it was more than that. It was May. I guessed that Natalie and Hannah had told them that I'd finally admitted that I had a sister who's dead.

After a few moments of silence, they forced themselves to chatter. Tristan lit a cigarette with his giant kitchen lighter. When he and Kristen had to leave to get ready to go to dinner with her parents, they both squeezed my hands, like they were trying to transmit a secret *I'm sorry*. But I didn't want any pity. I didn't deserve it. It wasn't a normal kind of thing where I could just cry and be sad and let them stroke my hair. There were too many mixed-up feelings— and what's starting to grow, more and more, is this ball of anger in my stomach that I can't control. I know that it's not what I'm supposed to feel. And I feel even guiltier for feeling it. But I can't help it.

When Tristan and Kristen left, I was about to go, too, so that I wouldn't be late again to meet Aunt Amy. But then Hannah said, "Hey. About your sister. I'm sorry that there's nothing good to say. And I'm sorry that we didn't say anything sooner."

The way that she said it, so kindly, made me wish that I could tell her everything. "I'm sorry, too," I answered, "that I didn't talk to you guys about it before."

Hannah said, "I mean, words can't be good enough for a lot of things. But, you know, I guess we have to try."

Then Natalie said, sounding very serious, "It's, like, really sad that people die."

We all laughed at once, because this was so obvious. It was an accidental, perfect example of what Hannah had just said.

"Are you drunk?" I asked her, which made us laugh harder.

When it finally got that after-laugh quiet, I said, "I'm so glad I have you guys." And I am.

I thought about what Hannah said, how words aren't good enough for a lot of things, but we have to try. And maybe I should try harder. I just don't know what they'd think of me if they knew what I told May that night. If they knew what I'd let happen the nights before that. I worry that I'd lose them, too.

The night you died, River, your brother and your sister and your girlfriend found you collapsed outside of a club. You'd taken too many drugs. Your sister tried to breathe life into your body. Your brother called 911. He shouted and shouted into the phone, begging for someone to come. Begging for someone to save you. But by the time the ambulance came, it was too late.

When they found May's body in the river, the coroner said it didn't look like her anymore. That's why Mom and Dad decided to cremate her. I never saw her. I've never seen anyone dead.

I guess you know what it's like to fail someone. To fail everyone. River, you were a star so bright. One that people made wishes on. Until you took so many drugs that you took your life. Do you think that everyone gets to be a star like that? Do you think that everyone gets to be seen? Gets to be loved? Gets to glow? They don't. They don't get to do it like you did. They don't get to be as beautiful as you were. And you just wanted to burn up.

Yours,
Laurel

Dear Elizabeth Bishop,

The art of losing isn't hard to master. I've done it. The days feel transparent, like I am walking through that kind of barely yellow sun coming through a shield of clouds—too thin. Empty light. It doesn't land.

Sky broke up with me three weeks and one day ago. After school this afternoon, me and Natalie and Hannah and Kristen were in the alleyway. They were smoking and talking. I wasn't listening. I was just looking at the flecks of late January snow, swirling in the yellow street lamp. The sky was glowing the way it does right before it's going to get really dark. I was holding Sky's sweatshirt that he'd let me borrow one night when we snuck out. I'd started wearing it to school back then and had joked that I'd never give it back. Now I never will. I finally pulled it out of my locker that day to take home and put in the back of my drawer where I keep memory things that make me sad. But it was snowing and I was cold, so I put it on. It smelled like him.

At that moment, Sky came out of nowhere down the alley. He looked startled to see me. He said, "Hey," and kept walking. I looked down because my eyes were filling up with tears, but I didn't want him to notice. When he passed, I whispered, "Hi," and watched his back. I loved him still and hated him all at once.

Then I saw. He stopped under one of the streetlights and put his arm around her. A girl with blond hair and big boobs that were bursting out of her shirt, which was super tight and pink with an anarchy symbol on it. She was only wearing that tee shirt even though it was snowing out. Sky took off his same leather jacket and put it around her. And they kissed. With his hands under the jacket. I knew I shouldn't look, but I couldn't move my eyes. My throat clenched so that I could barely breathe.

The girl saw me watching and pointed toward me, but before Sky's head could turn, I looked down. The next thing I saw, she was leading them off into this old yellow car, a cool car, and big enough to have sex in, I'm sure.

I wanted to scream. I wanted to jump in front of the stupid yellow car. I felt like I could burst into flames.

Hannah said, "He's an absolute asshole, Laurel. Do you want me to kill him? Because I will." Kristen offered me a cigarette, which I usually don't smoke, but now I did, if only to find a way to suck something in. I asked Kristen who she was, and Kristen said her name is Francesca, and she graduated last year, and she works at Safeway. While they tried to make me feel better by talking about how I'm so much prettier and cooler and nicer than her, I thought of her running people's ice cream and chocolate milk and hamburger meat and Jim Beam through the checkout line, and then running out through the snow in her uniform, where Sky would be waiting in his truck to take her home. And I thought of your poem.

—*Even losing you (the joking voice, a gesture*
I love) I shan't have lied. It's evident
the art of losing's not too hard to master
though it may look like (Write *it!*) *like disaster.*

Write it. Write it. Write it, Laurel.

Yours.

Dear Jim Morrison,

I played "Light My Fire" last night and tried to wake myself up from the fog I've been in. I bounced around my room a bit, but it didn't sound like it used to in the car with Sky, or at the Fallfest park, because I kept thinking about how they found you in a bathtub dead. Cause of death: unknown. It's hard not to know.

In the picture of you, the famous one that's on all those tee shirts and posters and stuff, your eyes are fierce. They burn into us, calling us forward and pushing us back at once. Your arms are out, making you into a cross. Your chest is bare, vulnerable, but strong like an animal's. I read about how when the Doors were recording an album, you would only sometimes show up to the sessions, and when you did, a lot of the time you were drunk. There would be piles of chicken bones and apple juice containers and empty rose wine bottles everywhere. And sometimes you'd yell at people. It's sad when everyone knows you, but no one knows you. I am guessing that you might have felt that way. They see what they want you to be. And if you wear leather pants, and have a beautiful body, and drink lots of expensive wine, and if your voice sounds like the edge you strike a match on, then these things are blocks that you have given them to build the person they want.

I thought May was what she wanted to be. I thought she

was free and brave and the world was hers, but I'm not sure anymore. Jim, I want people to know me, but if anyone could look inside of me, if they saw that everything I feel is not what it's supposed to be, I don't know what would happen.

Right now I am in Algebra. I think Evan Friedman is sort of playing with himself again. Britt is staring down into a compact she has hidden in her lap, trying not to look at him. They are broken up for the second time.

It's been five weeks and two days since Sky dumped me. I would like to say that I am getting over him, but obviously I am not. Sometimes after school I walk the long way to the parking lot around the track and I see him making out with Francesca near the bleachers, or getting into her car. I want to run and scream at him. I want to pound my fists against his chest as hard as I can, and I want him to put his arms around me and hold me so that I stop. I want him to kiss me again and make it clean. But now he's behind the thickest glass wall, like no matter how hard I ran at it I couldn't break it. I could only shatter myself.

Francesca is awful. She wants to beat me up. Yesterday, when I walked out of school through the alley, she was standing at the end of it with two other girls I've never seen before. When I saw her, I started moving fast with my head down, just wanting to get past, but they circled around me.

Francesca said, "I saw you watching Sky and me."

My heart was about to spring out of my chest. I was trying

hard to keep it in, because I didn't want it to land on the asphalt at her feet, next to the golden ring someone had dropped in the crack. And I really didn't want to cry.

"Let me tell you something, little girl," she said. "He doesn't want you anymore."

It wasn't fair of her. I knew he didn't want me. She didn't know how badly that hurt. I hated her. I could feel the tears burning in the back of my eyes, but I couldn't let myself cry in front of her. I couldn't.

So I said, "Don't you think it's a little lame that you still hang out at the high school?"

Her face turned red and she said, "I'll kick your little ass. I'll kick your ass so hard, no one will recognize your pretty little face."

I had to think fast. My body felt swervy and my brain was connecting all of these dots that shouldn't connect. But one thing I knew was she is bigger than me by far and definitely could beat me up.

So I said, "Why don't we play a game instead?" I pushed past her and walked out into the street. I called back to her. "It's called the dead game. Whoever lasts the longest when a car comes wins."

I lay down and closed my eyes. I heard a car coming from a ways away. I heard it getting closer, though it was not that close yet. I could last much longer.

I heard her say to her friends, "Oh my god. This girl's a total freak. Let's get out of here." And I knew then that I'd won. I knew that she was scared of me now, instead of the other way around.

I heard the car getting closer. And then I heard Sky's voice out of nowhere. "Laurel! What the fuck are you doing?!" he was shouting.

I rolled out of the way in time and I ran and I ran, and I remembered the night I got good at the game. May had always been the best, the bravest. Carl was almost as good as she was, but not quite. And Mark was just behind him. I had been last. As soon as I'd hear a car turn down the block, I'd want to run. I'd try to wait an extra second, but when I got up and pulled the blindfold off, I'd see the car was still so many houses away and feel stupid that I thought it was about to hit me. I knew that Mark would never love me because I was afraid, and they could all see that. I thought if only I could be fearless like May. If only I could be flushed and daring and beautiful in the twilight like she was. I thought if I wasn't such a wimp, then it would all be different. He might love me back.

Then something changed. It was after May started taking me out with her to the movies. We were playing the game, and I lay down for my turn. I felt a new kind of quiet. Like nothing could touch me. Waiting, just waiting for the car to come. And when I heard it turn down the block, I wasn't scared of anything. I could hear exactly where it was. I didn't need my eyes. I could see the street, the car traveling. It was in front of the Fergusons'. The Padillas', the Blairs', the

Wunders'—I knew just how close and just how far. It came in front of Carl and Mark's. I heard May screaming, "Laurel! Get out of the way!" But I didn't need to go yet. I waited one last second. Then I rolled and ran and saw the car whizzing right by. When I walked up to the sidewalk, May said, "Laurel! What's wrong with you?!" She looked really scared. The way I was always scared for her. I thought Mark would be proud. I thought we'd high-five. But he was white as a ghost. May hugged me.

She said, "Don't ever do that again!"

"But I won, right?"

May said, breathlessly, "Yeah. You won."

After that, I don't think we ever played again. And after that, I knew that Mark would definitely never love me. I'd changed.

I heard Sky's voice, echoing after me. *What the fuck are you doing?* I just kept running, faster than I knew I could, sucking the cold air into my lungs. Down neighborhood streets, through the shadows cast by crooked tree branches, past the houses in a row that seemed like they would be safe inside. Until all I could hear was myself breathing, as loud, it seemed, as an ocean.

Luckily for me, Aunt Amy was late to pick me up, so by the time I ran back to the parking lot, she wasn't there yet. Sky and Francesca and those other girls were gone. Aunt Amy felt bad for being late, so she asked me if I wanted to get fries. I did. And then I wished I could go home, home where

Mom would be making enchiladas for dinner and May would be setting the table, folding the napkins into diamonds like she would.

Yours,
Laurel

Dear Kurt,

You had a daughter, and now you'll never get to know her. You won't see what she's going to be when she grows up. You won't be there to make dinner together when she comes back from the pool in the summer smelling like chlorine. And when she rides her bike with no hands and flies over the handlebars, you won't make it better. You won't be at her chorus concert, with all the other parents on the sweaty gym floor, watching her face when she closes her eyes and lets her voice out. You won't watch her walk through new snow in your backyard or lie down to make an angel. You won't see her fall in love for the first time. And if her heart gets broken and she curls under the flannel sheets she just washed and cries, you won't hear her. When she needs you, you won't be there. Don't you care? How could you do that to her?

Do you know what she'll have instead of her father? Your suicide note. Did you think of that when you wrote it, that those words would shadow her whole life?

You wrote that you have a daughter, full of love and joy, kissing every person she meets because everyone is good and will do her no harm. You said that terrified you, because you couldn't stand the thought of her growing up and becoming like you were.

But did you think about the fact that when you wrote those words, when you took your life, you stole the innocence you loved her for? That you forever changed her heart full of joy? You were the first to do her harm. You were the first person to make the world dangerous for her.

I don't know why I've written you all these letters. I thought you got it. But you just left, too. Like everyone does.

I walked into May's room tonight, once Dad was asleep, and I tore your poster off the wall. I tore it to shreds and I threw it out. And I sobbed until I couldn't sob anymore. And now, that particular poster is gone forever. And I'm sorry.

It can't be undone. We can't put it back, and we can't bring you back to life, and I hate that. And I hate you for it, too. There, I said it, I do. I'm sorry. I'm so sorry. I wonder if your daughter has forgiven you, because I don't know if I could.

The truth is, I don't know how to forgive my sister. I don't know how to forgive her, because I don't deserve to be angry at her. And I'm afraid that if I am, I will lose her forever.

Yours anyway,
Laurel

Dear Heath Ledger,

The Dark Knight was on TV tonight. I watched it with Dad. One thing that we can still do together is watch movies. Those and baseball, but the season doesn't start again for another few weeks. When the movie ended and the credits came on, Dad said, "The world has changed, hasn't it?" before he got up to go to bed. That sentence seemed to carry the weight of everything we can't talk about.

Dad used to be happy. A man with a family. Superheroes used to be indestructible. They didn't lose the loves of their lives, or let good people die, or give up on their morals, or have to grieve. And storybook villains used to be simply evil. Not humans twisted into something terrifying. But *The Dark Knight* is like a grown-up version of a superhero story. Batman is broken, too—he loses the woman he loves, and he has to frame himself for murder in order to save hope for the city. You play the Joker, the evil figure, and you are brilliant at it.

The movie scared me, to tell the truth. You scared me. I want to say what I could take from it, but I can't. All there is is this deep-in-my-stomach feeling of terror, and this fear that there is no really happy ending anymore.

It's the second week of March. Spring should almost be here, but the air has held on to its cold, wind coming in gusts to scare off the buds that might want to start blooming. It's been a long time since I've written one of these letters—almost a month. I guess after I tore up Kurt's poster, I didn't feel like it anymore. Until I watched *The Dark Knight* and started thinking about you. I first got to know you from that movie *10 Things I Hate About You*, and I always remember that scene where you jump up on the bleachers and sing "Can't Take My Eyes Off You" to the whole girls' soccer team to capture the heart of the girl you like. But after that, even though you got a lot of offers, you wouldn't do any more teen movies. Instead, you ate ramen noodles in your apartment and waited. You didn't just want to be famous, you wanted to be true to yourself. And eventually you got more roles, better ones, and you became the kind of grownup that made growing up seem okay, like you don't have to lose your spirit in order to get older. You became the kind of father that any daughter would have wanted to have. When they found you in your apartment, dead from too many pills, I really did think it was an accident. I don't think you meant to go.

I read about how you were planning to buy a garage for your daughter in Brooklyn so that you could make it into your own private drive-in theater together. When I think about that, it almost makes me cry. How you would have parked there with her, the two of you in the front seat passing popcorn and eating Red Vines and laughing at a cartoon flickering on the screen—the sort of story that ends like it's supposed to, unlike the ones that haunt us as we grow up.

This month has passed by in a blur, but I guess there are a few new things to tell you about. One thing is that Hannah decided that she thinks bruises are pretty. She's started paint-ing them onto her cheekbone with eye shadow. They look real, too. Natalie tells her not to, but she loves her so much that she only kisses them and tells Hannah she'll make it better. Sometimes we want our bodies to do a better job of showing the things that hurt us, the stories we keep hidden inside of us.

The other thing is that Hannah got her provisional li-cense, and on Saturday we drove through the mountain roads to this guy Blake's house. Hannah met him at her new job at the Macaroni Grill. He's a busboy there, and she's a hostess. She got a new job because Natalie got so angry every time she talked about Neung that finally she swore she'd never see him again and quit Japanese Kitchen. But she still has Kasey, and now Blake, too. She doesn't like taking Natalie over to the boy-friends' houses anymore, but she still doesn't like to go alone, so I went with her.

When we parked in front of Blake's little mountain shack, I felt immediately nervous. It wasn't locked, so we walked right in. It smelled like cherry-flavored cigars, and all the windowsills were lined with glass bottles covered in dust.

When he came out of the bedroom, I froze. Hannah says he's twenty-two, but to me he looked even older. And not older-in-college like Kasey. Older like Paul was, May's boy-friend, and Paul's friend. His black hair was grown long into his face, and he had a midnight shadow, much darker than five o'clock.

He moved right past us and opened the fridge. He pulled out some Tecates and tossed them to us. I didn't catch mine. It flew past me and onto the carpeted floor, which I felt that I was sinking into. I tried to move my feet, but they wouldn't budge.

Hannah bent over and picked up my beer. I felt my fingers close around it.

"Laurel, are you all right?"

"What? Um, yeah. Sorry."

I watched Blake put his arm around Hannah, and all I could see was May, walking up to Paul. Watching her smooth hair swinging behind her. His eyes devouring her.

Blake's roommate was sitting on the couch, which was upholstered in brown velvet and looked like it had been there since the seventies. The roommate doesn't speak. Not because he can't, but because he took a vow of silence a year and nine days ago. He hasn't said a word since. After Blake explained this, he pulled Hannah off and they disappeared into his room, leaving me alone with the roommate, who was reading a book called *The Birth of Tragedy*. I guess Blake must have told me the roommate's name, but I forgot.

I forced my nail under the tab of the beer and popped it open with a crack that sounded as loud as an explosion. I sipped it. The roommate's eyes kept glancing up over the top of the page at me. I tried to count all of the little bottles sitting on the windowsill, but I kept losing track. My feet stayed just where they were, glued to the rug.

I wondered if where we were was like the places where May would go with Paul when he'd take her away those nights. It was so different than I'd thought when I pictured her driving off somewhere magical. I imagined her now in the room with the curtains drawn and fluorescent lights on, lying on the dingy cream-colored rug and smoking cigarettes, letting the smoke trail out of her dark lips.

The roommate moved his legs over, I guess to make room on the couch, and I got a sinking feeling, as if the carpet were quicksand. He patted the place on the couch beside him. All I could think was, *It will just hurt worse if you fight it.* As if my body were moving without me, I saw myself walk over. The world went quiet. Like we were being recorded on silent film. The roommate and the room and me. And I started just watching us in the movie. I watched his hand reach out and start to touch me.

My head was pounding. His hand—his hand was on my thigh. All of a sudden I was somewhere else. All I could think was *no. Please no. Make it stop.* I slammed my head against the wooden arm of the couch.

I felt the shock of the hurt and I let the colors start to come in at the edges of my eyes.

I don't know how long it was, but when I opened them, the roommate was staring at me, confused.

And then Hannah was standing over me in her bra. She looked alarmed as I opened my eyes. "I'm sorry," I said.

"What's wrong?" Hannah asked.

"Can we go?"

Hannah nodded and went to get her shirt. She promised to make it up to Blake later, because he was annoyed that I'd interrupted their hookup.

On the way to the car, I picked up some snow and rubbed it on my face to try to wake up. Hannah looked at me worriedly and asked, "Laurel, what happened?"

I could feel the bump growing on the back of my head. I started to cry. "Please, just drive," I said. So she did.

When we were partway down the mountain, she asked again. "What happened?"

"I never want to go back there," I said.

"Okay, you don't have to," she said gently.

"But I don't like Blake. I don't want you to see him again."

"Not you, too," she groaned. "That's Natalie's line."

"Please, Hannah, promise?"

"Why?"

I couldn't let anything happen to Hannah. "He just—he reminds me of this guy my sister used to date. Just don't see him again, okay?"

Hannah paused a moment and stared out at the road. "Okay," she said finally, "if it's really important to you." And then she asked, "Are you mad at your sister? For leaving you?"

My heart squeezed up. I started to panic. I thought somehow she knew. "What do you mean?" I asked.

"I mean, like, 'cause she died."

"But it's not her fault," I said.

"Yeah, but that doesn't mean you can't be mad. I'm mad at my parents for dying and leaving me with Jason, and I don't even remember them."

I thought about it. Nobody had ever said it like that before. "You're brave," I said.

She laughed. "What do you mean? I am not. I'm an idiot."

"No, you're so smart. I wish that you knew it."

And then it was quiet. We turned up the music and drove down the mountain roads, dark and shiny from March's melting snow.

The stories change as we get older. Sometimes they don't make sense anymore. I would like to write a new story, where Hannah just loves Natalie, and May comes back home, and I never tried to be like her but got the whole thing wrong.

Yours,
Laurel

Dear River Phoenix,

There's this part in *Stand by Me* where your character tries to convince Gordie that he could be a writer someday. You tell him that it's like God gave him a special talent and told him to try not to lose it. But, you say, "Kids lose everything unless there's someone there to look out for them." That hits me in the heart. It makes me think about everything there is to lose as you grow up. It makes me wonder if there was no one to look out for you. Or if there was and they just turned away for a moment.

I keep having this feeling, hot inside of me, that maybe there was no one to look out for me when I needed them to. It was May who I thought would always do it. But maybe there was no one to look out for her, either.

I think of Mom and the question she asked. "Did she jump?" I told Mom no, but I'll never know the answer. And I think of the question that Mom didn't ask, the question in her eyes. *Why didn't you stop her?* The question I can't get out of my mind. *Why didn't* you*?!* I want to ask Mom.

She called tonight. After I'd answered her usual questions about how's school, et cetera, with my usual one-word answers, she asked, "Is everything okay there?"

"Yeah, I guess."

"Are you sure? You never talk to me."

"I don't know what I'm supposed to say. You're not even here."

There was a long silence. Then she said, "I wanted to tell you. I finally went to the ocean yesterday."

"Yeah?"

"I hadn't gone since I'd gotten here. It's almost like I was waiting for you and your sister. But yesterday, I just . . . I got in my car, and before I knew it I was at the water. It's like May was pulling me. And it was so beautiful, Laurel. I could almost feel her there."

I wanted to say, *Well, how fucking great for you*. Instead I was quiet.

"Maybe you can come out for a visit sometime this summer and we'll go together."

All I could think when she said that was that it meant that she wasn't coming back. Instead of answering her, I blurted out, "Mom, why did you leave?" I wanted her to tell me the truth. If she left because she was mad at me, or because she thought it was my fault, or because I never answered her questions, I wanted her to just say it.

"Your sister's death shattered my heart, Laurel. Nobody knows what it's like to lose a child."

"Dad does."

Mom didn't answer.

"Nobody knows what it's like to lose a sister, either," I said.

"I know, sweetie. I know—"

"But Dad and I didn't run away. We stayed together."

"I know, Laurel. But staying together is not always the best thing when you can't be good for each other. Everything doesn't always work out exactly how we want it to."

"No kidding. Don't you think by now I've figured that out?"

I could hear Mom start to cry.

"No, Mom, please don't cry. Forget it, okay? It's fine. I have to go."

When I hung up, Dad walked in. "Hey, sweetie," he said. "Are you all right?"

I stared straight ahead and tried to wipe the tears away. "I hate her."

"No, Laurel, you don't mean that. I know you're angry, and that's okay. But you don't hate her."

I shrugged. "I guess."

I looked at Dad's shoulders, hunched over, and his face that was fighting to stay neutral. I think he was searching for something more to say, but when he couldn't find anything, instead he came over and gave me a half nelson, like he used to when I was a kid. I knew this was meant to make me laugh, so I did my best.

You grew up so fast, River. But maybe the little boy who needed someone to protect him never went away. You can be noble and brave and beautiful and still find yourself falling.

Yours,
Laurel

Dear Janis Joplin,

When you were alive you acted tough, shouting and drinking and singing your heart out. Giving it to everyone. All your fans. But the edge was too close. Your manager came to the hotel to find you one day when you missed your recording session. He saw your Porsche out front, painted bright and bold and psychedelic, with a night sky and a bright day, a land over the rainbow, a butterfly. The car was just there waiting, ready to go. But inside your hotel room, you were dead, sixteen days after Jimi Hendrix. The dream of the rock stars was ending. The dream of the sixties—where everything seemed possible, where there was everything and more to explore—didn't make sense anymore. The beautiful, the brave, were burning up. You had believed that the world could change. And then yours ended. An overdose of heroin. Some booze. It was an accident, everyone assumed.

I still love you, but I'm starting to realize that it's not a coincidence. That the people I most admire, the ones who seemed to be able to use their bodies, their voices, to fight away the fear, you didn't win, not really, in the end. It's gotten harder to write these letters, and maybe that's why.

But I wanted to tell you the only good news that I have had in a while, which is that Kristen got in to Columbia. For a congratulations present, Tristan baked her a cake with a New York City skyline that he drew on it with frosting, which I thought might have been the nicest thing ever. When we all met in the alley after school to celebrate, he cut the cake and passed it around. Natalie kissed Hannah's fake-bruised cheekbone and fed her bites of frosting. Tristan was smoking a cigarette in the middle of eating his and saying, "You're my big city girl, right, babe?" Kristen nodded and smiled a half-sad smile. "Right, babe."

Graduation is less than two months away. Afterward, Tristan is going to community college here. He already has an apartment picked out that he's going to move into this summer. And he got a job delivering for Rex's Chinese. They say that they are going to stay together, but they both know that they won't. She's leaving him, and he's happy for her, as much as he can be. Next year, he'll probably have a new girl-friend. A college girlfriend. Probably she'll have blond hair and her eyes won't stay still like Kristen's. They'll dance all around a room, and he'll miss the way Kristen looked at things, the way she looked at him, like there was nothing else to see.

Yours,
Laurel

Dear Amy Winehouse,

Aunt Amy asked me if I wanted to go to the mall with her today to get some spring clothes, including a dress for Easter, which is coming up tomorrow. She said she was thinking we'd have an aunt-niece day, like a mother-daughter day, I guess. I wasn't in the mood, but I didn't want to hurt her feelings, so I agreed.

We were in JCPenney, and I was browsing the tops, when she came back with an armful of dresses for me to try on, all of them too lacy and too long. I don't know how she even found so many church dresses in a department store, but she must have left the juniors' section, that's for sure.

When I came out of the dressing room to show her the first one, she looked at me in the mirror under the fluorescent lights. "You're so beautiful," she said, but she said it like it scared her.

I shrugged.

Then she said, "Be careful, Laurel." And out of nowhere she started to cry.

I put my arms around her, trying to make her better. I was shivering in the dress, the too-early air conditioner making goose bumps all over.

Finally Aunt Amy wiped her eyes on her flowered blouse and smiled at me. I wanted to get out. I didn't try on my other dresses. I just said I wanted the one I had on, with the long white sleeves and buttoned-up top.

So she paid for the dress and we went to have lunch. The smell of the food court in the mall is like an indoor version of the state fair. I got what I usually get—a Hot Dog on a Stick and lemonade. We sat near the fake trees under the white light from the skylight, where Mom and May and I used to sit. Aunt Amy looked at me picking the batter off the corn dog.

She said, trying to be casual, "So, do you have any crushes? A boyfriend?" As if she hadn't practically forbidden me from talking to any member of the male species. I wondered if this was a trick. I never told her about Sky, because I didn't want her freaking out about it. I shook my head no.

"Well, that's for the best . . ." And with that she trailed off.

She picked back up with, "You know, I am very proud of you. Your mother is, too."

I swallowed hard, the corn batter stuck in the back of my throat. I didn't believe that Mom had actually said that. But I guessed that she'd probably told Aunt Amy about our fight, and Aunt Amy was likely trying to smooth things over. I know I should call Mom and apologize, but instead I've been avoiding it for the past two weeks.

I didn't want to get into all of that, so I just tried to smile. "Thanks," I said. I couldn't imagine what exactly Aunt Amy was proud of anyway, unless it was the fact that I didn't have a boyfriend, which is only the case because I got dumped.

Then Aunt Amy asked me, "Do you remember my friend who I went on the pilgrimage with?" She couldn't keep herself from grinning. "He's coming into town next week."

She went on explaining, and what I got is that after all those months of not calling, the Jesus Man called Aunt Amy last week to tell her he was coming to visit. I guess they'll go to dinner at Furr's, and I will tell her she looks pretty before she leaves and pretend to be asleep when she gets home so she can do whatever God wills her to do with him.

Honestly, it makes me sad. Because she sent him cookies, and cards, and New Mexico chili, and messages, especially the messages where she would do the voices of Mister Ed and of the Jamaican bobsledders and she would be herself. Her hopeful self, like she was saying, *I'm here.*

But for the past year, she got no response, and finally she

stopped pressing her flowered dresses like she imagined someone was about to see her in them. She put her rose soap back in its box and back on the shelf where she'd never use it. She finally gave up.

And now she will take her rose soap out again, its rose petals rubbed down from all of the mornings of sitting in the shower waiting for something. It's not new anymore, but she'll take whatever she can get. She'll take even a night of iced tea with ice crushed the right way, and fake cherry pie, and maybe his hand on hers across the table. And if he wants more, she'll give it. If he says, "God means for us to do this," she'll believe him.

After lunch, we stopped at one of the kiosks where they sell tee shirts. Aunt Amy picked up one that said GOD MADE SOME MEN EXTRA CUTE. She found that hilarious. She laughed at it so hard that tears started running down her cheeks. I didn't get the joke. But she said she couldn't resist, she just had to buy it for him. I could see as she folded the shirt carefully into the bag, she's hooked on the promise again. I just don't want him to be gone in the morning and never call back.

After the kiosk, I took Aunt Amy into one of the cool stores, Wet Seal, where I secretly wanted to look around for something right. Something that would make up for the dress I had to get to make her happy, something that would feel like me—whoever I am right now. I hadn't bought any clothes in a long time. I'd been wearing May's for a while, but since Sky and I broke up I haven't wanted to. So mostly I just wear my old things and try to blend in.

At first all the clothes in the store seemed dressed up in the wrong way, like they were pretending. But then when I was looking in the back on the sale rack, "Rehab" came on the store radio. A lot of your songs, even the saddest or the maddest ones, sound happy, like you are telling a hard truth but backing it up with a dance tune. It's part of what I love about you, how you can be defiant, or heartbroken, or broken open, and still be bright about it.

And then I found this shirt. It's lavender crushed velvet. I felt like you were with me as I rubbed the fabric against my cheek and remembered how I love the way the new clothes in the mall smell sweet and pressed. Like very clean sugar. I tried it on and I felt prettier than I've felt since I had on May's dress at homecoming.

Tomorrow for Easter, I'll wear my scratchy white dress and we'll go to Aunt Amy's church, where they sing things like "Our God Is an Awesome God." And then on Monday, I'll wear my new shirt to school.

Amy, you were all over the covers of tabloids and stuff, doing what you did. And how the world is now, how we follow everyone and try to see everything, it changes the story. It makes your life into someone else's version of you. And that's not fair. Because your life didn't belong to us. What you gave us was your music. And I am grateful for it.

Yours,
Laurel

Dear Amy Winehouse,

Something terrible happened today. I wore my new lavender crushed velvet shirt to school, and in English, I saw that Mrs. Buster had on the exact same shirt. Mrs. Buster is not a young, pretty, hip teacher. She's old and she has bug eyes and ironed-out hair. It seemed impossible. I'd gotten the shirt at a cool store. A store for teenagers. Why would Mrs. Buster shop there? But her shirt was exactly the same, right down to the smooth gray shell buttons that I'd loved. That I'd been running my fingers over all morning. I know everyone noticed. My face was red all through class.

After the bell rang, Mrs. Buster tried to talk to me. "Laurel!" she called as I was walking out.

I turned around, barely.

"Nice shirt." She smiled.

She knew that our same shirts were not a good thing for me, so there was no reason to smile about it. I did not smile back.

"Laurel, how are you doing?" She said it the way she does, like a question that might as well be a loaded gun.

"Fine," I said. Though I wanted to tell her I wasn't doing well at all, if she must know. I also wanted to ask her what the hell she was doing ruining my life shopping at Wet Seal.

Instead, I mumbled, "I'm late," and ran out the door.

I knew I'd have to see her again in chorus, because she

co-teaches it with Mr. Janoff. And Sky's in chorus. When I got the shirt, secretly I had hoped that Sky would notice me in it and see who I could be. Maybe he'd feel a pang of regret over losing me. Now that clearly would not work. So I ditched. My grade in chorus is going to pretty much suck, between my mumble-singing and skipping class a couple of times. But at that moment, I didn't care. Tristan always ditches eighth period to get stoned, so I told him I wanted to come.

"Oh, the shirt thing?" he asked. Clearly everyone knew by then.

I just gave him a look. With Tristan, I never have to say anything if I don't want to. He always gets it.

"Well, in a who-wore-it-better poll, you'd smoke her. You look really pretty."

That was kind, and it made me laugh a little as I followed him out through the alley and down to the edge of the arroyo. It was still filled with shiny dry leaves leftover from winter that glinted below the budding trees.

I'd actually never smoked pot, so I think Tristan thought I was just going along to sit with him. But when he pulled out his pipe, I said, "I want some."

He raised his eyebrows at me, but he passed it over.

Before I started to try to figure out how it worked, I said, "Can I ask you something?"

"Hit me."

"Do you think it's true, what you said about being saved? Do you think Sky found someone better at saving him? Like

Francesca? Maybe I just couldn't do it. And maybe she can. Maybe he's happier now. Like really happy."

"You're too good for him, Buttercup. You deserve a better man. As for her, she couldn't save a ladybug from a rainstorm if you gave her a fifty-foot umbrella."

"But what about my sister? Why couldn't I save her?" My voice wavered, and I could feel myself tilt inside. Maybe outside, too. I never say things like that out loud.

Tristan paused for a minute and got very serious. But not quiet the way most people get about these things. He looked at me and said, "I was wrong."

"About what?"

"What I told you about saving people isn't true. You might think it is, because you might want someone else to save you, or you might want to save someone so badly. But no one else can save you, not really. Not from yourself," he said. "You fall asleep in the foothills, and the wolf comes down from the mountains. And you hope someone will wake you up. Or chase it off. Or shoot it dead. But when you realize that the wolf is inside you, that's when you know. You can't run from it. And no one who loves you can kill the wolf, because it's part of you. They see your face on it. And they won't fire the shot."

A long moment passed with me looking at him. I knew what wolf he was talking about. I feel its teeth all the time. And I understood, too, that even though Tristan seems tough, he is afraid, like me, that there is something inside of him that could eat him alive.

Then he said, "Laurel, you couldn't have saved your sister. But, love, you've got to save yourself. Do that for me, okay? Because you are worth it."

No one had ever said that to me before.

I realized I was still holding the pipe when Tristan said, "Do you want to pass that over here? You don't need it." So I did, and smiled at him. It was already almost three o'clock. Tristan was waiting for Kristen to come out, so I said bye and started walking back.

I went past the alley, on my way to the bus stop, and I nearly bumped into him. Sky. In the corner of my eye, I saw Francesca pulling away in her yellow car.

"Hey," I said, startled. I was closer to his body than I'd been since we broke up, and it hurt how badly I wanted him to touch me.

"Hey," he said back. He shifted awkwardly. "How are you?"

"All right." It was quiet for a moment. I knew that I should just walk away, but I couldn't do it. Everything in me that was angry at him for leaving started bubbling up to the surface. I thought of his arms around Francesca now, the way they'd been around me, and of his voice hot and gravelly, the way it would get when he said things that he meant. I kept telling myself not to cry, but the tears were already coming to the edges of my eyes. I wiped them away with the sleeve of the stupid lavender velvet shirt. "How could you do that?" I asked. "How can you just . . . be with her?"

I could see the muscles in his body get tense, and his voice was, too. "'Cause that's my way of dealing. You have these great friends. I don't. So yeah, it's nice to have someone around. It's nice to just be with someone who's easy to be with. I'm not proud of it. But that's what happens sometimes."

"But you said you love me. You don't just leave after that."

Sky was speaking low, like if he let himself go, he would explode. "Yeah, I did. You were the only girl I've ever said that to. You think it's just you who got hurt, but it's not like that. How do you think it was for me when I saw you climb up on the edge of that balcony? How do you think it was watching you cry all the time and not being able to do anything about it? I wasn't lying when I said I love you. How do you think it feels watching you in the fucking middle of the street waiting for a car to come and hit you?"

Sky was angry at me. Although maybe it's messed up to say, it felt good in a way, because it meant he cared. I guess when you love someone and they put themselves in danger, you are supposed to be mad.

I thought about what he said. That I'd hurt him. I'd never actually realized that. We do things sometimes because we feel so much inside of us, and we don't notice how it affects somebody else. I'd been selfish. I remembered the feeling of Sky's moths fluttering, looking for a light. I felt like a street lamp that had gone out.

"I'm sorry," I said. I reached my hand out to his chest. He didn't pull back.

"It's okay. It's just, I know that you love your sister, but it scared me, seeing you act the way that she would."

"What do you mean? How did she act?" And then I took a deep breath and asked, "How did you even know her?"

Sky paused a moment. "Do you really want to know?" He sounded nervous.

"Yes," I said. Although honestly, I wasn't sure.

"We had a couple of classes together freshman year. She was pretty much the life of any room she walked into. And she was the only girl in our grade who was always at all of the parties with upperclassmen. I never used to do that kind of stuff. Then when my dad left that year, I started going out, too. So we'd talk sometimes. She was usually drunk. She'd tell me about your family, and your parents getting divorced, and she talked about you, too. But she was always hooking up with these seniors. She got a reputation for being, um, wild, I guess. Maybe she needed the attention. I just thought that she'd get sick of all of that eventually . . ."

Sky trailed off. He was looking at me expectantly. I didn't know what he wanted me to say. I was trying to put it together, and the puzzle pieces fit, but the picture didn't make sense. I was trying to see May, but it wasn't the May who rushed off into high school like a new world was waiting to greet her. I guess it shouldn't have been so much of a surprise. I've known for a long time how she snuck out at night and came home drunk, about Paul and all of that stuff, but part of me still wanted to believe that there was something beautiful on the other side of it. That she was happy.

"What are you thinking?" Sky asked.

"I don't know. What happened after that?"

"Nothing really. By sophomore year, it's like she was somewhere else entirely. She'd sit in the back of the class, and she'd do her work, and she'd hardly talk to anyone. She was seeing that older guy. I saw them at a party together once. She was so drunk, and he was all over her. It was clear that she was out of it. They disappeared into some bedroom together. The whole thing made me sick. A few days after she died, I spotted him hanging around the parking lot at school. Maybe he was looking for her. I guess he didn't know yet. I was so pissed off. I beat the shit out of the guy. Once I started, I couldn't stop. When I got questioned about it afterward, I didn't want to say anything about who he was. I knew May had a family, of course, and I didn't want to cause any trouble. Anyway, that's why—I got kicked out of Sandia after that."

He finished talking, and then there was this gulf of silence. I wished that all of the words that Sky had said could go back into his mouth and never come out. Because there was one thing about the whole thing that was sinking in, that came through in his voice when he talked about her, and soon it was all I could hear. "You liked her," I said flatly.

"Yeah, maybe," he said reluctantly. "I mean, maybe I had a little bit of a crush on her."

Why did that hurt so much? I'd known it all along, anyway—when he looked at me, he'd only seen a shadow of May.

"So that's why you talked to me that first day. That's why you wanted to be with me. Because I was the next best thing."

"No," Sky said. "No, Laurel, it's not like that. I mean, of course I thought about May at first. But then I didn't. It's you I was in love with. You're actually . . . you're so different from her."

I shrugged. "Whatever. It doesn't matter now."

I started walking away, toward the parking lot. "Wait. Laurel!" Sky called, but I didn't let myself look over my shoulder. And he didn't follow me.

When I got home, I went into my room and I put on "Rehab" and turned up the volume. I tried to shout along, *"No, no, no,"* but I couldn't stop thinking about the irony of it. Amy, you were saying *I am who I am. Don't tell me what to do.* But now you're dead. Nobody did anything about it. You wouldn't go. You wouldn't get better. Happy in love, tripping on the stage, and we loved you for being yourself, but we let you go.

I shut off the music and the room got quiet. I tried to shake Sky's voice out of my head, but I couldn't get rid of it, no matter what I did. I kept hearing him telling me that both of the things I was afraid of were true—May felt shattered, too, and I'll never be as good or as beautiful as her.

After Dad went to bed tonight, I knew I couldn't sleep. I snuck some Scotch out of his liquor cabinet. I've never been drunk before without Natalie and Hannah. This time I didn't even mix it with cider or anything, I just swallowed up the burn of it.

When things started to spin, I lay down and put on *Back to*

Black again and listened to you sing the whole thing from the beginning. When I got up and went to brush my teeth for bed, I stood in front of the mirror, looking at my face and not understanding it. It was just me, plain and blank, and I didn't know what to see in it. I kept looking, looking for something else that I couldn't find anymore. I stared until there were just shapes that didn't figure into a person. But nothing reformed. I kept waiting for it to change, for May to be there, looking back at me. But I couldn't see her. I couldn't find her anywhere.

Yours,
Laurel

Dear Kurt,

I'm really sorry about the poster and about everything. But I need to talk to you. Since I got in the fight with Sky last week, everything has felt terrible. Then tonight, Hannah and Natalie and I went to this big party with Kasey. It was at the house of a football player who graduated last year, and he said that it was going to be a rager. When we walked in, Kasey started looking around for the booze, and that's when we saw that Hannah's brother, Jason, was there. Jason was not at all happy to see Hannah. In fact, he said, "What the fuck are you doing here?"

Hannah looked afraid. Kasey came over and put his arm around her. She'd kept him a secret from Jason so far, and she was trying to squirm away.

But Kasey said, "She's with me. And if you can't deal with that, we can take this outside." He was trying to be super tough for Hannah, blowing up like a blowfish.

Hannah muttered, "Kasey . . . don't . . ." but it seemed like her face had resolved into knowing that something bad would come.

Jason seemed like he was about to punch Kasey, but then one of Jason's buddies said, "Who gives a shit about that douche bag? Let's not waste the opportunity to drink some free beer." So that's what they did.

Hannah kept tucking her hair behind her ears and glancing back and forth between Kasey, Natalie, and the back door, where Jason and his friends had disappeared to the keg. I guess she thought the best way to deal with all this would be to get drunk. So she and Natalie and Kasey and the college boys took tequila shots, clinking glasses and sucking limes and cringing. Hannah started acting wild, slamming her glass on the table and asking for another. Finally, after the shots, she wandered off with Natalie, clinging on to Natalie's arm to hold her up.

I found a corner and tried to look absorbed in things, examining the sheen on the leaves of a houseplant, which was browning at the top, and inspecting the loose threads in the curtain. The party was a carnival of so many people, laughing and bouncing and blaring. It seemed everyone knew their place in it, but I was in the mood where I would rather be alone and look at the houseplants. Part of me kept wishing that Sky would show up, but I hated myself for even thinking about him.

Then, while I was arranging a bowl of M&M's by their colors, this guy Teddy, one of the soccer boys who's friends with Evan Friedman, walked up and said that I should come hang out. It was clearly just me and the M&M's there, and I couldn't think of an excuse, so I followed him. When I got outside, I saw Evan with some of the college guys, ex-baseball/soccer/football players, including Jason. Jason must have been really drunk, because he didn't seem to notice me. Evan said, "Hey," and sort of shifted back and forth from foot to foot nervously. "You look good," he said. I looked down. I was just wearing a tee shirt and a cotton skirt, and I didn't really agree. The world was all off its axis. I was confused about why he wanted to talk to me. A couple of the older guys nudged Evan, and he offered me some beer. The taste was like a yellow raincoat, but a dirty one. They also had caffeine pills. They said they wouldn't do anything, hardly, except wake me up. I would rather have been asleep, honestly, totally asleep.

I shrugged. "I don't know," I said.

The guys kept bugging and trying to convince me. Evan said, "Come on, it's a party."

Then I heard one of the college guys whisper, "That's her sister." I shouldn't have done it, but that's when I grabbed the pill and took it, whatever it was, washing it down with the beer.

Soon after, I wasn't feeling too great. Everything was starting to get fuzzy. Evan was putting his hands on me, on my back and stuff.

He whispered in my ear, "Let's go somewhere."

"I don't know," I said. "I have to find my friends." So I walked inside, and Evan followed me. As we were trying to make our way through the party, I kept asking, "Where are Natalie and Hannah?" I kept looking at the faces going by, looking for their faces.

I was really dizzy, and I felt like I was going to throw up. I was walking really slowly. Evan kept saying, "Let's go."

I said, "Wait," because I thought maybe I really would throw up. The whole party was dizzy, so many people, too many, all heavy, all sweaty. Finally I found the bathroom, and I guess there was a line, but I skipped it and opened the door, because I was about to be sick. Then I saw them there— Natalie and Hannah.

They were kissing like they couldn't get close enough. Like they wished they didn't have bodies to keep them apart. I caught Hannah's eye before I closed the bathroom door quickly, to hide them. But it was too late. People had started talking. Some guys were already pounding on the door. "Hey, ladies, open up! I want to join the fun!" I walked away, feeling sicker than before. The room was spinning. Finally Evan found me again and I said, "I don't feel good."

He said, "It's okay, come in here. Lie down."

So I did, because I didn't know what else to do. The room we went in was dark, with bunk beds, like May and I had when we were kids. I wanted to lie on the top bunk. May always got the top. I told Evan I wanted the top, but he put me on the bottom. I kept saying, "I don't feel good," and he kept saying, "It's okay," and rubbing me all over. When I tried to sit up, he pushed me back. I was swimming through the thickest fog. Everything that was happening seemed already to have happened before. He was rubbing everywhere, under my clothes. Under my skirt. What he was doing felt all wrong. I said no, but he wouldn't listen. All I could hear was my heartbeat and the cars outside. Evan kept doing what he was doing, and the cars got so loud, as if I were lying down on the highway. And I thought May would come in one of those cars. She would pick me up and take me away. We were going to the ocean. We were going to drive all the way there together. The waves would come and wash us over and over.

Then I started to hear it, "Heart-Shaped Box." It seemed as if they were playing it somewhere in the party, but no, maybe you were singing just for me. I couldn't tell. But I could hear your voice, full of anger. *Hey, wait . . .* It woke me up. It's like you were screaming from inside of me. I pushed Evan as hard as I could, harder than I knew I could, and he fell against the other side of the bed. He looked stunned and put his hand on his head, which had hit the wall.

That's when Sky came in. He was with Francesca.

When he saw me there, he stepped toward the bed. He said, "Laurel, what's going on?"

"I don't feel good" is what I said.

Sky told Evan, "Get the fuck outta here before I kick your teeth in." I've never seen him so mad. Evan got out, fast. Francesca lingered, but Sky turned to her and said, "Could you leave us alone for a minute?"

"Whatever," she said. "I don't need this shit." And she left.

"Are you okay?" he asked.

"I want to go on the top bunk."

"You should go home. Where are your friends?"

I started to panic, because I remembered Natalie and Hannah and how I opened the door so that everyone saw them.

"They were kissing." I tried to fix my skirt, which was pushed up and tangled around my shirt. I was so ashamed that Sky was seeing me this way.

"Come on. I'll take you home," he said.

When we walked out, there was a fight. Kasey was screaming at Natalie, "Get out!"

Natalie looked at Hannah with these wild scared eyes, but Hannah's eyes were down. She whispered, "Come on, Kasey. She's just a girl. It doesn't count."

Hannah was almost hidden behind him. I wanted to help them, but Sky wouldn't let me stop. When I wouldn't walk, he picked me up. The worst part was when we passed Jason standing in a corner. I saw what Hannah didn't want to see. His face was red and his veins were popping out. He was worse than angry.

Once we were in the car, I didn't look at Sky. I looked out the window at the treetops. I wanted to say something to make everything that was bad get better. But I couldn't think of a single thing. I guess Sky couldn't, either. So I closed my eyes until we got home.

I felt the car stop and heard the engine purring in stillness outside my house. I sat there, feeling so sick. Finally I said, "Sorry." And I reached for the handle.

"Did you do drugs or something?"

"I took some pill they gave me." They weren't caffeine pills, I realized now. Maybe I always knew.

"Why did you do that?"

I looked at him. "I don't know," I said.

I wanted him to kiss me. I wanted to go back to the fall and the night when I was dressed as Amelia and I could fly over everything. I wanted his hands to burn on me and make me new again. To erase everything else. Everything that was wrong and bad and dirty.

I put my lips near his mouth. Then I put them closer.

"You're messed up right now," he said.

He was right. I was too messed up, in every way. "I know," I said. "It's not supposed to be like this. We were supposed to be in love."

"Do you ever think that for one second you could forget about how it's supposed to be and just deal with the way it is?"

"You don't understand. She wasn't supposed to leave me. She was supposed to love me." I started to cry.

"Who? Your sister?"

I nodded. I tried to erase what I was feeling. I tried to get rid of the anger that seared me. I was sobbing now. I opened the car door. "I'm sorry," I said again. "I have to go."

His engine idled as he waited for me to crawl in through the window. And then I heard his car pull away. I felt sick with regret. I wanted him to come back. I wanted to tell him everything.

Yours,
Laurel

Dear Kurt,

May and I are going to go to the movies. She just got her driver's license, from Roadrunner Driving School, where they don't much care if you pass the test or not. The teacher just puts you on the highway to go somewhere to buy him fireworks. This is what May told me, but she didn't tell Mom and Dad. So Dad decided that she could drive me to the movies. It's his week with us. She and Dad get in a fight first, because May is wearing this lace-up shirt. Dad must think she is too pretty, because he says she should change out of it. He says she gives people the wrong idea when she dresses that way. He never usually says things like that. He usually lets her do what she wants. May cries, and I do, too, because this is our night together and I don't want Dad to ruin it. Finally Dad says softly, "Just change your clothes, May. And you can go."

May and I used to always do everything together, before she left for high school. But now I am thirteen, a for-real teenager. And now we are going to be friends again. In my head, I am begging May to do what Dad said so we can still go to the movies in her car together.

Finally May says, "Okay." And she goes to her room and puts on a giant sweatshirt. A Christmas one with puffy reindeer on it. It looks funny with the kitten heels she still has on. She wipes away the tears and she says, "Can we go now?"

"Go ahead," my dad says.

We are going to see *Aladdin* at the dollar theater. Lots of times they play old Disney movies there, which May and I still love. We are in the old Camry with May's pink beads hanging from the mirror. As soon as we are down the block, May pulls off her sweatshirt. She fixes the mascara smudged from crying and grins at me. I am wearing the shirt that I love, the one that I've had since fifth grade, with a picture of a rain forest and rain forest animals that snap on and off. I hope that it's cool to wear again, the way that Rainbow Brite and the Smurfs are. I wonder now if I should have worn something else. But my hair is clean, and I can smell the sweet green apple shampoo. I think that the night is not ruined after all.

It's the end of November, but we roll down the windows anyway and blast the heater, and May turns up the music. She sings along to "Heart-Shaped Box," and then she looks at me and asks, "Do you like it?" I nod that I do.

She kisses my forehead. She says, "I am going to meet

Paul at the movie, is that okay? You can't tell Dad, or Mom, either."

I nod. I am a little sad that it won't be just me and May, but the most important thing is that she let me in.

When we stop at the light before the movie theater, she tucks her hair behind her ears, and then ruffles it up, and then tucks it again. And then she puts on lipstick.

She turns to me. Her lips look grown-up, like the ones she cuts out of her magazines for collages, but her face is soft. She says, "Do I look okay?" I say she looks beautiful. I haven't ever seen anyone look like that before. Not even her.

When we get there, only a couple of people are left in the ticket line, and there is Paul with another man standing off to the side. Paul has on the same plaid shirt he wore the only other time I've seen him, at Fallfest. He looks a little cleaner than the other guy, who has jeans with holes and a shirt that says BACK IN MY DAY, WE HAD NINE PLANETS. When May sees Paul, she waves a little wave. She walks up slowly, her hair swinging behind her. I follow. When we get close, they don't touch, but from her look, I can tell they will.

I am playing with the frog snap on my shirt. I am snapping it on and off.

May talks in a grown-up voice and says, "Laurel, you remember Paul, and this is his friend Billy."

Paul says, "Hey, kid," which is what Carl and Mark, the neighbor boys, call me, and ruffles my hair. I don't want him to.

May says, "Paul and I are going to go somewhere, okay? Billy will take you to the movie."

I don't want to go see *Aladdin* with Billy, whose hair is long and dirty. I want to go with May. But I say, "Okay."

May says to Paul, "He'll take good care of her?"

And Paul says, "Of course he will."

May looks at Billy and says, "You will?"

"You bet."

May sounds very in charge when she tells him, "You are going to take her to *Aladdin*. Don't try to sneak her into something R-rated." He says he won't, but I start to feel like maybe he will. I am still snapping the frog on and off my shirt, on and off. The frog is my favorite. I am looking down at the shadows of the trees on the sidewalk.

May gives Billy Dad's ten dollars. She tells Billy that we love Sour Patch Kids. She makes him promise to get me some. And then May kisses me on the head and says have fun, and she says, "I'll be back right after the movie's over." And she walks off with Paul. I watch the car leave, taking May away, and I don't want it to go.

Billy says, "So what do you want to do?" My throat gets dry. I squeeze the frog in my hands. I try to swallow. I mean to ask if we are going to the movie, but I don't know if I say it out loud or not. I find the cherry Jolly Rancher in my pocket that I'd saved from the Village Inn where we had dinner that night. I start sucking on it, but somehow my mouth is still just as dry.

Billy says, "Do you talk?"

I shrug.

He says he forgot something in his car. He says come on. So I follow him over the long stretch of blacktop. The world is dizzy, like something happened to the earth under my feet. We get to a car at the edge of everything. He opens the door. He says get in. I don't want to. I just stand there. My mouth is really dry still. He says it again: "Get in." He sounds angry this time. It scares me, so I do what he says. He leans really close to me. I can feel his breath, which smells like something too sweet and wrong and hot and, now that I think of it, I guess maybe like booze.

The sky is dark already, and I wish that it wasn't. Billy says that he can tell I'm too old for a kid's movie. He asks if I want to go somewhere instead. "Ice cream?" he asks. I shake my head no. "Have it your way," he says, but he drives off anyway, and then he parks in an empty lot nearby.

The next thing I remember is that his hand is in my rain forest shirt. Underneath, I mean. I swallow the Jolly Rancher whole, and it hurts stuck in my throat, so I think I can't breathe. The frog is unsnapped, I remember, because I remember it in my hand, the plastic of it, and I remember thinking about the frog and wishing I could put it back on my shirt, because that is its home. Only now I never can. I would never be able to wear that shirt another time, and it wouldn't be safe for the frog. He would always be lost.

I try not to think of Billy's hand or where it is, so I just focus on trying to breathe. His hair is greasy, and his body is long. Too long. He tells me I am pretty.

I wonder if he means pretty like May is. I think of May with Paul and wonder if this is what is happening, if this is what's supposed to happen. Deep down I know it's not right, but I pretend, pretend I am like May with her pink cheeks and her lips that look like close-up pictures in a magazine.

I keep thinking she is about to come back. I can hear cars in the distance like ocean sounds. I am listening hard to engines rolling by like waves. Like the silence that isn't silence when you put a shell to your ear. And then sometimes something gets louder, and I hear a car, and I think it is getting closer. And I think it is May. She is about to come back. And it will stop. As soon as May comes, it will stop. But all the getting closer cars turn away. They go back on the highway. Maybe they are going to California.

When he is done doing that stuff, Billy drops me off outside the movie theater. The sign shines with the movie times. It still feels like there is a sliver of the Jolly Rancher stuck in the back of my throat. I am sitting there on the sidewalk, trying to concentrate on something. I look at the pale scattered stars in the sky, and then at the concrete and the pieces of glass glinting in it, like brighter stars. And then I read the numbers on the movie sign, over and over, trying to figure out what time it is so I could know when my sister would come.

People must be coming out of the movie, because there are voices around. When May jumps out of the silver car and it pulls away, everything is real again. She looks worried. She says, "Laurel! Why are you alone? Where's Billy?" I shrug. I tell her that he was late for something and had to go. "Were you waiting long?" she asks.

"No, not that much. He just left."

She tilts a little on her kitten heel, and when she thinks I am okay, she giggles like something good happened, but almost too much, like too happily. She says that Paul likes HardCore Cider, which is even better than the cider that we used to have at the apple farms in the fall.

When we are back in the Camry, I smile at her. And even though I don't feel well, I think maybe the world is back to normal again, because now we are in the car driving home, and May is my sister. I don't say what happened or anything about Billy. I know that it's not what was supposed to happen, and if May knew, she would always be sad. Too sad. She would go away from me. I didn't want that. And if only I'd never said anything, maybe she'd still be here.

Yours,
Laurel

Dear Kurt,

The day after the party was Sunday. I stayed in bed as long as I possibly could without Dad getting worried, and when I got up, I felt like I was walking through the thickest fog, like the kind that comes off of dry ice. I snuck into the bathroom and washed off the party makeup that was giving me black eyes.

Evan and Sky and May and the movies—it was all this frozen blur. I saw Jason's face in my mind. I called Natalie and Hannah a bunch of times, but neither of them answered. So I asked Dad to drop me off at Natalie's and said that I'd walk to Aunt Amy's from there.

When Dad pulled up and parked in front of her house, he hugged me and held on for a long time, which I thought was strange.

He looked at me and said, "Are you okay today?"

I worried that somehow he could see through me. "Yeah," I said. "Love you," and I hurried out of the car before he could ask me anything else.

When nobody answered the door, I went around to the back and found Natalie lying on the trampoline, crying. Hannah was sitting on the edge of it, her knees curled in a ball against her chest.

I stood toward the edge of the yard, listening. Natalie asked, through sobs, "Do you even love me?"

"Of course," Hannah said flatly. "But people won't understand. They'll take it apart and turn it into something else."

Natalie looked crushed. "Love isn't a secret. I can't act like it doesn't count. It counts, doesn't it?" Her voice went up at the end.

"You don't know my brother," Hannah said. "He flipped

out, and he'll flip out even more if he finds out we're, like, to-gether." I couldn't help thinking of the look in Jason's eyes. The kind of anger that could make anyone turn small.

"Are we even? You're with Kasey and whatever other guys. Like I don't even matter."

"That's not true," Hannah said. "Of course you matter." Then she said, more softly, "It's just better if I'm not around so much," and she got up. "I've got to get back. Jason thinks I'm at the library."

As Hannah turned around to walk out, she saw me stand-ing there. "Hey. What happened to you last night? You opened the door on us, and then you just disappeared after that?"

"I know. I, um . . . I'm sorry." I knew that I should tell them what happened with Evan. I knew that I should. But this horrible panicky feeling was all over me, and my voice felt choked.

"Laurel? Hello? Where did you go last night?"

"Sky took me home."

"Oh, great. So you open the door on us and then go off with Sky? Well, FYI, things are pretty much ruined now. Do you even care?"

"No, I mean, yeah, I . . ." May was falling off the bridge. I was falling with her. It was all my fault, all of it.

"Forget it," Hannah said. "It's done now."

She hopped over the low wall. Natalie watched her go, but Hannah never turned around to look back. Natalie cried harder. I tried to go and sit by her, but she curled into a ball.

"I'm sorry," I said before I got up.

On the walk to Aunt Amy's, I put your voice on my headphones and listened to you singing "Lithium." I shouted along with you, *"I'm not gonna crack,"* and it's exactly—not just the words, but how your voice sounded singing them—how I felt.

Yours,
Laurel

Dear Kurt,

When I got to Aunt Amy's, she wasn't home yet. She must have been out with the Jesus Man, I figured, who came into town last week. I lay on the couch and closed my eyes. I guess I fell asleep, because when Aunt Amy came in the door, she woke me up.

I asked her how her week was, trying to tell if she was happy now that the Jesus Man was back, but she just said, "It was good. How was yours?"

"Fine," I lied, and then she put on *60 Minutes*, which is pretty much the only show she likes other than *Mister Ed*. That little ticking stopwatch must be almost as old as he is. The episode was about free divers. They dive hundreds of feet underwater without any oxygen tanks, and if they're not careful, they can black out. I got sort of sucked into it, imagining what it would be like, trying to swim up from so far down with no air.

When the show was over, Aunt Amy called me to come eat. She'd made pancakes and bacon. That was May's favorite—breakfast-for-dinner night. I sat at the kitchen table and waited for the prayer. But instead, Aunt Amy just looked at me and asked, "Are you all right?"

"Yeah," I said. I wondered if I really looked that bad.

Then she said, "I know you must be thinking of your sister today. Should we pray for her?"

It hit me in a flash. It was a year ago today that May died. How could I have forgotten? I felt awful.

"Um, yeah. Can you do it?" I asked.

She squeezed my hand and then bowed her head and said, "Dear Lord, we ask that you keep May, our beloved sister, daughter, and niece, with you in heaven's care. We thank you for the blessing of the time we shared with her. We also pray for her sister, Laurel, who she's left on this earth, that you cherish her heart and stay by her side in her time of grief. In Jesus' name, Amen."

When she finished, Aunt Amy looked up at me with teary eyes. I didn't know what to say. I choked down a bite of my pancake and wanted to throw up.

After dinner, I tried to disappear into my room, except a couple of minutes later Aunt Amy came in to bring me the phone. It was Mom. Since we got in that fight last month, our few conversations had been about five seconds long.

"Hi, honey."

"Hi."

"How are you tonight?"

"Okay, I guess." I sat down on my bed and pulled the rose quilt around me and stared at the empty, pale pink walls.

"I know it feels like I'm far away, but I want you to know, my heart is with you today."

I couldn't swallow it. "That's nice, Mom, but it doesn't really make anything easier."

The other end of the line was quiet, until Mom said, "I'm sorry, Laurel. I just thought . . . I thought you'd be better off without my grief to deal with. I didn't know how to be strong for you after May died. I thought it would be worse, your seeing me cry all the time."

The words fell out of my mouth before I could think about it. "Nothing is worse than when someone who's supposed to love you just leaves."

The phone line filled with static that sounded like the ocean, both of us crying in our separate corners of the planet.

"Maybe you think it's my fault. Maybe that's why you left," I finally said.

"Laurel, it's not your fault. Of course it's not your fault."

"Well, maybe it is. I should have never told her . . ."

"Told her what?"

The room was spinning and spinning now, and I was breathing too fast. "I don't know. I have to go."

I let the phone fall to the floor. I couldn't stop crying.

Everything was flooding in, everything too fast. Hannah in her bra at Blake's, her face-painted bruise, Natalie's chipped tooth, don't tell, the door open with them kissing and it's my fault, I didn't save them, I couldn't save them, I couldn't save her. The soap in the shower that will never get it clean enough and the frog in the back of my drawer, I just left him there, and your poster torn to shreds and the bunk beds taken apart, I just want to climb the ladder and lie by May so it can be okay. Sky walking away, driving away, everyone away, and May rolling away from the car, how it was going to hit her, how she yelled at me when I tried to stop her, the car going too fast down the road, too fast, and now Mark the neighbor boy will never love me, the river flooding my whole head, the guy's hand reaching toward me, his hand on me, his hand under my shirt, sticky thighs on his seats, but just be like May, be pretty like her, be brave, this is what it's supposed to be, this is the world now, wake up, his hand on me, how it felt, and the night hot and sticky and sticking to me and your voice *I'm not gonna crack—*

Dear Kurt,

After the first night at the movies, I would watch *Aladdin* at home on DVD. I watched it over and over. Whenever I'd remember things I didn't want to remember, I would put it on so that I could replace Billy with the movie I was supposed to have seen that night, how Aladdin ran around the city, stealing things, saying, *"One jump ahead of the slowpokes."* How he and the princess rode on the carpet, singing, *"A whole new world . . ."* I would practice being like them, just soaring over everything.

The next time May took me to the movies after the first time, she walked into my room in Mom's apartment and asked, "Do you want to go to the movies tonight?" with a wink. At Mom's she could have just gone off by herself. When I used to ask her to take me wherever she was going, she'd say I was too young. But now she wanted me with her. I didn't know what to say. I felt like if I let her leave without me, I would never get her back. I told myself what happened with Billy wasn't that bad. I told myself that's what people do. If I pretended it never happened, I thought maybe it never would have.

So Friday nights became movie nights. It started late that fall after she met Paul and lasted into the spring. We'd go after the Village Inn dinners, with Mom's or Dad's ten dollars. When we'd be in the car on the way, May's lips would get dark as she put her lipstick on. She'd smile and pass it to me and say, "Do you want some?" I'd watch my lips turn dark, too, as I smoothed the crayon-tasting color over my mouth. It was like make-believe. I thought if I stayed close enough to May, the power of her would rub off. So I'd try to use the crimson as an eraser, to take away the feeling of being scared. For both of us. We'd listen to songs and sing loud. I would ignore the sick feeling in my stomach. I would try to be happy. I was with my sister. She liked me, and we were friends again.

And sometimes, May and I really did go to the movies. Sometimes there was no Paul or Billy to ruin everything, and we'd buy Sour Patch Kids and sit in the back of the theater and whisper.

But other nights, when we'd walk up and I'd see Billy standing outside with Paul, my heart would go sick with dread. May and Paul would go off in Paul's car, and once they were gone, Billy and I would get into his car, parked on the field of blacktop, and he'd drive off somewhere. I got good at it after a while, riding on the carpet above the earth, or riding with the car engines to the ocean.

Billy would start to touch me and say, "I can't help it. You cast a spell on me." I wondered if I did cast a spell on him by accident. What if somehow I made him do it, by wishing to be like May, by wishing that she'd take me with her when she used to leave at night?

Sometimes Billy would hang around with me outside of the theater, waiting for May and Paul to come back, so that I wouldn't look like I was always alone, I guess. When May would ask me if I liked the movie, I would rush past my answer, asking her for stories instead, imagining parties she'd been to with the music so loud that it got into your heartbeat. A lot of times, her breath would smell like alcohol, or her eyes would be glazed over. But she was always smiling, so I thought she was happy. I wanted her to be happy.

When I would come home and get undressed at night, I pretended like I was peeling off my skin. Taking away the dirty parts so I would be new again. Soon there weren't many clothes left to wear anymore, and I kept asking Mom for new shirts. I felt bad about it because we weren't supposed to get that many new shirts, on account of not having a lot of money, and she kept asking what about your old shirts, and I said that in middle school they didn't wear rain forests or deserts or even tie-dye. And I didn't tell her that they were all thrown away, balled up in the trash of the McDonald's near the apartment.

But the frog I couldn't throw out. I saved him, in the back of my secret drawer. He was the only one who knew what happened. And the frog was my favorite. The shirt he used to live on was gone now, but he still had the bottom half of a snap on his belly to remind him of the home he got broken off from.

The night May died was after a movie night. Things were different with Billy that time. "You're getting to be a big girl," he had said. "Let's try what big girls do." It used to be that he would just want to touch me places. And then he'd want me to watch while he did something. But this night, he wanted me to do it. He said I couldn't stop until it was done. I kept waiting for it to be done, but it seemed like it never would be. I couldn't go anywhere else in my mind. All I could see was that, waiting for it to be over.

After, I was waiting outside the theater. Paul's car pulled up, and May got out. Her breath smelled like liquor, and she looked like she had been crying. But when we got in the Camry, she tried her best to smile and turned up the music.

She said let's not go home yet. She said let's go to our spot. And when I reached out to touch her arm, she stopped singing and turned to me.

She said, "Laurel, don't ever let anything bad happen to you, okay?" She looked back at the road and said, "Don't be like me. I want you to be better, okay?"

I swallowed and nodded. I didn't know what to say. When we got to the bridge and crawled out into the middle, I looked at her. "May?" I said. "I'm scared." I wanted her back.

"What are you scared of?" she asked.

"I—I don't know."

"Here," May said. "Do you want to make a spell? Go get one of those flowers."

I crawled across the bridge, and pulled one of the little blue flowers out of its crack, and brought it back to her. May pulled its petals off, one by one, and held them in her hand. "Beem-am-boom-am-witches-be-gone!" her voice slurred as she flicked her fingers, scattering the petals to the wind. She laughed a little and looked at me like she was searching for something.

I tried to smile back. But then I blurted out, "Billy says that I am going to be pretty like you."

"What do you mean? When does he say that?"

"Just, just when you leave sometimes. When he—he takes me in his car with him."

I could see her face change. She was scared. It made me even more terrified. She started crying. She grabbed on to me and held me too tight. "What happened, Laurel?" she whispered. "What did he do?"

"No. Never mind," I said, desperate to push it away. "It's okay." I was grasping for anything to make her stop crying. I just wanted her to be magical again and protect me from everything. "May, remember? Remember when you could fly?"

She looked at me with a little smile. "Yeah," she said softly. And then she stood up. She started to walk across the track, her arms out like make-believe wings. I kept looking for my voice. I wanted to call her name, but I was somewhere else. Not there, not all the way. And then—it's like the wind blew her away from me. When I screamed, "May!" it was too late. She didn't hear me. She was gone. She was gone already. "May! May!" I screamed her name over and over, but my voice was drowned out by the river.

When she went somewhere I couldn't follow, I sat frozen. Waiting for her to come back. To come and get me. I heard the river like the sound of distant traffic, like the sound of the far-off ocean, same as ever. But no cars came. The road was as empty as a night sky without starlight.

Dear Kurt,

Aunt Amy is snoring now in the next room. After I got off the phone with Mom, she came in, and I was crying and crying. When I finally calmed down, she made me tea and tried to talk to me. I told her that I was just sad tonight and asked if I could go to bed. But I couldn't actually sleep, so I wrote you letters. And then I didn't know what else to do. The spring air was coming in through the window. It smelled just like it did the night she died, blossoms in the dark, new weather trying to break through the cold. I couldn't be alone.

I picked up my phone and saw that I'd missed a call from Sky. I kept almost pressing the button to call back and then taking my finger away. But finally, I let it ring. I told myself there was nothing left to ruin.

It was late, midnight, but he picked up. "Hey," he answered.

"Hi."

"I was worried about you."

"I kind of have to . . . I'm at my aunt's and I just . . . I can't be here right now. Could you come and get me?"

He paused a moment. "All right."

So I crawled out the window, shivering in my sweatshirt, and waited for his truck to pull up. When I got in, Sky didn't really look at me. He was staring straight through the windshield.

"Where do you want to go?"

"The old highway." Right then, I knew I had to.

"Are you sure?" Sky asked.

I nodded yes.

So we turned onto the road, which I hadn't been on since, except in my mind. I was breathing way too fast.

When we got by the bridge, I said, "Stop here." I forced

the door handle open and stepped out. I walked toward the edge of the bridge. I kept walking forward. I put one foot on the ledge. I held my arms out. The night was still. No wind. Nothing to push me one way or the other.

I could feel my one foot on the slim line of metal. The balance beams of our childhood. And the other foot still back on the earth.

I saw May walking out, her slender arms reaching out through the air on either side. I saw her fairy wings come out. I saw them trying to flutter to keep her up. To take her back. But I'd broken them. I saw the wings like tissue paper break off and float into the sky as she fell. I saw them falling after her, slowly like leaves. But her body. Her body had density. It was gone before I could hear it splash. Her body that I used to sleep next to. Her body that would steal the covers and roll like a burrito so that I would shiver and then give up and scoot closer, just to get a little warmer. I remembered how she smelled like apples and mint and earth in the summer. I wanted to go with her.

And then I heard Sky. "What the fuck are you doing?"

I pulled my foot off of the ledge. I could feel him grab me.

"Don't get that close," he said. "You're scaring me."

I heard the sound of the river moving on, as if it hadn't stolen my sister's body. I turned to him. And I just talked. Because everything was already lost. "She left me. She'd leave me alone at the movies with this guy who used to do stuff to me. I know she didn't mean to—but I was so—I'm so mad at her." I'd said it. I'd said it out loud.

"Laurel," Sky said, and reached out to me again. "Of course you are. What guy? Who did that?"

"It doesn't matter now. A friend of Paul's. And I tried to tell her what happened, and then—she was so upset, and I'm afraid, I'm afraid it killed her."

"Why would you think that? What happened?" Sky asked.

I told him the whole story. When I was finished, he looked at me and said, "Laurel, it wasn't your fault."

"But maybe if I never let it happen in the first place, or maybe if I never said anything, maybe she'd still be here."

"Stop it," he said. "You can't blame yourself. Maybe she'd still be here if she hadn't been drinking. Or if the wind were blowing a different direction that night. Or if she'd leaned another way. You'll go crazy thinking like that. She made her own choices. You have to look out for yourself now. That's the best thing you can do for her. That's what she'd want for you."

I looked at his eyes, and it started to sink in. I'd told Sky, and nothing bad was happening. Nothing worse. He was still right there. Just standing in front of me.

"You don't hate me?"

"No."

"You're not scared of me?"

"No. I just want you to know that you don't have to let that stuff happen to you anymore."

He put his arms around me, and something burst open. I started to cry. "How could she just leave me here to live without her? I miss her so much. I love her. I want her to grow up and become who she was meant to be. I wanted her to grow up with me."

Sky let me cry, and when I finished, he led me away from the bridge and opened the door to his truck. "Come on," he said, "let's get out of here."

We got in together, driving the other way on the road. He drove fast but never too fast. Just right the whole time, the way he always had.

Yours,
Laurel

Dear Amelia,

Sometimes it feels strange that the sun just goes on rising, as if nothing happened. When I woke up today, the birds were chirping their oblivious chirping, and cars were starting down the block. I'd hardly slept last night after I got home from the bridge, and my eyes would only open into little slits. As I tried to pull myself out of bed, I thought of you for some reason. I thought of you on the tiny island where you might have landed and lived as a castaway.

I imagine what it would have been like, waiting and waiting for someone to come and rescue you. Building fires, making smoke signals that disappeared into the clouds. How long could you have lived there, you with your navigator? Which one of you died first and had to mourn the other?

They've found artifacts on Gardner Island, which lies near Howland—the place you meant to land that morning, in the middle of the Pacific between Australia and Hawaii. They found pieces of Plexiglas that matched the kind on the windows of your plane, the heel of a shoe that could have belonged to you, bird bones and turtle bones, the remains of a fire, shards of Coke bottles that seemed as if someone had used them to boil water to drink. And then, most recently, they found four broken pieces of a jar, the shape and size of one used for a cream made to fade freckles in the era when you were alive. Everyone knew that you had freckles you wished you could erase. As I got dressed, I carried the thought of that little jar, left behind as evidence. It seems so vulnerable, compared to your brave face meeting the world.

At school this morning, everyone knew about Natalie and Hannah kissing at the party. I saw Hannah walking down the hall, and one of the soccer boys called out, "Yo, wanna have a threesome?" His friend said, "Four boobies are better than two." I told them to shut up, and I tried to go over to Hannah, but she turned and rushed the other way.

In English, Natalie kept the hood of her hoodie on all through class, and when the bell rang, she hurried out before I could talk to her.

At lunch, our table was empty. I stood there for a minute, wondering where to go. Finally I went and sat by the fence, like I used to. I remembered watching the leaves fall from the trees at the beginning of the year and stared at the green buds starting to grow back now.

Then Sky walked up and handed me a pack of Nutter Butters. "Here," he said. "I thought you might want this."

"Thank you," I said, and smiled at him. I took it, and he sat down next to me. I gave him half, and we just sat like that, crunching and not saying anything else.

After school, I called Aunt Amy and told her I had a study group and that I would get a ride home after. I stayed in the library alone for as long as I could, thinking about Natalie and Hannah, and thinking about May, and thinking about you on your island. I thought about how I tried so hard to be brave this year. But maybe I've been getting it wrong the whole time. Because there's a difference between the kind of risk that could make you burn away and the kind you took. The kind that makes you show up in the world.

Finally, when it started to get dark out, I walked back to Aunt Amy's. I took a deep breath and turned the knob to the front door. She was sitting on the couch, waiting for me. She had a kaiser roll sandwich cut in half on a TV tray.

"Are you hungry?"

I wanted to say that I wasn't and disappear into my room, but the sandwich waiting like that made me sad and made me love her all at the same time. So I dropped my backpack by the door and sat down.

"Thanks," I said.

I waited for her to make us pray, but instead she said, "Laurel, you were so upset last night. I'm worried about you."

"I'm doing better today," I said carefully. It wasn't a lie.

"I know that you miss May," she said, "and I know that you looked up to her. But I can see you becoming your own person, Laurel. And I am proud of you. The Lord Jesus is, too." She squeezed my hand and looked at me. Then she said, "And so is May, from where she is in heaven."

Although I still didn't know what exactly Aunt Amy was proud of, and I didn't really think that Jesus would be, it was a really nice thing for her to say about May.

I wonder what it was like, Amelia, in the final moments of your life. Did you stare up at the clouds that you had soared over? Did you wonder if you were going back there, to live in your beloved skies forever?

Yours,
Laurel

Dear Jim Morrison,

There is something that you said once: *A friend is someone who gives you total freedom to be yourself—and especially to feel, or not feel. Whatever you happen to be feeling at any moment is fine with them. That's what real love amounts to—letting a person be what he really is.* Thank you for saying it, because I've been thinking about that. I think that I've been trying for a long time to feel like I am supposed to, instead of what I actually am.

Since what happened at the party, I'd been missing Natalie and Hannah painfully. The week passed, and they'd been avoiding me, and each other, and pretty much everyone.

Then when I got to school today, Monday, I saw Hannah in the parking lot, getting out of a car. The passenger door was silver, but the rest of the car was painted black. She stumbled, her pointed heel stuck in a crack, as she turned to wave bye to the driver. It was a half-fingered wave that looked like it was meant to be flirty, but she could barely muster it. And when I followed her gaze, I saw him—it was Blake with the mountain house. He peeled out of the lot, dodging the minivans and mom cars and darting into traffic.

When Hannah saw me walking toward her, she looked at me like she wanted to disappear. Her red curls were coming uncurled, and her makeup was heavier than normal. She had one of her eye shadow bruises painted on her cheek.

"Hey," I said.

"Hey."

"Was that Blake?"

"Yeah."

"Why was he dropping you off at school?"

"I stayed at his place last night."

"Hannah, you promised you wouldn't see him."

"I know," she said. "But I had to get out of my house. And it's over with Kasey, of course."

"You could have called me."

"I've never even been to your house before, Laurel."

"Well, it could have been the first time . . ."

Hannah looked down. I could tell she was still angry.

Then she just laughed, suddenly, although nothing was funny. She laughed like she was making the only sound that could cover everything up. "I really can't be here today," she said. "Do you want to go somewhere?" The first bell hadn't even rung.

"Okay."

So we snuck off campus and walked to Garcia's and ordered taquitos for breakfast, sitting on the stoop of a drive-in spot. We used my cell phone and each called the office, pretended to be the other's parents calling us in sick. That's not the kind of thing that you can get away with often, but we'd only ever ditched eighth period before, and we hoped we'd get lucky this time. We made sure to wait a few minutes in between so that it would be less suspicious.

When our order came, Hannah pulled a little airplane-sized bottle of vodka out of her purse and started to unscrew it. "Wanna spike your limeade?" she asked.

"No," I said, alarmed. "It's barely nine o'clock."

"It's five o'clock somewhere," she said, and laughed. "Like in Norway. Think it's five o'clock in Norway? I wish I were in Norway. Or Iceland. Or somewhere really far away." She started to try to pour the vodka into my drink and said, "Come on. Lighten up."

"Stop it," I said, and grabbed the bottle.

"Since when did you get all high and mighty?" she asked, annoyed.

"I just—I'm not really drinking now," I said, "after what happened at that party."

"You mean after you opened the door on Natalie and me and then decided to ditch us?"

"The reason that I disappeared was that I was messed up." Then I blurted it out. "Basically Evan Friedman almost raped me. I took some pill that he gave me. He said it was a caffeine pill, but obviously it was something else."

"Laurel. Oh my god. Why didn't you tell me? Are you all right?"

"I guess so," I said. "Finally I shoved him off. And then Sky came in."

"I think I have to murder Evan," Hannah said. "I'm so sorry. I didn't know."

"I'm sorry that I didn't tell you before. I mean, I'm sorry I don't talk about stuff that much." I paused a moment. "Honestly, it's because of something that happened with my sister."

Hannah listened as I told her what happened with Paul and Billy and the night that May died. She hugged me when it was over and said how sorry she was. Tears were running down her face.

Then she said, "I guess I'd be a hypocrite if I didn't tell you the truth after you told me all of that." She looked away for a moment and took the sleeve of her sweatshirt and started to wipe away the fake bruise she had drawn on her face with eye shadow. Her hand was shaking. Underneath there was a real one, yellow and fading. I reached out to touch her arm.

"Was it Jason?" I asked softly.

Hannah nodded. "He was so angry after the party."

"Has he done that before?"

She shrugged. "Not in a while."

"We have to do something, Hannah."

"There's nothing to do."

"Have you told your grandparents?"

She shook her head no. "It would just hurt them. My grandma's sick, and my grandpa has to take care of her. He can hardly even hear when I try to talk to him. I never wanted anyone finding out, because what if they put me in a foster home or something? Or else I'd have to go back to Arizona to my aunt, and then I'd lose Natalie for good, and you, too, and everyone. Jason's finally going to the Marines in a few months. It's better just to wait."

"Natalie doesn't know?" I asked.

"I've never told anyone."

"You should tell her, Hannah."

"She'd freak out. She'd want me to talk to someone. Besides, she hates me now anyway."

"No she doesn't. You know that. She's in love with you. Her heart is broken, that's all."

"Do you think that I can unbreak it?"

"I think all she wants is for you to love her back, like she loves you." I paused. "Do you?"

"Yeah," she said softly.

"Then tell her. Please?"

Hannah nodded. "I'll think about it."

"Do you want to spend the night tonight? If you need somewhere to stay, you can always stay at my house."

"Really?"

"Yes. Lucky for you I'm at my dad's this week, so you won't be subjected to any questions about whether you've accepted Jesus."

Hannah agreed to throw out the vodka, and we passed the day walking around with our limeades. I still didn't know what we'd do about Jason, but Hannah said that she wanted to forget about it for a little bit, so we went to the park and swung on the swings and jumped off into the dirt. She sang for me the whole time, a mix of Amy Winehouse and old country songs—"San Francisco Mabel Joy" and "I Fall to Pieces." Her voice sounded beautiful, in the way that a voice does when you need it. Then we went to Walgreens and unwrapped the lipsticks in secret and tried on nearly every color, until we each picked one out and Hannah bought them for us with her Macaroni Grill money. When we went to check out, the cashier asked us why we weren't in school. "Mental health day," Hannah said, so confidently that the cashier just nodded in response. And then toward the end of the day, we took the city bus to my house. I'd texted Dad and asked him if I could have Hannah spend the night. I said I knew it was a school night, but she needed to stay in town. He said yes.

When we got there, I started showing Hannah around—the living room, the kitchen, the bathroom, Dad's room, and my room that is still completely dorky.

Then we passed by May's room, with its door closed. I paused a moment, almost walking past it, but then I went back and turned the handle to open it.

"And this was my sister's room," I said. We walked in, and Hannah started looking around, at May's half-burned Virgin of Guadalupe candles on the dresser, her collection of heart-shaped sunglasses, her jar full of seashells, her Sunflowers perfume. Her pictures on the bulletin board, the picture of River on the wall, the little globe lights strung around the room. "Wow. Your sister was so cool," she said.

I smiled. "Yeah. She was."

Then I heard the front door open. "Dad?" I called.

Hannah seemed nervous suddenly. "Do you think he'll like me?" she whispered.

"Of course," I answered as we walked into the living room to say hi.

"Hey, Dad," I said. "This is Hannah."

I'd never seen Hannah that way before. She was like a little girl, shifting from foot to foot, wiping her palms on her dress. I guess she cared a lot what he thought. It made me sad, realizing how she probably didn't have a lot of experience with parents. She extended her hand. "Hello, sir."

My dad smiled. "Call me Jim. I'm so glad to finally meet you!"

"You too."

"Are you girls hungry?" Dad asked. It had been forever since we'd really done anything for dinner other than microwave food, and it was usually me who made it. But then he said, "I was thinking of making Jim's famous tacos."

He was showing off for Hannah, I thought, and I smiled. I guess having my friend over brightened him up. He wanted to make things good for us.

So Dad cooked tacos, and we ate them together and then made Jiffy Pop and watched a movie on the couch. Dad let us pick, and we chose *Midnight in Paris*, which we all loved. The whole thing was surprisingly fun.

When we went to get ready for bed, Hannah borrowed pajamas. We were lying in my bed under the plastic glow-in-the-dark stars on the ceiling, trying to fall asleep, and then Hannah turned over and said, "I guess it's, like, Jason's just really pissed off at the world. Our parents are dead, and we got stuck with our grandparents, and he was supposed to get out on a football scholarship, and that got ruined. And I think that he gets scared for me, like I'll fuck up and I'll get stuck here. The weirdest part is that I know I should hate him, but I don't. I mean, of course I do in certain moments. But, you know, he's my brother. And I still love him, too. Do you think that makes me crazy?"

"No," I said. "I think that you can feel all of that stuff about him at once." I thought of your quote, about how with real friends you can feel however you do.

"Hold on one minute," I said. "I'll be right back." I wanted to do something nice for Hannah, and I had an idea. I tiptoed out of my room, pulled the attic stairs down from the ceiling, and climbed up into the dark, where May and I used to pretend that we were stowaway kids, hiding on a ship. I found the box marked *Halloween* and pulled it down. I opened it and found the matching pairs of wings that May and I wore, perfectly shaped and stretched over with gauzy panty hose, painted with patterns in glitter. I took May's pair.

I brought them down to Hannah. "Here," I said. "I thought you might need these. They'll make you brave."

She sat up in bed and stretched the elastic over her shoulders and smiled. "I love them."

Yours,
Laurel

Dear Jim,

As we were getting ready for school this morning, Hannah put the wings on and announced, "I'm wearing these today." And when we walked into the hall, she ignored everyone who stared at her.

I'd texted Natalie, and she agreed to meet us in the alley at lunch. Hannah had promised she'd talk to her. Hannah and I got there first, and when Natalie came up and leaned against the wall, the two of them just looked at each other for a long moment.

Finally Hannah broke the silence. "I do love you," she said in a burst. "And I'm sorry. But it's just scary. I'm not good at it. And I hate the way people talk. I don't know if I want everyone to know, I mean, if I am ready to be together or something. But I promise that I'll stop seeing other people."

Natalie looked back at her. "Really?"

Hannah nodded, and then she went on quickly, as if her voice was trying to outrun the sob that wanted to break into it. "Something happened with Jason after that party. I mean, if you thought he was mad when he knew I was there with Kasey, you should have seen him after he found out about us in the bathroom. He was like, 'That's fine for dykes, but not my sister.' I actually tried. I tried to stick up for us. He hit me. Anyway, he's leaving sometime this summer."

"What? He hit you?"

Hannah nodded. "Yeah. It's okay. I mean, I'm okay."

"It's not okay. I hate him. I hate him so much. I hate anyone who hurts you. I love you." Natalie rushed over and put her arms around Hannah. Hannah eventually let herself collapse into Natalie, her shoulder shaking as the tip of the fairy wing bumped against Natalie's cheek.

Then Hannah reached her arm out in the direction of where I was standing. "Come on, Laurel, you can, too." It was a joke-reference to when they used to tell me I could join in if they were making out. We all laughed as I went over to hug them both.

When we stopped hugging, I looked at them and asked, "What are we going to do?"

Natalie turned to Hannah and said, "Come live at my house for a little while. Until he's gone. Will you?"

Hannah wiped the tears from her eyes and looked at Natalie nervously. "What will you tell your mom?"

"I'll just tell her that you need somewhere to stay."

"But what if she wants to know why? What if she wants to talk to my grandparents or something, or what if she finds out about Jason?"

"Someone has to find out, Han. He's hurting you."

"But what if I get sent away somewhere?"

"We won't let that happen. No way I am losing you. My mom won't want me to, either. She, um, she more or less knows about us now, because I more or less told her, after the party when I got super depressed. So you might have to stay in a separate room or something." Then Natalie added, with a little smile, "But you know, there are always her date nights."

Hannah laughed at this. Then she asked, "Are you sure it will be all right?"

"Yeah, I promise."

So after school, we went to Natalie's house to talk to her mom. Hannah kept wiping her palms on her dress, and her eyes were darting everywhere, but Natalie's mom stayed calm the whole time, and eventually Hannah started to relax. Natalie's mom said of course Hannah could stay there until Jason left for the Marines, or for as long as she needed. But she wanted to make sure that Hannah's grandparents knew what was going on, and that Hannah understood that if necessary they could get a restraining order against Jason. She said that as long as Hannah was safe, she would respect her wishes about whether to report him, because she understood how complicated things could be. She said that the most important thing is that Hannah was taking steps to get herself out of a bad situation. And she told Hannah that she knew how hard it could be to do that, especially when you are afraid, and that she was proud of her. Natalie's mom is a great mom.

She offered to talk to Hannah's grandparents, but Hannah said that she thought it would be better if she was the one to do it. Of course none of us wanted to let her go alone, so Natalie and I drove with her on the highway toward the red dirt hills. We were hoping that by the time we got to her house, Jason would be on a workout. He usually goes late in the afternoon, Hannah said. But as Natalie pulled up to Hannah's driveway and parked, Hannah didn't want to get out.

"This is a bad idea," she said, breathing fast.

"You can do it," Natalie said. Then she got out of the car, and I followed, and finally Hannah did, too.

We went in, and after Hannah looked around to make sure Jason was gone, she knocked on her grandpa's bedroom door. He opened it, looking like he was only half-awake. Hannah pointed to her cheek, but not a word came out. Her grandpa squinted at her, confused, until finally he saw it.

"Jason did it," Hannah whispered.

"What?" he said, and turned up his hearing aid.

Hannah kept whispering, and her grandpa kept not hearing, until finally Hannah shouted, "Jason did it!"

Hannah's grandpa shook his head at first, like he didn't understand. "Was there an accident?"

Hannah just looked back at him, tears running down her cheeks. She said, loudly, "It's okay. I'm going to stay at Natalie's house for a while. Until it's time for him to leave, okay? I don't want you to worry."

Her grandpa's face turned pale, and he nodded, bewildered.

"Will you make sure to take care of Buddy and Earl? While I'm gone?"

Her grandpa promised that he would.

After Hannah said bye to him, we went to her room to help her pack. Natalie got to work, folding clothes really carefully into the suitcase. She put the shirts with the shirts and the jeans with the jeans and the soft pants with the soft pants and the lacy tops with the lacy skirts. And every time she found something fragile, like a perfume bottle, she rolled it up into something soft. Sometimes, the smallest gestures take up the most room.

When we were done, we carried Hannah's suitcase out through the hall. That's when Jason came in the front door. His eyes flashed from Hannah to Natalie and me.

"Where do you think you're going?" he asked.

Hannah flinched. "I'm going to stay at Natalie's house for a while."

"Like hell you are. I told you not to see her," he said, glaring at Natalie.

Hannah's hands were shaking, but her voice steeled itself. "I am. And Natalie's mom said that if you come anywhere near it, we will get a restraining order."

Jason's face turned a little bit pale. "Is that so?" He tried to sound angry, but there was a tinge of fear underneath his voice. "And on what fucking grounds would you do that?"

"On the grounds that you hit me!"

"Oh, come off it. It's called discipline. Obviously no one else around here is taking care of that with you. Someone's got to watch out."

"No, it's called abuse. You're lucky I didn't tell the cops."

Jason stared at her, disbelieving.

"I know you're pissed off at the world," Hannah said, "but you can't just go around yelling and being a jerk. And you can't take it out on me anymore."

"So you're just taking off? Just like that?"

"Until you're gone," Hannah said. "And if you break a restraining order," she added, "then it's a crime, and I bet that will mess up your chances in the Marines."

Jason's voice wavered. "Have it your way. I'm going to shower."

"I won't see you before you go, then," Hannah said, more softly now. "Good luck."

They didn't hug or touch or anything else. Jason just walked out of the room.

We carried Hannah's stuff to the car, and she said, "Wait." Natalie and I followed as she ran to the barn, the little fairy wings still on and flapping behind her, to see Buddy and Earl the donkey. When Buddy came over to greet her, Hannah nuzzled her face against his and kissed his nose. She said, "Don't worry, Buddy, I'll be back soon. I promise." Then she wiped her tears away and turned to us. "Let's go."

In the car on the way back, I put on your album, the first one, and as you started shouting *Break on through*, we rolled down the windows and screamed along, and for a moment we forgot about everything that's hard and just let ourselves feel what we wanted to, which was free.

Yours,
Laurel

Dear Kurt,

Things have gone sort of back to normal after last week. Hannah's been staying with Natalie, and we've been eating at our table again, Natalie and Hannah trading Capri Suns, and me with my Nutter Butters. Instead of going off campus for lunch, Tristan and Kristen have sometimes been eating with us, too, because they are getting nostalgic about the end of high school, which is only three weeks away. Today was the first day that it was real shorts weather. I wore my cutoffs just above my fingertips that I made at the beginning of the year.

Since the night at the bridge, Sky and I have hung out a

little bit at school. I'm not exactly sure what's going on between us, but one good thing is that he's not seeing Francesca anymore. And then today, I ran into him in the alley, and he asked me if I'd come over later. It was the first time he'd asked me to go to his house during normal hours. Unfortunately, it was an Aunt Amy night, and I had no idea how I'd get to go. I've been avoiding Mom entirely, so asking her to tell Aunt Amy to give me permission was out. And I didn't feel like making up an elaborate lie. That left only one option—try telling Aunt Amy the truth. She's been extra nice to me ever since I got upset that night, and I figured I had a shot.

When she picked me up after school, I asked her if we could go get French fries. On the way to Arby's, I kept opening my mouth, and then closing it again. Finally, after we got through the drive-thru line, Aunt Amy turned to hand me the bag. I took a deep breath and said, "So, there's this guy . . ."

She looked at me with a mixture of curiosity and concern.

". . . who I like. His name is Sky. He was actually, well, he was my boyfriend for a while." I waited to see if Aunt Amy would freak out.

Instead of pulling back onto the street, she parked in the lot. Then she asked, "Why didn't you tell me that sooner?"

"I thought you'd be mad. I mean, it's just that you never want me to do anything. You hardly let me spend the night at a friend's house."

Aunt Amy sighed. "I know that I've been a little bit strict

with you. There are just so many dangers in this world, Laurel. I never want to see you suffer. Being a teenager was a really painful time for me. And I wanted to protect you from it. From all of it."

When she said it like that, everything seemed different. She was the way she was not just because she believed in God and sin and all of that, but because she wanted to protect me, and suddenly, I felt thankful that she cared that much. "That's really nice, Aunt Amy, but don't you think everyone has to go through stuff?"

She paused a moment, and then she said, "I can't stop you from growing up. But Laurel, you have to be careful . . . Of course I would recommend against a sexual relationship, certainly at your age, as would Our Lord, but I want you to know that if you do get into a situation where you—"

Oh no. A sex talk with Aunt Amy. I cut her off. "Right, well, we're not. Having sex. I haven't. We're not even together anymore." I ate a French fry and offered her the bag.

"What happened?" she asked. "Why did you break up?"

"It's sort of a long story. Basically, I wasn't really ready to be with him. There was a lot of stuff I still couldn't say. And then I found out that he used to like May, which was awful, of course."

Aunt Amy's face melted with sympathy. "Yes," she said, "I imagine that was really difficult."

"Yeah. But on the other hand, he's been a great friend, and I think I still like him, and I think he might like me again, too. And he asked me to come over tonight so that we could talk. So, do you think I could go?"

She looked torn. "Will a parent be home?"

"Yes," I said. "His mom. She's always there. And I promise not to be out late."

Finally Aunt Amy said, "Okay." Then she said, "I'm glad that you felt like you could talk to me."

I saw that it really had made her happy. "Me too." I smiled.

So later that evening Aunt Amy drove me to Sky's. When she let me off, I kissed her cheek and thanked her for letting me go, and then I walked up to his door. The bulbs we'd planted in the fall were blooming now—tulips craning their necks all in the same direction, toward where the sun comes up.

I ignored my pounding heart and knocked.

Sky answered. "Hi," he said. His body in the doorway was like a wall, protecting the house. We stood there in silence for a moment, and I wondered if maybe he'd changed his mind about asking me over.

"So, can I come in?"

Over his shoulder, I could see the shadow of his mother, peering toward the open door. "Skylar, who's there?"

Finally I just ducked under his arm and stepped inside. The television was on, talking about someone's dream house. Sky's mom walked over. She had on her same bathrobe, and her hair was in the same frayed bun. She pointed to the cut tulips from the yard that stood proudly in a vase amid the clutter.

"Did you know if you put a penny in the water it keeps them straight?" she asked.

"Oh," I said, "no, what a good trick. They're really pretty."

She smiled the kind of smile that made it seem as if it had honestly occurred to her to be happy in that moment. But then she just kept looking at me, like she was trying to figure out who I was.

"Mom, it's Laurel," Sky said. "You met her before. Outside, when we were planting the flowers."

"Oh," she said, "silly me." But her eyes didn't flash with recognition. "Can I get you a cup of tea?" she asked, a bit bewildered.

I followed her to the kitchen while she made it. Sky tried to help, but she swatted him away. She performed the ritual with careful, measured steps, as if she had memorized the motions as handles to hold on to, to keep her upright.

When I took the cup and smelled the peppermint steam, she said, "Skylar, I'm going to lie down. I'll leave you two alone."

I followed Sky across the squeaky floors to his bedroom. Unlike in the rest of the house, everything in his room had a place. The furniture and posters lined up in straight lines, like they were working hard to form a kind of sense. He had one of your posters, the one from *In Utero*, and one of the Rolling Stones.

Sky propped a pillow against the bedpost and gestured for me to sit down. I arranged myself on the edge of his bed.

"So . . ." I said.

"So," he answered.

"So I never really thanked you for the night at the party. And the night at the bridge. And all of that. Thank you. For being there."

"You're welcome. I'm glad that you let me."

"Can I ask you something?"

"What?"

"Do you see her when you look at me? I mean May?"

"No. I see Laurel."

"Really?"

"Yes."

"Then why do you even love me? I mean, why did you?"

"Because—because you remind me of my first concert. The one I told you about on New Year's. You remind me of the feeling of wanting to make something."

My heart twirled around in my chest when he said that, and it wanted to leap into his arms.

"Listen," he went on, "I'm sorry that I took so long to tell you all of that stuff about May. And I'm sorry that I said it the way I did. But I don't want you to think . . . I mean, the way I felt about you, I've never felt that way about a girl before. Not your sister or anyone."

"You know how you said May didn't have an easy time in high school or whatever? I just always thought that it was different from that. Why didn't she ever tell me?"

"You were her little sister. She probably wanted to protect

you from all of that stuff. She probably wanted you to look up to her."

Maybe he was right. I thought about the lengths that she went to to make me believe she had wings when we were kids. Maybe May had needed me as much as I needed her. She needed the way I saw her, the way I loved her. "Do you think that I didn't know her?" I asked. "What if I didn't really know her?"

"Of course you knew her. You knew her for your whole life. Nothing changes who she was to you. Maybe it's just when you get older, you understand things that you couldn't before."

"I think that after my parents split up, she must have been really angry at them. I mean, my mom spent May's whole life telling her how she brought our family together. So she must have felt betrayed. Even though of course it wasn't her fault, maybe she felt like it was. So maybe she was angry at herself, too."

Sky said, "When she used to talk to me, she'd talk about you sometimes. How she hoped that growing up would be so much easier for you."

I smiled to think of her saying that, but of course it wasn't easy. I guess it's not for anybody. The truth was too sad to feel right away. May couldn't see how she was letting me get hurt, because she was hurting, too.

"I just want to go back in time and tell her that she could talk to me. That I would understand. That it could get better."

"I know," Sky said.

"The only thing I liked about that story you told me," I said to Sky, "was Paul getting beat up. But I'm sorry that you got kicked out of school. That wasn't fair."

"Yeah," he said. "It wasn't fair what happened to you, either. Or what happened to her. A lot of things aren't. I guess we can either be angry about it forever or else we just have to try to make things better with what we have now."

I looked at him. "Yeah," I said. "You're right."

I didn't know if I would ever kiss Sky again or not, but it was nice to be able to talk about May with someone who knew her.

I looked up at your *In Utero* poster, with the picture of the winged woman with the see-through skin, watching Sky and me from the wall. I thought about how for a long time, I wanted to be soaring above the earth. I wanted Sky to see me as perfect and beautiful, the way I saw May. But really, we all just have these blood and guts inside of us. And as much as I was hiding from him, I guess part of me also always wanted Sky to see into me—to know the things that I was too scared to tell him. But we aren't transparent. If we want someone to know us, we have to tell them stuff.

Yours,
Laurel

Dear Allan Lane,

On the way home after school today, Aunt Amy turned to me and asked, "Would you like to come to dinner with Ralph and me tonight?" (Ralph, aka the Jesus Man.)

He never comes to the house, at least not when I'm there, but she's been seeing him, and the rose soap in the shower has turned into a diminishing pink disk. Maybe after I told her about Sky, she wanted to open up to me, too. Maybe inviting me along was part of her trying to be closer with me, I thought, so I agreed.

When we got home, Aunt Amy went about getting ready, dabbing rose oil behind her ears and taking a faded flower dress out of the dry cleaner bag.

We met Ralph at Furr's. I thought it was weird that he didn't pick us up or something, but I didn't ask any questions. We got there first and waited for him by the door. Finally he walked up with a swagger and kissed Aunt Amy on the cheek. He was wearing knockoff Birkenstocks, jeans with a suit jacket, and had long hair that was scraggly and wavy, as if he were literally trying to look like Jesus.

He shook my hand and said, "You must be Laurel."

I tried to be polite. "Nice to meet you," I said with my best smile.

We went through the cafeteria line, and he got chicken fried steak, Salisbury steak, and fried chicken—all at once!

Plus cornbread, mashed potatoes, okra, and three kinds of pie. And then, when we got to the end, he let Aunt Amy pay. I mean, he didn't even try to take out his wallet or something. He didn't even pretend like he was trying.

When we got to our table, I was poking my fork at my Jell-O, and he said, "Uh-uh. What do you think you are doing, young lady? No eating your food before we pray."

"I wasn't eating, I was poking," I mumbled. But Aunt Amy eyed me nervously, so I didn't make a fuss.

Then he took Aunt Amy's and my hands and bowed his head and said, "God bless this food we are about to receive. In Jesus' name we pray. Amen."

That was the lamest prayer ever, I thought, for a Jesus Man. Aunt Amy always says something that's relevant to what's going on, like she mentions me or our family or May, or what she has to be grateful for, in particular.

Once we started eating, Ralph turned to me and said, "So, how's school?"

"It's all right."

"This is a very difficult time in a young person's life. A time when the Lord gives you a lot of tests."

"Yeah, I hope I'm not failing," I joked.

But I guess it wasn't that funny. He didn't laugh. Neither did Aunt Amy. She still looked nervous. Finally he said, "The pitfalls of sin are not something to make light of."

I won't bore you with all of the rest, but it went on like that, more or less. I tried to keep up some kind of conversation and to figure out what exactly he was doing here. I guess he's staying in a church and showing up to all of these services to talk about his journeys. The thing is, Aunt Amy didn't even seem that happy around him. She didn't do any Mister Ed impressions, or anything like that. She was just really quiet. And I don't know if it's because I was there, but mostly she seemed nervous, like she felt like he was going to get up and leave at any minute.

We finally said good night and got in the car to go home. It was too quiet for a while, until we came to a stoplight and Aunt Amy said, "Thank you for coming, Laurel." She paused, and then she asked, "What did you think?"

"Do you want me to tell you the truth?" I asked.

"Yes," she said thinly. "Of course."

"I think you are too good for him. I mean, way too good for him. Like, he doesn't even hold a candle to you. I think just 'cause you love God definitely doesn't mean you have to love him."

She didn't get mad or anything. She kept her eyes on the road. And then she finally said, "Thank you for giving me your honest opinion. I appreciate that."

"You do?"

"Yes." The light turned green, and she drove down the street, turning into the quiet dark of the neighborhood. She pulled up to the little adobe house that she's lived in for so many years and turned the car off, but she didn't get out. I waited to see if she wanted to say something else.

"He's been asking me for money," Aunt Amy finally said, "to help fund his next pilgrimage. But I've been thinking that I don't want to give him any more. I could be saving for you instead, for college."

It felt like one of the most generous things that anyone has ever said to me. Not just because of the money—I know I'll need a scholarship anyway. But because it meant that she really cares about me, and maybe that she was starting to care about herself in a different way, too. I knew that I couldn't even imagine what it would be like to be lonely for that long, and I wanted her to have someone. I just wanted it to be someone who would really see her.

When we got inside, I asked Aunt Amy, "Do you want to watch *Mister Ed*?"

Aunt Amy smiled and said she did. The theme song came on, and without her even having to ask, I did the horse hoofs on the table and the horse noise with my lips, until she started to laugh.

Yours,
Laurel

Dear Judy Garland,

I always thought of you as a kid. The little girl tap-dancing in the air-conditioned movie theater in the desert. The little girl whose daddy clapped for her and then carried her through the summer night heat to the station wagon. The girl who sang to stop them from fighting. The girl who sang herself to sleep. And then the one who got signed by the movie studio, where they put fake teeth on her and told her she wasn't pretty. The girl who took the pills they gave her and wore pigtails and did one picture after another. The girl whose voice broke into sobs as she sang "Somewhere Over the Rainbow," over and over again. You were so tired. But they gave you more pills and told you to keep singing. You kept singing. You were the girl who was about to become a star, just when your daddy died. The little girl whose voice was too big for her body.

But I didn't know that you grew up and hurt your own kids, too. I watched this movie about you on TV yesterday—a replay of something they made years ago. I know that not everything they say on TV is true. I know. But there you were, with your little girls, girls little like you used to be. You taught them to get up and sing with you. You taught them that applause was the closest thing to love. You taught them that people love you for what they want to see in you, not for what you are. That's a sad thing to learn. You could have made it different for them.

I guess maybe even though you got older, you never stopped being the little girl who needed someone to take care of her. So you wanted your own little girls to take care of you. And when they couldn't—how could they have?—you left them finally, for good.

Sometimes I wonder if it's the same with my mom. Like she started her life so young that she never got to finish growing all the way up. And maybe that's why she needed us— May especially—so much.

She called today, and Aunt Amy tried to hand me the phone. I've been avoiding Mom for almost three weeks now. I said that I'd call back later, but Aunt Amy insisted that I really needed to speak with her. So finally I took it.

It started out normal. "How are you, honey?" she asked.

"I'm actually pretty good, I guess."

"Are you looking forward to summer?"

"Yeah. It's weird that the year is almost over."

Then she launched into it. "Laurel, the last time we talked, you mentioned that there was something—something that you'd told your sister . . . I'm worried about you."

I wiped my palms on my dress. "I don't really want to get into it on the phone, Mom."

"I've been thinking about how you said you feel like I'm not there for you. And I know that you aren't eager to take a trip out here. But it's been too long since I've seen you. So I think that I'll come back for a few months this summer. If not for good, then at least for a visit. I can stay with Amy."

"Okay . . ." I said. I wasn't sure what to make of this. "But you know I still have to be at Dad's every other week. I can't just ditch him 'cause you're coming back."

"Yes, I know, sweetie." Then she said, "I can't wait to see you."

"Yeah," I said. "You too, Mom."

I know Mom coming back is what I've wanted this whole time, but now that it's really happening, I'm not sure how I feel about it. It's like I've finally gotten used to just being with Aunt Amy and Dad. But mostly, I am scared that she's only coming back to try to get some story out of me. So that I can tell her the whole answer about what happened to May and confirm her suspicions that it was my fault. *Fine*, I keep thinking, *if she wants to know, I'll just tell her this time. And then she can disappear forever.* I'll feel like I am starting to get better, but with Mom, suddenly I turn into a little kid again, who got left behind somewhere.

Judy, you took the pills the studio gave you. The pills the doctors gave you. You started so young that you could never stop, and then you were gone. I can't help but wonder if nobody ever really grows all the way up. I look at you in *The Wizard of Oz*, on that yellow brick road that you just hope will lead to home, and I know you always wanted to get there.

Yours,
Laurel

Dear Amelia,

This morning at school, something great happened. I saw Hannah standing with Natalie, getting books out of her locker. Hannah zipped up her bag, and then I watched her lean into Natalie and give her a kiss on the lips. Right there, in front of everyone passing, anyone who wanted to look. She grabbed Natalie's hand and walked with her down the hall, as they weaved through the soccer boys staring, the science nerds pointing, all of them talking and whispering and saying what they would. Natalie and Hannah were beautiful, both of them, like their own constellation.

You once said that you thought people are too timid about flying their own Atlantics, and I think it's true that all of our lives are full of oceans. For Hannah, the Atlantic was standing up to her brother. And I think that now that she's on the other side of it, she's realizing how brave she can be.

For me, maybe the Atlantic has been learning to talk about stuff, even a little at a time. But I think the thing that takes me the most courage is realizing that as many oceans as I might cross, the stupid simple truth will always be on the other side. May was here and then she was gone. I loved her with all of my soul, and she died. And no guilt or anger or longing changes that. There's a new sadness now, as I open the fist I've been clenching shut and realize that there's nothing there. I don't know how to keep her anymore. Sometimes I'll be doing something normal, like standing in the alley with my friends, or getting ready for bed, and suddenly the pain of missing her will come up and nearly knock me over.

But sometimes, there are things that help. Tonight was a good night. Sky came over and watched baseball with me and Dad. He liked it so much when I had Hannah over, I figured I'd try to do that kind of thing more. And he and Sky seemed to be getting along. I was more or less tuning out while they were talking about players and trades and stuff. It's still early in the season, but I know that the Cubs are doing pretty well so far. In this particular game, however, they were losing by a lot, and Dad just shut it off all of a sudden and said, "What do you say we go out back and have a little ball game of our own?" It's funny how he comes alive with other people around. Maybe he feels like it's a sign that I'm letting him into my life, or that I'm not ashamed of our family. Or maybe it's just been forever since the house hasn't felt totally quiet.

It was sort of a crazy idea, because it was already almost dark out—the dead game time of dusk—but I thought, why not? So Dad pulled out his old gloves and bat and a wiffle ball, and he pitched for Sky and me. I kept missing, but Dad gave me more than three strikes, and finally I got a good hit. Then Sky pitched to Dad, and he hit the ball clear over the roof! He loved this so much. "Your old man's still got it!" Dad told me as he ran around the yard, crossing the imaginary bases, and finally calling out, "I made it home!"

It was pretty much totally dark by then, so we figured it was a good note to end on. Dad went to bed, and he was in such a good mood, he didn't even kick Sky out before he said good night. Sky came into my room with me, and we both sat down on my bed.

"Your dad is really cool," Sky said. "We should hang out with him more."

"He likes you. I think it made him happy, you being here."

"Yeah?"

"Yeah. Thank you for coming."

"Of course." He smiled.

I lay down on my pillow. Then I said, "So, my mom's coming back. Next weekend. At least for the summer."

"Oh, wow. Are you happy?"

"I don't know. I want to be, but it's like I don't know if I trust it."

Sky nodded. "I get that. When parents ditch out, it's pretty hard to forgive them."

He lay down next to me, and I reached out and let my hand fall onto his chest. "Was he good while he was around?" I asked. "Your dad?"

"Not really. He had his moments, but not so much." Sky paused, and then he said, "I don't know what will happen to my mom after next year, if I want to go away to college or something. I'm scared sometimes that I'll turn out like him. Like I'll always be the kind of person who leaves."

I looked at him. "You're better than your dad. But maybe it's not your job to make up for him forever."

His lip that falls a little crooked to the left straightened out when I said that. He was thinking about it.

We lay there next to each other on my bed, quiet for a while, looking up at the bumps in the ceiling that turned to shapes. I remembered lying in May's top bunk and looking up, trying not to fall asleep so that I could see if she went out to fly.

"Look," I said to Sky, pointing up. "That's a face. She's half girl, half ghost. You can see where she's split—she only has long hair on the one side." I pointed to the place where the paint gathered into tresses. "And there, that's a hand. It belongs to a man living inside the wall. He's collecting raindrops. He wants to come out and give them to the ghost-girl. She'll fight off the spirit in her. And then they'll go together and swim in that ocean"—I pointed—"over there."

Sky laughed and nuzzled his face into my neck. I put my hand out and stroked his head. He seemed like a little boy just then, in a way that he never had before. Maybe because I felt stronger now, strong enough to hold him.

We didn't kiss or anything else. We just lay together like that, breathing. I felt something between us shifting, like the hidden plates of the earth. You think you know someone, but that person always changes, and you keep changing, too. I understood it suddenly, how that's what being alive means. Our own invisible plates shifting inside of our bodies, beginning to align into the people we are going to become.

Yours,
Laurel

Dear Elizabeth Bishop,

At school, everyone is buzzing with the energy of the coming summer, a week and a half away. I went up to Mrs. Buster's desk today after class. I'd never really spoken to her voluntarily before. But there was something I had to tell her. "You know the assignment from the beginning of school? The letter?" I asked.

"Yes?" She looked surprised.

"Well, I'm still working on it." And then I added, "Actually, I've been working on it all year. I have a whole notebook full of them. I just wanted you to know."

"Oh, well, I'm really happy to hear that, Laurel." She lit up when she said it, but then she kept looking at me in that way that she does, like she was waiting for something. Like she wanted me to say something about May. So finally I asked, "When May was in your class, what was she like?"

"She seemed like a girl who was struggling to figure out who she was, kind of like you are. She was very bright, in both senses of the word. I thought that she had a lot to offer. I think that you do, too." She paused, and then she said, "I know what it's like to lose someone, Laurel."

"You do?" I asked.

"Yes. I had a son—he passed."

"Oh my god. I'm so sorry." I was searching for something better to say. It made my chest crush in to think of that happening to Mrs. Buster. "When—when did it happen?"

"He was young," Mrs. Buster said. "It was a car accident."

I stared at her big blue eyes, and they didn't seem like bug eyes anymore. They seemed sad. It's like all of a sudden she'd turned from a teacher into a person. I guess when you lose someone, sometimes it feels like you are the only one. But I'm not.

"I'm sorry about your son," I said again. "And I'm sorry that I wasn't nicer this year. I think you are a really good teacher. I loved all of the poetry you gave us. And I am—just really sorry—I wish there were something good to say. I guess there aren't really any words for it, huh?"

"There are a lot of human experiences that challenge the limits of our language," she said. "That's one of the reasons that we have poetry." She smiled. "Here." She fished something out of her desk. "I wanted to give you this. I'd copied it for you at the beginning of the year, since you seemed to like Bishop so much. But then—well, maybe you weren't ready for it yet."

I took the poem. "Thank you," I said.

Then she said, "I'm proud of you. It's not easy, and you've done a great job this year." She didn't have to be that nice to me, but she was.

I thanked her again for the poem. I was anxious to read it, so I found a bench and sat outside before I went to lunch. It was your poem called "The Armadillo." I loved the poem so much, it stopped my heart. And I knew why Mrs. Buster had given it to me. It was about a certain kind of beauty we aspire to and how fragile it is. The poem starts out talking about fire balloons that people send off into the sky. *The paper chambers flush and fill with light / that comes and goes, like hearts* as they rise toward the stars. When the air is still, they *steer between the kite sticks of the Southern Cross*, but with a wind, they become dangerous. The end of the poem shows the tragedy that happens.

Last night another big one fell.
It splattered like an egg of fire
against the cliff behind the house.
The flame ran down. We saw the pair

of owls who nest there flying up
and up, their whirling black-and-white
stained bright pink underneath, until
they shrieked up out of sight.

The ancient owls' nest must have burned.
Hastily, all alone,
a glistening armadillo left the scene,
rose-flecked, head down, tail down,

and then a baby rabbit jumped out,
short-eared, to our surprise.
So soft!—a handful of intangible ash
with fixed, ignited eyes.

Too pretty, dreamlike mimicry!
O falling fire and piercing cry
and panic, and a weak mailed fist
clenched ignorant against the sky!

I couldn't stop thinking of it, our flushing hearts, trying to climb to the stars—how with the wrong wind, we can fall. I'm not sure if this is what you meant by the poem, but it made me think of how we all have both parts in us. I think maybe we all carry both the fire balloons and the soft animal creatures who could be hurt by them inside of us. It's easy to feel like the bunny rabbit frozen in terror. And it's easy to feel like one of the fire balloons, at the whim of the wind, either rising up out of sight or burning down. Blown one direction or another.

But there is a third thing in the poem—your voice. The one who saw it. The one who could stand and witness, the one who turned the pain and terror into this beautiful lyric. So maybe when we can say things, when we can write the words, when we can express how it feels, we aren't so helpless.

I thought after reading your poem today that I might want to try to be a writer, too. Even though I don't think I can ever write a poem as good as yours, it made me think that maybe I can do something with all of the feelings in me, even the ones that are sad and scared and angry. Maybe when we can tell the stories, however bad they are, we don't belong to them anymore. They become ours. And maybe what growing up really means is knowing that you don't have to just be a character, going whichever way the story says. It's knowing that you could be the author instead.

Yours,
Laurel

Dear Judy,

Mom got here four days ago. Of course she had to come back on the last weekend before school is over. Part of me wished I was out with my friends, but instead I was at the airport with Aunt Amy, waiting on the bench and watching the bags turning on their carousel, nervously balling up the fabric of my dress.

Then I saw Mom, riding down the elevator as if she'd walked out of another life. She was shifting her travel purse from shoulder to shoulder, the same one that she used to pack up with snacks to sneak into the movie theater when we were little. Her soft brown hair was pulled back into a ponytail. When her eyes met mine, she waved and put on a big happy smile. Then there was this awkward moment where we weren't actually close enough to say anything yet. I didn't know if I was supposed to run up and hug her, but I stayed frozen in my seat.

When she was standing in front of me, I got up and let her pull me against her body. She smelled the same, like our brand of dryer sheets and the lavender perfume she always dabs behind her ears, and something else—a smell like falling to sleep.

"Laurel," she said. "I missed you so much."

"I missed you, too, Mom."

Then she and Aunt Amy hugged, and we stood around, waiting for Mom's suitcase and making awkward small talk—how is school, how was the flight, how about the weather. Never mind how was the whole past year when I didn't see you. It felt like a canyon between us, the time that had passed.

And it stayed like that, the first couple of days. Like we were still in the in-between space of the airport. Like we weren't home anymore, but we hadn't arrived anywhere else. I mostly stayed in my room studying for finals, and Mom kept busy, as if she was trying to make up for the year of mom stuff that she'd missed. She made me waffles for breakfast, packed lunches with sandwiches on perfectly toasted bread, and made her famous enchiladas for Aunt Amy and me for dinner. Aunt Amy did a lot of the talking, actually. She'd tell Mom stuff about how well I'd done in my science class, or how Mom raised a good daughter because I always helped with the dishes. Mom would ask me the most basic questions. "What was your favorite class this year?" I felt like we were tiptoeing over a sheet of ice that could break any minute. We'd gone a whole three days without actually saying May's name.

Then this morning, as Mom was putting down a waffle in front of me, the syrup neatly poured into each square, I said, "No offense, Mom, it's really nice and all, but I usually just eat cereal for breakfast now. I mean, I've had to do all of this stuff without you for a year. You don't have to be, like, the world's greatest mother now."

But then her eyes got teary, and I instantly felt bad. "I'm trying, Laurel," she said.

"I know," I said softly, and started to cut the waffle along its lines. It just seemed strange to me, if she cared so much about all of this, that she'd gone so long without doing any of it.

Mom wiped her eyes and said, "I have an idea. Do you want to go out to dinner tonight? Just the two of us?"

I agreed, and so after school this evening, Mom and I went to the 66 Diner and ordered burgers and fries and strawberry shakes.

I was doing my best. "What was it like at the ranch?" I asked.

"It was pretty," Mom said. "It was peaceful."

I still couldn't picture it. "Were there, like, palm trees and stuff?"

Mom sort of laughed. "No, not on the ranch. But there were in the city."

"Oh," I said, sucking my shake out of its straw. "You went to LA?"

"Yeah," Mom said. "For the first time in my whole life."

"What did you do there?"

"Well, I went to see the Walk of Fame. I found Judy Garland's star. I wanted to stand on it."

"Was it cool?"

"I don't know," Mom said. "It was actually a little strange. You think of the Walk of Fame—I always did, anyway, when I used to dream that I'd be an actress—and you imagine it glittering and gleaming. But the truth is, the star was just on the sidewalk. Where people walk right over it. Next to a parking lot." She sounded sort of bereft when she said this, like a little kid who learned that Santa Claus was made up.

"We should find a star, like, in the sky," I said to Mom, "to name after Judy instead."

Mom smiled. "Let's do that."

Then it was quiet for a moment. I dipped a French fry in the ketchup and started nibbling on it.

Finally Mom looked up from her plate and said, "Laurel, I owe you an apology. I am sorry that I was gone for so long."

I didn't know what to say back to that. *It's all right*? It wasn't. And I wanted to try to be honest. "Yeah," I said. "It was hard." And then, "I mean, I know that you left because you were mad at me. I know you think that it's my fault, and that's why you wanted to go. You can just say it."

"What? Laurel, no. Of course I don't think it's your fault. Where would you get that idea?"

"Because," I said, "because you left. I thought that was why."

"Laurel, if I left because of someone's failings, they were my own, not yours. I really just—I must be the world's worst mother." Her voice started to break. "How could I have let that happen? How could I have lost her?"

I didn't realize that Mom felt guilty, too. "But Mom," I said. I reached out to take her hand across the table. "It wasn't your fault."

"Yes, it was. I was supposed to protect her. And I didn't."

"Well," I said quietly, "maybe you didn't know how."

Mom shook her head. "It's like when you guys were little, you needed me. I was the sun that you'd orbit around. But as you got older, and the orbit got wider, I didn't know my place in the universe anymore. I thought, *That's what's supposed to happen. They're growing up.* I thought the best thing I could do was to try not to hold on too tight. But you two were my reason to be."

"But what about Dad?" I asked. "Why didn't you love him anymore?"

"I'll always love your father, but we got married so young, Laurel. When May started to have her own life, and you did, too, your dad and I started having more trouble. It felt like we had so little in common, besides our daughters. But I shouldn't have left him. I don't think May ever forgave me."

Mom was shaking now. She looked down at her burger that

had only one bite out of it. She seemed so fragile, like a little girl. I saw why May thought that she had to keep all of the hard stuff secret from her.

"And look at you," she said. "You're doing so well. I can't help but think that I was right. That you were better off without me."

"Mom," I said. "I love you, but that's dumb. I still need you."

"Do you want to tell me, Laurel? Do you want to tell me what happened?"

There it was. I knew it was coming. I couldn't help the surge of anger that rushed into me. "That's why you're really here, right? So that you can find out finally? So that you can have an answer to everything? And then you can feel better?"

"No! No. I just want you to know that you can talk to me, if you want to."

"Well, I don't. Not about that. We can talk about something else."

She looked like I'd stabbed her in the heart when I said it.

"Fine, Mom. Look. When we were supposed to go to the movies, mostly we didn't go. May was seeing an older guy. And she went off with him. She thought I went to the movies with this friend of his who was supposed to take care of me, but I didn't go, either, because the friend molested me instead, and when I tried to tell May that night, she was already drunk, and then she was so sad, and when she got up, she started pretending to be a fairy, and she slipped or tripped or fell off the bridge or something. There you go. You can go back to California now."

I got up from the booth and walked out. I was crying in the parking lot, and hating myself for crying, and for being so mean to Mom, and for everything. It's supposed to get easier when you say it out loud. But it didn't feel that way. I was searching the sky through my bleary eyes, trying to find you, to find May, to find some sign that things weren't as lonely as they seemed.

Then Mom walked out. She was crying, too, but I could tell she was trying not to. She put her arms around me. "I'm so sorry, Laurel. I'm so sorry I let that happen to you." And I don't know what it was, the way that she smelled like Mom or the way that she stroked my head like she had when I was a kid trying to fall asleep, but I felt little again, and I put my head against her chest and just sobbed. I wasn't the same person she'd left. But she was still my mother. And the memory of the way that felt, to have a mom, it took me over.

People can leave, and then they can come back. It sounds simple, like an obvious thing. But when I realized that, the truth of it seemed important. My mom wasn't perfect. And she didn't even always take care of me. But she wasn't gone forever.

When I finished crying, I looked up at the sky and pointed to the star in the middle of Orion's Belt. "That one," I said to

Mom. "That's the Judy Garland star." And then I pointed to the one at the handle end of the Big Dipper. "And let's give that one to May."

Yours,
Laurel

Dear Kurt, Judy, Elizabeth, Amelia, River, Janis, Jim, Amy, Heath, Allan, E.E., and John,

I am writing to say thank you, to all of you, because I think this will be my last letter. It feels right like that. Yesterday was our last day of school. When the final bell rang, the halls filled up with woohoos. I walked past the screams and cheers and out to the alley to meet my friends. The air hung open in that way where we weren't sure if we should be somber or celebratory, but when Tristan got there, he walked up to Kristen and slapped her butt and said, "How's my New York babe?" She smiled. It was their last day of high school, forever. Tristan said that this called for a ceremony, and Kristen agreed.

So we all drove up to Kristen's house, and Tristan made a tent of little sticks in the yard that he lit up with his kitchen lighter. It would be like New Year's, but this time we were supposed to burn things we wanted to let go of. Tristan pulled the contents of his emptied locker out of his backpack—algebra quizzes and lab reports and tests with red *68*s circled on them—and he started putting them in the fire. Then he pulled out his English paper, one he had gotten an A on, called "I Lost Paradise," but before he could throw it in the fire, Kristen grabbed it and said, "I'm keeping this."

"You want my English paper, babe?"

"It was really good."

He looked at her for a moment and smiled. "Okay," he said. "Well, who's next then? I can't be the only one with something to burn!" The little fire was getting hungrier, eating up the pages. The sun was low and miming the blaze.

Hannah threw in her tests, and then she threw in her dried flowers and cards from boys, and she looked back over her shoulder at Natalie. The fire lit up both of their faces, and Natalie beamed back. Kristen threw in her locker pictures of New York, because now that she's really going there, it's not just a dream anymore.

I wanted to take a turn, and I thought about my notebook filled with my letters to all of you. I thought about how they would look, burning in the fire. I wondered if the flame would carry them up to you, wherever you are.

But when I reached for my notebook, I couldn't do it. Somewhere, it seemed, in my letters to you, was a story I had told. Something true. So I decided that I'm going to turn all of my letters in to Mrs. Buster. School is still open for a few days for teachers to finish their grades, so tomorrow or the next day, I'll go and leave them in her teacher's mailbox. For some reason, maybe because she gave me the assignment in the first place, I want her to read what I wrote.

So instead of burning the whole notebook, I took the last blank page out and threw it into the fire. I watched the white page, with its fine blue lines, as it burned. It made me cry for all of you who should have had more time. And for May.

After the fire was done eating my blank page, everyone was looking at me. "I miss my sister," I said simply, and it was nice to be able to just say it out loud. Hannah put her arm around me as I wiped the tears from my eyes. "She would have loved you guys," I added.

"If she was anything like you, we would have loved her, too," Tristan said, and smiled.

When the moment was over, we looked down and noticed that the fire was still getting bigger, so Tristan went to get the garden hose to put it out. He squirted Kristen and made her squeal, and then he squirted us all, and we tackled him for the hose and squirted back. All of our clothes were wet after that, but none of us cared, because it was summer-night warm out.

As the sun fell over the horizon, we went to sit on the deck, and I texted Sky to ask if he would come and meet us. When I saw his truck pull into the driveway, my heart leapt. He walked up wearing his same leather jacket, even on the brink of summer. He looked as beautiful as he did the first day I saw him, but more than that even, because now I knew him.

He came up to sit with us, and the sky opened wide, the way it does in summer, to let a lightning storm in. We all watched it for a while, and Kristen brought out a bottle of her parent's champagne and popped it, and we toasted each other. I took a sip, but I gave the rest of mine to Tristan.

Then I said, "Hey, Tristan?"

"Yes, Buttercup?"

"I think that next year in college, you should start a band."

He smiled a soft sort of smile that didn't go with his normal pointy edges. "You're right. I should."

"You could name it the Regular Weirdos."

He laughed. "I love that." It was quiet a moment. Then he said, "Well, no need to wait for college, right?" He turned to Hannah and said, "Are we going to do a song together, or what?"

Hannah got a spark in her eyes. This was maybe going to be the first time that she would sing for people, other than me or Natalie. She swallowed and nodded. We followed Tristan as he went to get his guitar and set it up in the living room and pulled up a stool for Hannah to sit on. "What do you want to sing?" he asked. Hannah wiped her palms on her dress and thought about it for a long minute. She said, "'Sweet Child O' Mine,'" which was all of our New Year's song. Tristan grinned and started right away with the first strings of the guitar that vibrate through your body. Hannah's voice shook for a moment, coming out quiet, but as she kept singing she got louder and louder, until the song was pouring out of her. She looked at Natalie as she sang. Tristan looked at Kristen as he strummed the guitar hard and mouthed along with Hannah. And I looked at Sky.

I grabbed his hand and whispered under the music, "I really want to kiss you."

He took my face in his hands, and it was a different kiss than it's ever been. I didn't feel like a light that he was crowding toward anymore, like a street lamp, or even like a moon. I felt like we both had the sun inside of us. Our own ways to stay warm. So when our bodies came together, it was the hottest thing I'd felt.

As Tristan and Hannah got to the end of the song, we all bounced up and down and shouted along, *"Where do we go now?"* Hannah was beaming, and Tristan played the end again. I can't describe how it felt, being there right then, so close together, on the edge between who we were and who we wanted to be.

Sometimes when we say things, we hear silence. Or only echoes. Like screaming from inside. And that's really lonely. But that only happens when we weren't really listening. It means we weren't ready to listen yet. Because every time we speak, there is a voice. There is the world that answers back.

When I wrote letters to all of you, I found my voice. And when I had a voice, something answered me. Not in a letter. In a new way a song sounded. In a story told on a movie screen. In a flower shooting through a crack in the sidewalk. In the flutter of a moth. In the nearly full moon.

I know I wrote letters to people with no address on this earth. I know you are dead. But I hear you. I hear all of you. *We were here. Our lives matter.*

Yours,
Laurel

EPILOGUE

Dear May,

I had a dream about you last night. I watched you walk on the tracks, your moonlit arms balancing you like thin white wings. I saw you turn to look back at me. I felt your eyes catch mine. I saw you fall. And I saw you hovering there, midsky, like you were standing on air. I kept begging myself to move my feet. But I couldn't. They were stuck. I kept thinking you were waiting for me. There was still a moment. If I could just walk forward, I could reach out and take your hand and pull you back across the tracks to the land. But my body was frozen. I tried with all my strength, but lifting my foot was as hopeless as shoving a mountain. It was the most awful feeling. I was in a panic, trying to get to you.

Then I heard you whisper, "Laurel," as you turned your back to me. "Look." And that's when I saw it. I saw you take your wings out. I saw them, paper-thin but stronger than anything, glittering like water. They weren't broken. They were carrying you into the sky. You got smaller and smaller, until you turned into a pinpoint of light, same as a star. And I knew you were there. And everywhere.

When I woke up, I went into your bedroom. Aside from your clothes that I borrowed (but always put back) and your Nirvana poster I tore off of the wall (sorry), everything was just where it was the last night we left for the movies. I sat on your bed for a moment. And then I took some of your Mexican candles to burn in my room, and your collection of seashells that I wanted to spread on my desk. This time, I wasn't afraid of moving things and making new places for them. My room is pretty much the same as it's always been, too, ever since you moved out of it when you got to high school. And I want it to be more like who I am now. I want it to have some pieces of you, together with other things, like the Janis Joplin record Kristen gave me before she left for New York, and the heart that Sky carved me for Christmas, and the glow-in-the-dark stars that have been there since we were kids.

When I was looking on your bookshelf, I found an E. E. Cummings book. You had a bookmark in it, the one you'd made yourself in third grade. *May* was written in blue glue glitter, laminated over. I read the poem you'd marked, and really, it was so beautiful I started to cry. I loved the whole thing, and the last line was perfect: i carry your heart(i carry it in my heart).

I brought the book into my room with the bookmark still in it. I read that poem again and again, and I knew somehow you'd marked it for me to see. I knew I was supposed to find it. May, I carry you in me.

Still, it doesn't change how much I miss you. Every time something happens, any little thing, I wish that I could tell you about it. Sky and I got back together. Sometimes my mind races, and I worry about what will happen after next year, when he leaves for college. But I try to take a deep breath and stay where I am. I have my first job this summer, at the city pool snack bar. My friends Natalie and Hannah come to meet me sometimes when I get off late in the afternoon. Hannah reads magazines and Natalie draws and we all drink Cokes and eat Goldfish. They don't ever get in, but I love to swim like I always did. I love how you can push water away and it always comes back. I run into Janey there sometimes, too. You'd be surprised if you could see her now. She comes with her boyfriend and wears a pink and white polka-dot bikini. It was awkward at first, because she was mad at me for disappearing on her after you died. But it's getting better. Now she'll sometimes come over and sit with me and Natalie and Hannah. Today, we were talking about the time when you taught us to flip off the diving board. We were both terrified until you made it look so easy.

I wrote all of these letters for school this year, and it helped me a lot. When I finally gave them to my teacher (I left them in her mailbox at school), she called me to say she was proud of me for handing them in. I thanked her for reading them. Then she said that I needed to get help to deal with all of it. But I told her Mom and Dad already started making me see this therapist. The therapist is actually nice, and she talks to me like I am smart. I'd told Mom what happened when she got back from California, and after that Mom told Dad. "I'm sorry we let you down, Laurel," he said. "I'm sorry we let your sister down, too." He looked like someone had shot him in the heart. I just hugged him. I didn't know what else to do.

May, I realize this now—it's not that I shouldn't have tried to tell you about Billy. It's that I should have told you sooner, and maybe then you could have told me things, too, and neither of us would have ever had to go back there. I think that if you were still here, we could have helped each other. I think that you would have walked away from the ledge you were on, and everything bright in you would have kept glowing. I can't bring you back now. But I forgive myself. And I forgive you. May, I love you with everything I am. For so long, I just wanted to be like you. But I had to figure out that I am someone, too, and now I can carry you, your heart with mine, everywhere I go.

Today I decided I had to do something. I knew it was time. After I went through your room, I went to find Dad, who was listening to baseball like usual. He turned down the volume right away when I walked in.

I asked, "How are the Cubs doing?"

"Three games out of first. Cross your fingers for us."

I smiled and showed him that my fingers were actually crossed. Then I said, "Dad?"

"Laurel?" he teased.

"I want to scatter May's ashes."

He was not expecting this. He swallowed. "Oh." And then he tried to recover. "Well. What were you thinking?"

"I think in the river."

I know I could have saved your ashes to put into the ocean, but I wanted you to have the journey, all the way with the currents, to the open sea. And I know that when I finally get to see the waves washing on the shore, to hear them, I will feel you there.

Dad said, "Okay. I think that's a nice idea."

"Can we go?" I asked.

"Right now?" His voice jumped.

I nodded. "And we have to go get Mom."

Dad swallowed. "Okay," he said, and he got up, the baseball game still murmuring in the background.

I called Mom at Aunt Amy's house, where she's still staying. When I told her we were coming, she didn't argue, or ask any questions even. She just said, "Okay." Aunt Amy was out for the afternoon with this guy Fred who she met at her church. He's really nice, much better than the Jesus Man. I nicknamed him Mister Ed in my mind, because he has long white hair that he wears in a dignified ponytail and a horse nose.

Mom and Dad were quiet with each other in the front seat as we drove. I sat in the back, holding the jar of ashes tight, mostly noticing how heavy it felt, and thinking of what it contained. What's left of what your body was—once the girl with bare shoulder blades, giggling, once the girl galloping an imaginary horse, once the girl sleeping in her sequined red dress—was now ash in a jar. Grains of bone. But then, I knew it wasn't you anymore. You were somewhere more.

After we parked at our spot, Mom and Dad followed me out onto the tracks. And as I walked across them, it became the place it had always been while you were alive. The place we first discovered when we came for walks with Mom and Dad, the two of us running ahead of them and chasing the sky. The place we spent hours sitting, talking, and playing Poohsticks. The river we'd loved in every season was moving quietly now for summer. I handed Mom the jar first, and she reached in and took the ashes in her hands. As she let them go, her eyes filled with tears. She reached out for me as she passed the jar to Dad. He scattered a handful and said, "May, this land is your land."

Remember? That song he'd sing us? *From California, to the New York Island, From the redwood forest, to the Gulf Stream waters* . . . He was right. It is your land, all of it. You are everywhere in it. The whole big world we dreamed of.

When Dad handed the jar to me, I poured out the rest of the ashes and watched the wind carry them down to the water. Little bits still stuck to my fingers. I said, "She's free now."

And then Dad started sobbing like a little kid. I've never seen him that way before. I went to hug him. Mom stood off to the side, but eventually she came over, too, and all of our bodies were shaking together.

When it was over, Dad ruffled my hair and said, "I love you, Laurel."

"I love you, too, Dad."

"You're strong, but you're still our baby girl," Mom said. Her eyes met Dad's and held on to them for a moment. "We're proud of you. Your sister is, too."

I smiled at them and asked, "Do you want to play Pooh-sticks?"

They laughed. Dad said, "I haven't thought about that game in years."

"May and I still used to play together," I said, "after you taught us here. We'll do one for her, too."

So we crossed the tracks onto the forest side to look for sticks. Mom picked one with a pretty knot on the wood. Dad's was like a walking stick. I got myself one with the bark still on, and I got you a smooth one, straight and strong. We went back on the bridge and leaned over the edge, and "One, two, three, drop," Dad counted. And as we ran to the other side to see, yours won! I told them it's because you were hurrying toward the sea.

I imagined your stick, washing in the waves for hundreds of years, turning to driftwood, smooth and hard like stone. I imagined a little girl finding it on a beach so many years later. Saving it on her shelf, where she put the things that made her feel like the world was magical.

May, I decided that I might want to be a poet when I grow up. Which is pretty much now, because I guess this is what growing up is like. So, I wrote my first poem this week. I wrote it for you. Before we left the bridge, I read it out loud to you.

A Love Letter for My Sister

A ghost cannot open an envelope. Still I address
this to you—I am saving this world for you, see.

River water runs. Fields fill with golden.
Apples bitten. *A ghost cannot open*

an envelope. A ghost cannot run.
The road travels its forever distance.

Two girls pause by a bridge, to notice.
The fall leaves don't fall hard.

The spring lasts forever, after a storm.
I am opening this envelope for you, see.

An open blue flower. A paper bag holds a candle.
I am letting the world open me.

A leaf falls. A lead smudge
leads to a girl in a red dress.

I am reading the letters you meant for me to see.
I hope that you will open the envelopes,

so I am opening the world inside of me.
I am sending my letters to you.

The river goes to the ocean.
The ocean sounds infinite.

We are big enough to hear it.
Both of us.

Love always,
Your sister, Laurel

ACKNOWLEDGMENTS

When I think about the fact that *Love Letters to the Dead* is now a book that exists not only in my head or heart or on my computer screen, but in the world, gratitude feels like an understatement. I offer my most full-hearted *thank you!* to everyone who made it so.

To Stephen Chbosky, my dear friend and mentor, who told me I should write a novel to begin with, then gave it his boundless support: thank you for letting me be a part of telling your stories and for helping me learn to tell mine.

To Liz Maccie, who was the first person to read the very first draft of this book: thank you for seeing what it could become and for your unconditional love and encouragement that gave me faith to carry it through. Your friendship is a true guiding light.

To Hannah Davey, who shared my first days of high school and who has been my forever best friend ever since (and who is happily also a genius reader): thank you for making memories with me that become stories, for sharing stories with me that become memories, and for growing up with me for so long.

Doug Hall, my love, I am so grateful for you every day. Thank you for not only helping me to become a better writer, but for helping me to become who I needed to be to finish writing this story.

I have been astoundingly lucky to work with the brilliant Joy Peskin, who is a dream of an editor and who has treated Laurel and her family and friends with the utmost attention and generosity. Joy, thank you for seeing what I'd kept hidden and helping me to bring it onto the page and into the light.

To my wonderful agent, Richard Florest, thank you for believing in this story from the beginning and fighting for it with such vigilance and compassion at every step along the way. A book couldn't have a better friend.

To the people at FSG: I am wowed by you all and so grateful that you have embraced this story and lent it your hearts and amazing minds. Thank you especially to Katie Fee, Molly Brouillette, Caitlin Sweeny, Holly Hunnicutt, and Andrew Arnold for all that you have done to shepherd *Love Letters to the Dead* into the world.

To my friends and early readers, Anat Benzvi, Kai Beverly-Whittemore, Michael Bortman, Matt Bradly, Sean Bradly, Willa Dorn, Lauren Gould, Lianne Halfon, Will Slocomb, Katie Tabb, and Sarah Weiss, thank you for your support, inspiration, and insight. This book wouldn't be what it is without you. Thank you also to all of my wonderful teachers at the Iowa Writers' Workshop, the University of Chicago, and the Albuquerque Academy, who changed my life and made this book possible for me. Thank you to Carol Hekman. And thank you to my stepmom, Jamie Wells, for her support and kindness.

To Kurt Cobain, Judy Garland, Elizabeth Bishop, Amelia

Earhart, River Phoenix, Janis Joplin, Jim Morrison, Amy Winehouse, Heath Ledger, Allan Lane, E. E. Cummings, and John Keats, thank you for your beautiful lives and work, which continue to inspire me and so many others.

To my father, Tom, thank you for your endless supply of love and encouragement, honesty, guidance, and wisdom. For a lifetime of love and our lives together. I am so proud to be your daughter.

And most of all, to my sister, Laura, my fellow fairy and partner in all things magical: I am so grateful that I get to grow up with you and for all that you've taught me along the way. I love you more than the whole universe.